D1087503

Peaches and Schemes

Also available by Anna Gerard

Georgia B&B Mysteries

Peachy Scream

Peach Clobbered

Black Cat Bookshop Mysteries
(writing as Ali Brandon)

Twice Told Tail

Plot Boiler

Literally Murder

Words With Fiends

A Novel Way to Die

Double Booked for Death

Tarot Cats Mysteries
(writing as Diane A.S. Stuckart)

Fool's Moon

Leonardo Da Vinci Mysteries
(writing as Diane A.S. Stuckart)

A Bolt from the Blue

Portrait of a Lady

The Queen's Gambit

Peaches and Schemes

A GEORGIA B&B MYSTERY

Anna Gerard

CROOKED
LANE

NEW YORK

Copyright © 2021 by Diane A.S. Stuckart

Published in the United States by Crooked Lane Books, an imprint of The Quick Brown Fox & Company LLC.

Crooked Lane Books and its logo are trademarks of The Quick Brown Fox & Company LLC.

Library of Congress Catalog-in-Publication data available upon request.

ISBN (hardcover): 978-1-64385-584-4
ISBN (ebook): 978-1-64385-585-1

Cover illustration by Brandon Dorman

Printed in the United States.

www.crookedlanebooks.com

Crooked Lane Books
34 West 27th St., 10th Floor
New York, NY 10001

First Edition: May 2021

10 9 8 7 6 5 4 3 2 1

I lost two fine friends recently, Steven Kerry Brown and Al Hallonquist. Both were unstintingly generous in sharing their lifetimes of law enforcement knowledge when I needed "just the facts" about police procedure in one of my stories. This book is for them.

Chapter One

U nlike most women I know, I've never much cared for weddings. Heck, I barely managed to get through my own nuptials almost twenty years ago. It's not that I wasn't excited about marrying my husband-to-be, a good-looking golf pro working at a small country club in Atlanta. At the time, I was in love and thought it would last forever. You know, the whole *better or worse, richer or poorer, till death do us part* thing. (We actually made it to "richer," which eventually led to the "parting" part of our union.)

Nope, marriage wasn't the problem . . . at least, not at the beginning. What was too much for me was all the wedding planning. Pre–internet and social media, I didn't have wedding blogs and websites and Facebook pages for guidance. Thus, I was more than a little overwhelmed deciding on venues and menus and flowers and cakes and a proper dress. It didn't help that my mother was consumed with the impending birth of my sister's first child. My niece ended up arriving a week before my wedding, and so both Sis and Mom were mostly absent from their respective matron-of-honor and mother-of-the-bride roles. As for my groom, he shrugged and said he was good with whatever I chose.

In the end, however, the license was signed, birdseed in lieu of rice was thrown, and a honeymoon commenced. And I vowed that it would be my last wedding, except as a guest. I even turned down a couple of bridesmaid stints, just because the entire prospect gave me the willies, as my grandmother used to say.

But weddings and their related festivities can be lucrative business if you happen to own a bed-and-breakfast, which I do. Which is why I agreed to take part in the third annual fall Veils and Vanities Bridal Expo here at Cymbeline High School.

And which is also how I came to be hiding in the downstairs girls' restroom of CHS overhearing a heated argument that I later would realize was a motive for murder.

But let me back up a bit.

My name is Nina Fleet, that first name pronounced NINE-ah, like the number nine. I clock in at pretty much the average female height and weight, with brown hair and brown eyes. Mine are the sort of regular features that rank as cute rather than beautiful (think Sandra Bullock versus Sophia Vergara), which is okay by me. I'm divorced, as I noted, but have a full-time partner in my sassy Australian shepherd, Matilda aka Mattie. Together we own Fleet House, a bed-and breakfast retreat here in Cymbeline, Georgia, about an hour west of Savannah.

I kind of fell into innkeeping by accident after my impulse buy of the place a few months ago, but things have worked out surprisingly well for my fledgling business. Of course, it helps that Cymbeline is considered a little gem of an antiquing and arts enclave. Founded in the 1890s, the town was named after the Shakespearean comedic tragedy. The result is that numerous local businesses have names that reference the Bard's works, adding to the town's funky vibe.

Tourists and creative types travel here from all around the state of Georgia and beyond. This includes brides, who see Cymbeline as a fun place for a destination wedding that won't break the bank. Fortunately, they and their guests like to rest their heads in quaint rooms rather than chain motels. Fleet House definitely falls into the former category, being a pristine three-story Queen Anne house with a green-and-yellow color scheme. Add immaculate landscaping thanks to my gardener, Hendricks, and the place is perfect for intimate outdoor weddings.

While I've been to my share of trade shows over the years as an attendee, I had never been on the other side of the booth before Veils and Vanities, so this was definitely a new experience. My buddy Roxanna Quarry was the one who had convinced me to give the show a try.

"You've got a fine online presence," she assured me, "but when it comes to weddings, brides want to see and touch and talk in person. Trust me on this."

And, since Roxanna was the queen of all things wedding, I did.

We'd met at a Chamber of Commerce event a couple of months earlier and had struck up an immediate friendship. For one thing, we both were dog lovers—me with Mattie and Roxanna with her Goldendoodle, Gustopher. We both were divorced female entrepreneurs about the same age. Roxanna, however, had grown up in Cymbeline, though she'd returned home only a couple of years ago after moving to Savannah right after graduating college and later ending up in Atlanta. In looks, we were opposites, her being tall and model thin, with hair bleached to a platinum hue that contrasted rather oddly with her dark-brown eyes.

An event planner who specialized in weddings, Roxanna had already sent a bachelorette weekend and two bridal showers my way. In turn, I passed out cards for her business, Your Big Day, to future brides who stopped by Fleet House for a look-see. And both of us never hesitated to recommend our mutual friend Gemma Tanaka, who, with her husband Daniel, owned Peaches and Java, the nearby diner/bakery that catered for my B&B.

But Roxanna's enthusiasm for everything bridal wasn't limited to individual weddings. She and Virgie Hamilton— the sixty-something owner of Cymbeline's sole bridal shop, Virgie's Formals—were in their third year of showcasing all manner of local businesses related to the wedding industry. Their seasonal expo—hosted in both the spring and the fall of each year—was now a Cymbeline tradition. And not even the fact that the event was held in the gymnasium of the local high school took away from its professionalism.

I must admit to having been darned impressed when I arrived at the old-fashioned brown-brick building earlier in the morning to set up. Picture your senior prom night—except with yards of white tulle ribbon replacing the cascades of colorful paper streamers hanging from the ceiling. Pale-blue industrial carpeting covered the basketball court striping on the wooden floors, while lacy white draperies in lieu of balloons and painted poster board blocked off the bleachers.

The floor area had been divided into two sections for the expo. The first half as you walked in through the gym's double doors was the vendor area where I had my booth. There, three rows of white-clothed tables featured everything from flowers to jewelry to cruises to makeup. By my count, close to thirty exhibitors were taking part—not too shabby for a small-town event.

I was relieved to see that most were dressed for comfort like me, with my white denim jeans, black loafers, and pale-yellow oxford shirt. My new Fleet House logo—a stylized Victorian home encircled by the words *Fleet House Bed & Breakfast*—was embroidered in dark gold over the pocket. The laminated exhibitor's badge hanging from a lanyard around my neck made me official.

The remainder of the gym floor space had been designated as the expo's demonstration area. A temporary curtained stage was set up at its far end, with rows of folding chairs arranged on either side of a raised catwalk that stretched into the audience. For now, the stage was empty save for one of those giant prop cakes, the kind you'd expect to see a scantily clad gal or guy leap out of to general hilarity. This one, however, was elegantly covered in fake white frosting and decorated with piped ribbons and curlicues of white and silver and pink faux icing like an actual wedding cake.

Later in the day, the stage would play host to the expo's main event, a full-blown fashion show featuring bridesmaid and mother-of-the-bride dresses, followed by the latest fashions in bridal gowns. Lukewarm as I was about the whole wedding thing, I was rather looking forward to seeing the dresses, if only to take a break from my booth. For, from the minute the gym doors opened at nine AM, the place had been filled with a steady stream of excited brides-to-be accompanied by relatives and friends.

"This whole trade show thing is a lot harder than it looks," I confided to the guy in the next booth over, after barely an hour of it. "I haven't stopped talking since the doors opened. I don't know how I'm going to last until four o'clock."

John Klingel, owner of Midsummer Night's Flowers—another of Cymbeline's Shakespeare-themed business names—let loose with a boisterous laugh.

"You're doing great, kid," he assured me, running a hand over his thinning, slicked-back blond hair. "Don't look at the clock and time will fly. Believe me."

Tall, pink cheeked, and round faced, the man looked a good decade younger than his actual age of sixty-something, in part because he had been smiling from the moment he walked into the gym. And it wasn't just his attitude that was cheerful. From his purple button-down shirt to the electric-yellow sneakers he wore, his whole persona exuded good-natured fun.

Not surprisingly, he also was a seasoned pro at the trade show game. In fact, he had already given me a few tips as an expo newbie.

Stand, don't sit, when there are people around.

Don't spend time chatting up obvious non-prospects.

Seriously, don't graze out of your booth's candy bowl.

As we currently had a lull in the action, however, I figured I could ignore rule number one for a moment. I let myself flop onto my folding chair with an exhausted whoosh of breath.

"I'm sure you're right. I guess I'm just out of practice being 'on' nonstop," I told him, going on to break rule number three by reaching for one of the individually wrapped truffles filling my booth's candy dish. Through a bite of gooey chocolate heaven, I continued, "At the B&B, I usually only see my guests in the morning at breakfast and in the afternoon at happy hour. During the day, it's pretty much me and my dog, and Mattie isn't that big of a talker."

John let out another laugh.

"Another couple of hours here, you'll be ready to give advice to next expo's first timers. Oh, and speaking of first times, here's your credit card back," he said, and handed over my Visa. "You're all set for the workshop on Monday night."

"Thanks for squeezing me in. I'm really looking forward to it."

As a bit of payback for John's coaching, I'd signed up for his upcoming seminar titled *Flower Arranging for First-Time*

Florists. It was one of those fun classes for amateurs, and I'd figured what the heck. My current skill level in the floral arts began and ended with ordering from online flower sites.

But I have foliage and blooms aplenty in my own gardens. Various climbing heritage roses—white, yellow, pink—are planted alongside my garage's outer wall, serving as a fragrant border to the west end of my backyard. The centerpiece of the landscape, however, is my Shakespeare garden—a formal series of herb and flower beds containing only plants mentioned in the Bard's works. Mine is situated in the backyard just beyond the brick patio outside my back door, slightly raised above the level of the sloping yard.

The main garden is circular, with a splashy three-tiered concrete fountain in its center, though the outer pathways have been squared off on all sides. Graveled paths divide the circle portion into four pie pieces of closely planted beds that, depending on the season, burgeon with fragrant herbs and colorful blooms just begging to be picked. And so it made sense to learn how to put together nice arrangements for my B&B guests to enjoy.

I tucked the credit card back into my purse; then, seeing a woman striding our way, I scrambled to my feet again.

"Prospect," I playfully told him, since I recognized the woman headed toward us.

John glanced in the direction I'd been looking, and to my surprise, his ever-present smile froze. Which didn't make sense, since the strider was the expo's cofounder, Virgie Hamilton.

I'd met her a time or two already as part of our Chamber activities, though I wouldn't have called us friends. Virgie tended to stand out in a crowd—literally. She was several inches taller than my five foot five, and her ever-present high heels added even more height. She wore her steel-gray hair in a complicated confection of upswept curls that gave her an endearing mother-of-the-bride look and added another few inches on top. Virgie favored pastels—today's outfit was a pale-blue suited skirt paired with a dark-blue silk camisole, which, combined with her hairstyle and honey-soft Georgia accent, completed the whole modern southern belle package.

But as with most southern belles, refined didn't mean she was a pushover. From what I'd heard, the woman was a consummate pro, whether she was calming nervous brides-to-be or cutting deals with vendors. Putting on an expo would be a piece of cake—I know, bad choice of cliché, as it would turn out—for a woman like her. That's why I was surprised to see that her usual genial expression today reflected vague peevishness even when she smiled. Which she did as she paused at my booth.

"Good morning. You're Nina"—she pronounced it NEE-nah—"aren't you? You're the one who bought the Lathrop house and turned it into a B&B. How are you enjoying our little event?"

"So far, so good. And actually, it's NINA-ah," I cheerfully corrected her, smiling a bit at the reference to my home's former owner, Mrs. Daisy Lathrop.

Another fact I'd already learned about small-town Georgia life: most places were known by their original names or owners even decades after the property changed hands. Which was why I'd added a brief paragraph about Mrs. Lathrop to my brochure and website to placate the locals. But I suspected that for a certain contingent in town, even twenty years from now Fleet House would still be known as old Mrs. Lathrop's place.

Virgie, meanwhile, was nodding as she gave my booth the once-over. In addition to my candy bowl, I had the aforementioned brochures in neat holders, plus some poster-sized photos of the B&B pinned to my booth's backdrop. My table also held a couple of white lace decorated binders filled with more photos showing my guest rooms and my gardens. And, at Roxanna's suggestion, I'd printed off excerpts from a few of my glowing online reviews, which I'd framed and displayed alongside the binders.

Compared to John's booth next to me, which he'd turned into a replica flower shop, it was a modest effort. Still, Virgie gave me an approving nod.

"I see you are collecting names for your mailing list," she said, indicating my sign-up sheet, which already held a dozen email addresses from various expo attendees. "If you get nothing else from today, you have prospects for later. Good job."

With that, she marched over to the florist's booth.

"Over the top as always, John," she observed with a cool smile at odds with her honeyed Georgia drawl. She ran her hands along the fronds of a fountain-like greenery arrangement that spilled out of a tall standing urn. "You do know that some-times less is more."

"Oh, I agree. The less time I spend with you, the more I like it," was the man's equally chilly response.

I couldn't help staring at him in surprise. From the moment I'd met him, the man had been bubbling over with positivity—a chummy guy who smiled more than a toddler playing with a puppy. What had happened here?

Equally surprising, Virgie didn't seem shocked by his response. Still, I waited for a pithy comeback from her as she moved to the table overflowing with an array of both fresh and dried displays. But instead she gave a shudder and practically leaped back.

"Ugh! First Roxanna and now you. You do this deliber-ately to torment me. I know you do!"

She pointed dramatically at an arrangement of dried lotus pods—decorative floral elements resembling flat circles of wood a few inches across and with a pattern of holes on their surfaces. These had been spray-painted gold and were mixed with dried silver eucalyptus and some sort of tall, fluffy green-ery. I thought the display had a certain understated elegance perfect for a wedding reception. Virgie, however, had averted her gaze with a look of horror, as if John had speared a bunch of baby bunnies and stuck them in a vase.

What was threatening about a lotus pod?

John, meanwhile, gave a rather mean-spirited chuckle. "Maybe you should get some professional help for that irratio-nal fear-of-holes thing you've got going," he said, unwittingly answering my unspoken query. "So tell me, Virgie, are you just here to manhandle the exhibits, or did you stop by for a reason?"

"Oh, I always have a reason," she retorted, turning her back on the table and focusing on him. Just as John had abruptly gone from cheery to churlish, the southern belle had morphed into a battle-ax.

Uh-oh. Gonna get ugly, I told myself, and promptly scooted to the far end of my booth. How and why John and Virgie knew—and apparently disliked—each other, I couldn't guess, but I wanted no part of their dispute.

As slapping my hands over my ears and singing *la-la-la* to block out their conversation wasn't an option, I swiftly busied myself with thumbing through my binder while pretending I couldn't overhear the pair.

"Let's keep it short and sweet," the woman went on. "I received the letter from your attorney, and the answer is still no. I'm not selling you my share in the shop. So you can stop asking."

"But why not sell?" John countered, and even with my ears figuratively closed I could hear the faint tone of desperation in his words. "It's been twenty years. You've made your profit already. And you know as well as I do that the floral business isn't what it used to be. Everyone is shopping online these days. Buy me out and let's be done with it!"

"Nope," was her flippant response. Then, as I furtively glanced their way, wondering if fisticuffs were about to break out, I saw her cool smile broaden into a spiteful grin.

"Sorry, Johnny boy. If you really want the whole shop to yourself, you'll just have to outlive me."

With that final jab, she strode off in the other direction. Fortunately, at that same moment a bride and her mother rushed up to my table, which spared me from having to awkwardly pretend I'd not witnessed John and Virgie's mutual lapse into nastiness. I saw another group swoop over to chat with John about floral arrangements. By the time both of us had a moment to breathe at the same time, almost thirty minutes had passed.

I glanced over John's way. The smile he'd turned on again after Virgie's departure was flagging. Feeling a flash of sympathy. I grabbed a couple of truffles and crossed the few steps to his booth.

"You doing okay?" I asked and handed over the candy. "Here, chocolate can fix just about anything."

"Not this," was his gloomy response, though he unwrapped one of the truffles and popped it in his mouth.

"Sorry you had to overhear that little tiff," he added once he'd swallowed the sweet. "I don't usually air my dirty laundry in public like that."

"Don't worry, I don't think anyone else knew anything was going on," I assured him. Which was likely true, given the gym's questionable acoustics, along with the undercurrent of chatter from the milling attendees. "So you two are business partners?"

"Not by choice. One of the terms of our divorce settlement was that in lieu of alimony, she became an automatic partner in any business I might start."

"Divorce?" I echoed in surprise. "Sorry, I didn't realize the two of you had been married."

"For ten years," he confirmed. "Not that we were very well suited from the start. Ours was what those old Gothic romances called a *marriage of convenience*."

He gave the words air quotes, smiling a little now as he continued his explanation.

"You have to realize that this was almost forty years ago, back when Cymbeline was still small-town in every sense of the word," he said. "Virgie had no interest in being a housewife, but local society said otherwise. I hadn't found the right person myself, and being a florist, some people assumed I wasn't interested in women. Not that either of us cared what people thought, but it got irritating after a while."

I nodded. "I can imagine."

"We already were good friends from school, so we decided by getting married we could shut everyone up but still live our own separate lives. And our arrangement worked out quite well for the first few years. But then one of us decided to change the terms of our marriage."

"I know how *that* goes," was my rueful response. "My ex pretty much did the same thing. The only positive was that we didn't have any children to traumatize with custody arrangements and such. You?"

John grimly shook his head. "No. That was part of the terms."

What exactly those terms were, and which of the pair changed them, I didn't find out. Roxanna's voice abruptly came over the gym's loudspeaker, interrupting his confession.

"Good morning, brides-to-be and your bridesmaids, friends, and relatives. Welcome to the third annual fall Veils and Vanities Bridal Expo. As our greeters told you when you arrived, we'll be having contests and giveaways all day. Up first is a chance to win a custom bridal veil from Virgie's Formals. You have ten more minutes to get your wedding bingo card stamped by twelve of our exhibitors and turn it in at the front table for our drawing!"

Of course, that announcement led to ten minutes of shrieking and running as the brides rushed to get the final stamps on their cards. By the time Roxanna's disembodied voice called a halt, my stamping hand was smeared with bright-blue ink and I'd worked up a bit of a sweat. Not exactly the professional vibe I was going for.

I looked in John's direction again. A cluster of young women had remained at his booth, earnestly debating the merits of baby's breath in a twenty-first-century bridal bouquet. I caught his gaze and pantomimed with a walking-fingers gesture that I was leaving my booth for a minute. He nodded back, and so I propped up my *Back in Ten Minutes* sign, grabbed my purse, and headed across the gym and out into the hall.

A few moments later I found the restroom. I slipped past the heavy door, with its glass transom above and metal placard below proclaiming *Girls*, and entered the 1960s.

The door slammed shut behind me, and I stared about me in amazed appreciation. Black-and-white penny tiles covered the floor, and the white subway tiles on the walls were accented by a broad black-and-red zigzag that raced horizontally along the entire room. Six individual stalls took up the wall to my left, while an equal number of porcelain sinks with mirrors lined the wall to my right. Sandy from the musical *Grease* would have been right at home touching up her lipstick here.

Since I was the only one currently in the restroom, I had my choice of sinks. I scrubbed my hands with industrial liquid soap until only a faint hint of blue remained and used one of the old-fashioned air dryers, which, in the emptiness, sounded loud as a jet engine. Then, since I was already here, I figured I might as well try out the rest of the facilities.

The one drawback to all the restroom's retro vibe was a lack of decent lighting. Vintage metal fixtures hanging over the sink area gave sufficient illumination for primping, but the remaining lighting was adequate at best and a bit creepy at worst. Having seen enough horror movies in my time, I chose the very last stall, which statistically should be the safest to use.

Instead of the typical painted metal partitions with matching doors found in most public facilities, these stalls had actual tiled walls with wooden louvered doors for privacy. They were deep enough that sitting on the porcelain throne would put you several feet back from the door. Somewhat surprisingly, no juvenile graffiti marred their inner walls. Either high school girls were classier now than back in my day, or the CHS janitorial staff were sticklers for cleanliness.

That, or it was just too darned dark within the cell-like stalls to bother scribbling dirty limericks and cell phone numbers.

I hung my handbag from the sturdy hook provided and went about my business as swiftly as I could. I finished up and had opened the stall door to exit when I realized I had left my purse behind. Before I could retrieve it, I heard the main restroom door slam open. The sound of rapidly moving high heels echoed off the tile, along with a familiar outraged voice.

"You're a real piece of work, Virgie Hamilton," my friend Roxanna declared, her usual soft drawl stretched taut. "Did you really think I wouldn't find out that you grabbed all those web domains so you could redirect brides looking for me over to your website?"

"Is it my fault you weren't smart enough to buy up all the other domains of *yourspecialday* besides dot-com?" Virgie shot back. "Talk about an amateur mistake. You snooze, you lose."

I froze.

Last thing I wanted to do was overhear another verbal brawl featuring Virgie, but no way did I want to walk out right into the middle of one either. On the other hand, it would be worse to stay where I was and walk out once they were finished fighting; I didn't want a reputation as an eavesdropper. But before I could choose the lesser of the two social evils, I heard heel clicks coming my way.

"Wait," Virgie commanded as the sound of her footsteps grew nearer. "I already had one public disagreement this morning. Let's make sure this isn't another."

Darn it!

As there was no graceful way out of the situation now, I made a swift decision. The stall was dark enough to offer a bit of cover should someone take a cursory look within. I hurriedly squeezed into the gap between the wall and the louvered stall door and hoped I'd never have to explain how I came to be hiding in the downstairs girls' restroom of CHS.

Chapter Two

I held my breath as Virgie's footsteps paused in front of my stall. Given that the door opened inward, the only way Virgie could spot me would be if she walked into the stall and turned around. *Go away, go away, go away* became my sudden new mantra.

And it worked. A moment later the heel clicks started back in the other direction.

"They're all empty," I heard the woman declare as I quietly breathed again. "Okay, so let's have it out. If someone types in the wrong URL for you and ends up redirected to my site—well, too bad, so sad. I only did what any good businessperson would do."

"But not what a partner would do," the other woman shot back. "Seriously, I can't believe you'd stab me in the back like that, not after all these years. So enjoy squatting on those domains. I'll just set up a new website under a new business name and buy up the dot-biz and dot-net and dot-com and any other dot that's out there."

Even I knew that was an empty threat. Roxanna had her entire business tied up in the Your Special Day name. Rebranding her company would cost her thousands in advertising, not to mention the legal paperwork and lost business.

"I have an idea," Virgie said, and I could almost hear her purring in satisfaction. "Why don't I sell you the domains? There's, what, five of them—so, let's say ten thousand dollars for all."

"You have to be kidding! That's highway robbery. Besides, where am I supposed to get that kind of money?"

"Here's a thought, *partner*." The purr morphed into a genteel growl. "How about you start with the ten thousand bucks you skimmed off the top from our joint expo account?"

From my hiding place, I stifled a gasp. *Skimmed?* As in, illegally took? Was Virgie really accusing Roxanna of embezzlement?

"What are you talking about?" the other woman growled right back. "I didn't steal anything!"

"I have to say, you were pretty darned clever about it. It took me almost a year to realize that money was missing, and I still haven't figured out how you did it. But since we're *partners*, I'll give you a chance to make things right. Pay it back to the account, and we'll pretend none of this happened. And I'll even let you buy the domains at a reasonable price."

"Virgie, you're talking crazy. I can't pay it back because I never took any money that wasn't mine."

Roxanna's tone had taken on a hard edge, and I frowned. Although I considered her a friend, the truth was that I'd known the woman for only a few months. Still, I found myself believing her. Besides, my gut feelings about people tend to be correct.

On the other hand, why would Virgie lie about money being missing?

Unless Virgie had done the skimming and was trying to shift the blame to her partner, I answered myself. But that didn't make any sense either.

Before the argument could escalate, I heard the main restroom door slam open again. In marched what had to be at least four women, their echoing footfalls accompanied by a wave of equally noisy chatter that would have done a posse of high school girls proud.

From my hiding place, I heaved a silent sigh of relief. No way would Roxanna and Virgie continue their argument in front of paying customers. As proof of that, I heard Virgie's equally hard-edged parting comment to Roxie—"We'll talk later"—followed by more echoing footsteps and the sound of the restroom door opening again.

Had they both left?

I tried peeking through the gap but couldn't see more than a sliver of the sink area. Gambling on yes, I swiftly closed my stall door before one of the newcomers could inadvertently barge in.

I waited a respectable few moments more, using the continued commotion as cover. Then, telling myself it was now or never, I slung my purse over my shoulder and casually walked out of the stall.

Fortunately, neither Roxanna nor Virgie was still lurking about the sinks. Still, I took my time washing my hands and checking my hair and makeup before I slipped out the restroom door and into the hallway. No Roxanna or Virgie there either. Which meant that neither woman knew I'd overheard Virgie's accusations.

Which also meant that I could put the incident out of my head and enjoy the rest of the expo.

Easier said than done, I told myself, lapsing into cliché. And then I promptly proved the adage wrong when I took an alternate entry back inside the gym again and spied a booth I hadn't noticed earlier.

At first glance, the setup wasn't much to look at. On the plain white backdrop hung an equally uninspiring white sign with the words *Plus One* along with a logo that I couldn't quite make out at a distance. I couldn't tell anything about the booth's contents either, since women were gathered three and four deep in front of it. Obviously, whatever was being hawked there was popular with brides-to-be and their friends, never mind the lackluster presentation.

Curious, I walked closer and smiled as I finally made out the logo on the sign. Done in black and white, it featured a cartoonish, droopy-eared rabbit wearing a tux and top hat and leaning against a plus sign. I had to admit it was cute; still, I frowned as I noticed that something about the character looked vaguely familiar.

And then, like a scene from a romantic comedy, the crowd of women parted long enough for me to finally see the exhibitor casually posed behind the table.

Not a rabbit, I promptly realized, torn between a laugh and a groan. *A hare*. Which happened to be the favorite insignia and likely personal spirit totem of my BFF—best frenemy forever—one Harold A. Westcott III, aka Harry Westcott.

Harry saw me, too, and sent a grin and breezy wave my way. Simultaneously, a dozen pairs of suspicious female eyes whipped about in my direction to see who deserved this attention from him.

Have I mentioned that Harry is an actor? And not just a wannabe. He's had major roles in a couple of really bad made-for-cable horror movies, at least one having to do with swamp werewolves. Your basic C-lister, but not for lack of talent. Almost a month ago during Cymbeline's annual Shakespeare festival, he served as both director and lead in *Hamlet*. That production received stellar reviews from as far away as Atlanta.

Of course, the fact that one of the play's actors had been murdered in my B&B might have had something to do with the newspaper coverage received.

Unfortunately, circumstances beyond Harry's control had kept him here in Cymbeline afterward. But what any of that had to do with his presence at the expo, I couldn't guess.

As I debated whether or not to battle through his hangers-on to find out just what in the heck Harry was doing at the expo, a voice came over the gym's PA system again. This time it was Virgie.

"Good morning again, brides," she said. Her amplified tones were honeyed and reflected none of the anger or snark

I'd heard during her arguments with John and Roxanna. "It's almost time for our next giveaway. This prize is for a free week-end stay at the Cymbeline Manor Resort. If you haven't done so already, please find the pink ticket that was in your wel-come bag, take it to the stage, and deposit it in the giant wine-glass next to the pop-out wedding cake. We'll be drawing our winner in fifteen minutes."

The prospect of two free nights at what for Cymbeline passed for luxury accommodations was enough to clear the decks around Harry's booth. As the women hurried to drop off their tickets, I took the opportunity to see what he was up to this time.

I should explain that Harry and I have history. No, not that kind—there's never been anything romantic between the two of us. I first made his acquaintance remotely soon after I bought my house, when he began calling and sending fevered letters accusing me of stealing the place from him.

Not that the allegation had come totally out of left field. It turned out that Mrs. Lathrop had been Harry's great-aunt, who'd given him a verbal promise that the house would be his upon her death. Unfortunately, the old woman had died before she'd had a chance to change her will. As a result, her executor—who happened to be Harry's estranged father—had put the house up for sale without Harry's knowledge.

In the months since, Harry and I had managed a truce that culminated in a contract of sorts following the Shakespeare festival. I'd let him stay at the B&B for thirty days rent-free until he got his literal and figurative act together again. In return, he would quit pursuing any claim to Fleet House.

Harry had agreed and installed himself in my tower room, which had also been the room where he'd stayed summers as a kid when visiting his great-aunt. Actually, the arrangement had worked out rather well. If nothing else, it had been nice to have someone besides Mattie to chat with on the occasional quiet days when no guests were registered at the B&B.

But my concern now was what he was doing here at the bridal expo. I'd been talking to him about the event for a couple of weeks now—as well as about rearranging my guest schedule to be sure I'd have no one checking in or out on expo day. And never once had he mentioned that he'd paid for a booth at the same event.

"Fancy meeting you here." I greeted him with a timeworn idiom. "If you'd told me you were taking part, we could have ridden in together."

"It was a last-minute decision, so I didn't think it was worth mentioning," he replied with a noncommittal shrug.

Which in Harry-speak probably meant there was something just a bit shady about the situation. But since that would be Virgie and Roxanna's problem, I let that pass and instead gave a nod toward the sign. "So what's this, some sort of spin-off of your tour company?"

One of his non-acting gigs was Wild Hare Tours. Harry—the aforementioned "hare"—served as guide and official driver to various offbeat destinations around the state. At my insistence (backed by Cymbeline's code enforcement department), his half-scale tour bus, a school district reject repainted with a similar cartoon bunny logo, was parked for the duration at the Heavenly Host Baptist Church a few miles away.

Harry shook his head. "A whole new venture. Welcome to Plus One," he said, and handed me a surprisingly expensive-looking flyer.

Can't get a date for your sister's wedding? Dread showing up to the next family picnic minus a boyfriend? Need someone to cheer you on at that awards banquet? What you need is a professional Plus One. Hire an award-winning actor to play the role of your date, colleague, or BFF at your next event. Choose whichever Plus One persona best suits your needs:

Suave Man of the World
Brainy yet Handsome Nerd
Former Pro Athlete
Successful Businessman

Or work with your Plus One associate to create a custom character. Hourly rates, will travel. Go to our website for details.

The URL was at the bottom of the page, followed by a disclaimer in bold print: *Your Plus One's services are limited to public appearances only.*

By the time I'd finished reading his flyer a second time, my mouth was hanging open in disbelief. I sputtered wordlessly for a few moments and then finally burst out, "Y-You're a male escort!"

Which would explain why he'd neglected to mention the whole expo thing to me before.

Meanwhile, Harry gave me a disapproving look.

"Really, Nina. Escort sounds so . . . smarmy. I prefer *professional companion*. Or perhaps *hired associate*. Or even *compensated colleague*. And for your information, people are clamoring for this service. I've already booked an event for tomorrow afternoon. Now, would you like to review my portfolio of suggested personae?"

As I've previously said, it wasn't a lack of talent that had kept Harry from greater things in the acting world. Neither was it his appearance. Because the man looks like what my mom back in Texas would call a matinee idol.

We're talking thick hair so dark it's almost black and artfully razored so it has a tendency to fall gracefully across his tanned brow. Combine that with features that are neither too sensitive nor too craggy and eyes so blue you'd swear he was wearing colored contacts and you have definite leading-man material. He's a couple of years younger than me, which means he has at least another decade before he makes the transition from hottie to distinguished. It also helps that he stands six feet tall and hits the gym just often enough to look good in a tight T-shirt and snug jeans. He was wearing a pair of the latter now, along with one of his favorite nubby-textured,

untucked linen shirts in deep forest green. His was a decep-
tively casual look, made more so by the eighties-throwback
stubble on his chin and cheeks.

Harry, meanwhile, had flipped open a thick white binder
similar to the one on my booth's table. But rather than featuring photos of guest rooms and flowers, this one was filled with
professional head shots as well as what appeared to be candid
set photos from his various films.

"As you can see, we have all manner of looks for your Plus
One for you to choose from." He began his spiel as he turned
the pages. "Here is our Successful Businessman, if you'd like
to impress a certain someone who thinks he's an investment
genius. And the PhD who plays first base for an amateur soft-
ball team on the weekends—this one is perfect to stick it to a
boss who lies about having an MBA. Oh, and the ever-popular
Boy Next Door to bring to your grandmother's birthday party.
Of course, each character has his own backstory, which we
can customize for our clients."

"We? Our?" I echoed, looking around. "Is that in the Sybil
sense"—referring, of course, to the famous psychiatric case of
supposed multiple personalities—"or is someone else in on
this besides you?"

"Actually, it's the royal *we*. One of our characters is a distant relative of the Windsors," he coolly replied, turning
another page. "But I must say that this one is my favorite. I
call it the Retired Secret Agent."

I suppressed a smile. This version of Harry did look like
something out of a James Bond movie. He was wearing a

perfectly fitted tux, hand casually tucked in a pocket and hair slicked back, sternly gazing away from the camera as if contemplating how best to deal with the latest crop of supervillains.

My smile broadened. "I have to say that I agree with you. In fact, if I ever attend another wedding, this is the guy I'd want to bring with me."

"Let me know next time an invite comes around, and I'm there. I'll even give you the friend rate."

"Oh, okay, sure."

Abruptly discombobulated, as—despite the reference to friends and discounts—his offer had sounded uncomfortably like a date, I hurried to regroup.

"So, why are you doing this Plus One thing, anyhow? You've got the tour company already. And shouldn't your agent have something new for you by now?"

"You should know the reason better than anyone else," he replied.

Dropping the sales pitch, Harry flopped gracefully into his chair behind the table. I noticed that he didn't have one of those ubiquitous candy bowls. Apparently, truffles weren't necessary when the exhibitor himself was eye candy.

His gloomy expression as he stared back at me now only made him look more attractive, assuming one went for the moody "Twilight" sort of male.

"Our thirty-days'-free-rent agreement is almost up," he reminded me, "and I'm still too broke to fill up the bus for the trip back to Atlanta. And no way can I scrape up enough for first and last for a new apartment there. I've done exactly one tour in the past month, and that went to pay my current bills. I talked to my agent yesterday, and the situation hasn't changed. No one's willing to touch me right now because of that whole thing with my series."

That "thing," I knew, not being Harry's fault.

Apparently the director of *John Cover, Undercover*—which new cable series Harry had been confident would be his break-through role—had been accused of sexual harassment by some of the female crew as work on the first season ended. At least one lawsuit had ensued, prompting the production company to yank the show before it ever aired. And, as Harry had the starring role, even though he'd not been accused of anything inappropriate, he was still suffering the fallout.

"Hang in there," I awkwardly reassured him, not able to think of any better platitudes. "Another scandal is bound to happen before too much longer, and the powers that be will all forget all about you."

"That's what I'm afraid of."

It didn't take binoculars to see that the gloominess was rapidly morphing into full-blown self-pity, Much as I wanted to help, I wasn't being paid by the hour to serve as Harry's therapist. So I did the next best thing.

"Harry, about that moving-out deadline," I began, hoping I wasn't going to regret what I was about to offer, "let's just say it was merely a suggestion. If you need more time to save enough rent money for your own place, you can stay a while longer."

"Really?"

He perked up at that. Straightening in his chair, he put a hand over his heart and gave me the old matinee-idol smile. "You're a lifesaver, Nina Fleet. I promise I won't abuse your hospitality for any longer than I have to."

"I'll hold you to that."

My reply was a bit more stern than necessary, but only because it had hit me that I was actually glad he was staying. Which was not at all the reaction I'd expected of myself. But I didn't have time to dwell on that now, especially as it had also occurred to me that I'd been away from my own booth for far too long.

"All right, gotta go now," I told him. "Otherwise the guy in the booth next to mine is going to think someone kidnapped me. Maybe I'll see you at the fashion show after lunch."

I'd meant that last as something of a joke, but to my surprise, Harry nodded. "Wouldn't miss it for the world. If you get there first, save me a seat. I'll do the same for you."

By now, the expo attendees were making their way back to the vendor area, having dropped off their tickets for the drawing. I left Harry talking to a pink-haired middle-aged woman who had swooped in the moment I turned away. Smiling, I started back to my own booth. If the fashion show proved boring, I could entertain myself by imagining scenarios between Harry's various Plus One characters and random members of the audience.

I had a couple of brides-to-be waiting at my table. I hastily apologized for having stepped away and, plying both women with truffles, pitched them on the benefits of choosing Fleet House over any other B&B in Cymbeline.

What was left of the morning passed speedily. Even lunch, a tasty-enough boxed sandwich meal eaten in bites between conversing with potential guests, was a hurried affair. During a momentary lull, I ducked as low as I could behind my table to finish my final bite of dessert—a white-iced petit four with a piped yellow rose on top—only to look up and see Roxanna standing at my booth.

By design or accident, she was wearing a reversal of Virgie's outfit, hers a dark-blue skirted suit with a pale-blue silk top. Her ensemble was topped by a striking purple-and-blue scarf, its tiny circle pattern reminding me of the lotus pods Virgie had so disliked. The length of silk hung around her neck and was tucked loosely under either lapel rather like a religious stole.

Her bright-pink lips stretched in a genuine if weary-looking smile.

"So, how's it going? Are you getting lots of prospects?" she asked, and held out her arms for a friendly embrace.

I hopped out from behind my table to give her a quick hug. "So far, so good, for a first timer. I have to say, I'm really glad you talked me into taking part."

While the sentiment was true, my smile was forced, awkward as I suddenly found myself feeling in her presence. *She doesn't know you eavesdropped on her argument with Virgie*, I reminded myself. But even with that self-reassurance, it was hard to meet her gaze.

Roxanna must have noticed something was up, for she asked, "Nina, is everything okay? You look distracted."

"No worries. Everything's fine," I lied.

She nodded. "Sorry, I guess it's just me. I had a little confrontation with Virgie earlier, and I'm still upset."

"Oh no, that's too bad. Would it help to talk about it?"

If she recounted their argument, then I'd have a legitimate reason to know about it and could face her without feeling guilty. Unfortunately, it seemed Roxanna shared John's reluctance to air unclean washing in public. She shook her head.

"It's just a business disagreement. We'll work it out."

Then her smile slipped. Lowering her voice, she glanced either way and leaned closer to add, "Seriously, sometimes I'd just like to strangle that woman."

"I think they put you in jail for that sort of thing," I told her with a wry smile as I resumed my seat. "Working things out is probably the better strategy."

"Well, all I can say is that before she starts accusing me of dirty deeds, she'd better clean up her own house." With those cryptic words, she glanced at her watch and then pulled back on another smile. "Gotta go. The fashion show starts in about an hour. Be sure you take a break and watch at least a little bit of it. We've got a lot of surprises planned."

"I will. Can't wait," I promised, though she had already scurried off before I'd finished the words.

I spent the next half hour chatting with a bride and her mom who were considering an outdoor wedding the following

April. Once they'd wandered off with one of my brochures in hand, I saw that it was almost one thirty. And according to the expo schedule, that was when the show would start.

Sure enough, Virgie's voice came over the PA system again.

"Attention, brides and friends and family. Our Veils and Vanities fashion show will begin in just a bit. If you've not already taken a seat at the expo stage, I suggest you do so quickly. You won't want to miss this collection of fabulous bridal and wedding fashions coming from Atlanta, New York, and even London!"

That was my cue to pull out my *Back in Ten Minutes* sign again and gather my phone and purse. The other nearby exhibitors seemed to have the same idea. In fact, John had already left his booth, though in his case I doubted he was headed for the fashion show. More likely he was taking a well-deserved break.

The seating area around the stage was already almost full by the time I'd walked to the other side of the gymnasium. The stage was empty now too, the multilayer faux cake gone and leaving only the curtained backdrop.

With most of the expo attendees gathered in one spot, the noise level from the accompanying excited chatter had risen significantly, amplified by the gym's uneven acoustics. Not surprisingly, the seats closest to the runway were already filled on either side. Remembering my promise to Harry, I found two empty chairs together not far from the action. I hurriedly plopped into one seat and stuck my bag on the other. Then, hoping it wouldn't prove too awkward to watch a parade of bridal gowns while sitting alongside arguably the most eligible bachelor in the place—especially in my current unsettled state—I glanced about the crowd for him.

Chapter Three

As Harry was taller than most of the predominantly female throng, I spied him almost immediately. He was surrounded by a small knot of teenage girls who'd apparently appointed themselves his personal posse. I knew that, on the one hand, Harry adored the attention, but on the other, a crowd of hangers-on could become a major annoyance. And given the demographic of said posse, I figured things had already reached the aggravation point.

Allowing myself a grin at his predicament, I stood and waved.

"Harry, over here," I called, doing my best to be heard over the babble of conversation.

He caught sight of me and nodded. I saw him say something to the teens, and then he started in my direction.

"You're welcome for the rescue," I told Harry a few moments later as he took the seat next to me. "I was afraid I was going to have to run over there and pry you away from your new friends."

He gave an airy wave. "They were glad to let me leave once I explained the situation. If anyone asks, you're my spinster cousin here to experience planning a wedding vicariously, since chances are you'll never walk up the aisle yourself."

"Thanks." I shot him a sour look. "You know darned well I've been married before. You even worked with Cam once."

Yes, my ex-husband is *the* Cameron Fleet, rising star on the professional golf tour circuit and current media darling. And small world that it is, it had turned out that several months before Harry and I met, he had been hired for an allergy medicine commercial featuring Cam.

Things had not gone well. Apparently, after a few takes, good old Cam had managed to get Harry booted off the shoot. Probably for being too good-looking, I had privately decided when Harry related the story, knowing how my ex hated to share the spotlight.

But that was last year. Now, and to mix sports metaphors, Harry tossed me a curve ball. "Speaking of your ex-husband, I meant to ask you how you were handling it."

"Handling what?"

"You know, his big announcement."

Announcement? The pro golf tour had ended in August, giving us civilians a respite from televised tournaments. Frankly, I'd deliberately avoided keeping track of Cam's standing on the leaderboards, though I knew he had won a couple of tour events early in the season. And so I shrugged and shook my head. "Guess I'm going to need a few more hints."

"It was all over the sports section the other day," he replied. "I even saw a couple of stories online about it this morning. Apparently, everyone's favorite professional golfer is engaged to be married."

"Cam is engaged?"

I wasn't sure which shocked me more: the news that my ex-husband was tying the knot again or the fact that Harry actually perused the sports page. Ignoring the latter revelation, I concentrated on the first bombshell.

"Engaged?" I repeated, struggling to keep my tone even. "When? To whom?"

"Yes. Just this week. Some female sportscaster." He answered my questions in quick succession. "And that's the extent of my knowledge. Anything else and you're going to have to pick up a newspaper yourself."

Still, his expression was sympathetic as he added, "I really did think you already knew. Are you okay?"

"Yeah, sure. Just give me a minute to get used to it."

Though, of course, I would need more than sixty seconds to merely digest the news. Accepting it would take even longer. To be honest, it felt like someone had socked me in the gut. It wasn't that I still loved the man, but we *had* been married for almost twenty years. And though we'd parted on less-than-friendly terms, on some level a connection remained between us.

Which had to be why a little voice inside me was suddenly crying, *How could he love anyone besides me-e-e-e!*

I summoned a smile. "Really, I'm fine. And I have to say, I'm not surprised, now that I've had a moment. Cam's the type of man who needs a woman hanging around. That was pretty much the reason we got divorced—all those extra women."

Harry smiled back. "If it helps, I think Cameron Fleet was an idiot for not being satisfied with the woman he already had."

I waited to see if a punch line would follow, but he sounded sincere. Feeling warmed by the compliment, I replied with equal sincerity. "Thanks. That helps."

And then, because I still hadn't reached the acceptance stage, I added, "You know, maybe I'll skip the fashion show after all."

"Are you sure? I think you might find it more entertaining than you expect."

As if on cue, the overhead lights dimmed, while a series of small white spotlights illuminated the stage and catwalk. The chattering crowd promptly settled itself into relative silence. And then over the PA system came a familiar male voice.

"Welcome, brides-to-be, relatives, and friends, to the third annual fall Veils and Vanities bridal fashion show!"

I whipped about to stare at Harry.

"That's you!" I exclaimed as the crowd broke into applause. Or rather, it was the announcer-guy version of him. The recorded voice was a little more theatrical, a little deeper than the actor's everyday, only-slightly-Georgia-accented tones.

The real-life Harry gave me a smug smile. "What can I say? Virgie offered me a free booth if I'd do their voice-overs for the fashion show. Her son, Jason, has a recording studio on the other side of town."

I raised my brows a little at this new tidbit of gossip. John had told me previously that he had no children, so this Jason had to be the product of a second marriage for Virgie.

"He's the one handling the lights and sound for the expo too," Harry continued. "Now, sit back and enjoy the show."

The disembodied Harry voice went on to recognize Virgie and Roxanna and to acknowledge various sponsors, along with the high school administrators and staff. I sighed and settled back into my seat. While I wasn't in the mood to ogle wedding dresses, it might be amusing to listen to Harry's description of same.

The show began with the sound of eighties-era pop, starting with Madonna and morphing into Michael Jackson with a little segue into Rick Springfield. The women who strutted out one after the other from behind the curtain and onto the catwalk were old enough to have listened to that music when it was first released. I already knew from the expo promo material that the models were not professionals but volunteers from the Cymbeline Chamber of Commerce.

All were wearing mother-of-the-bride (or mother-of-the-groom) dresses. Roxanna had chosen women of various sizes and ethnicities to show off the dresses, which ranged in style from cocktail length to actual ball gowns. While they strolled, the disembodied Harry voice named styles and colors, reminding the audience that all the dresses were available from Virgie's Formals.

I joined the applause as the last model, with a saucy bounce of her size-sixteen hips, whipped back behind the curtain.

"Don't go anywhere," Harry beside me murmured as the music switched over to hip-hop. "The bridesmaid dresses are next, and there are a few doozies."

And a couple *were* the dreaded stereotypical bridesmaid gowns with puffy sleeves and ruffles and in various sherbet hues. Most of the dresses, however, were modern and sleek and something that could actually be worn to another event later. Modeled by a group of young women who, per Harry's next prerecorded introduction, were CHS students, they ranged from a sweet, slip-like creation in baby-pink satin to a Goth floor-length number in black-and-red lace.

I saw in surprised approval that one of the teen models was Daniel and Gemma Tanaka's daughter, Jasmine. She came out wearing a knee-length silk sheath the same bronze shade as her riot of shoulder-length curls, the dress topped with a dark-green lace shrug. From the applause that greeted her appearance, I wasn't the only one who thought she looked stunning.

"Wedding gowns up next," Harry warned me once all the teens had exited back through the stage curtain to even more clapping. "You going to be okay with that?"

"Yeah, I think so. If nothing else, I'll enjoy the music," I added as Adele's distinctive, emotional vocals came over the PA system.

Harry's prerecorded patter for this collection differed from the earlier scripts. The other dresses had cycled down the catwalk at a swift pace. The bridal gowns, however, each received a more leisurely stroll, so that the entire audience had time to ooh and aah over every bit of lace and beading.

And the first couple of dresses were indeed lovely, being traditional gowns with plenty of lace and pearls and long satin trains. But by the time the third model had made her way around the catwalk and Adele had been replaced by Lady Gaga, I'd reached my limit.

"Sorry, Harry," I said, leaning closer so he could hear me over the applause. "I don't think I can take any more brides right now. I'm going to get a little fresh air."

"Understood," he replied. "There's another eight or nine dresses to go, so probably another fifteen minutes left in the show. But you might want to come back for the finale. Virgie and Roxanna have some sort of dramatic finish planned with that big cake. They wouldn't tell me exactly what it was, but I gathered it was some sort of floral 'four-and-twenty blackbirds' kind of thing. You know, roses or something spilling out all over the place."

Not sure I was in the mood for nursery rhymes either, I shrugged. "I'll think about it. See you later."

I stood and made my way as unobtrusively as I could over to the exhibitors' side of the gym. Not that there was any way to escape the cheers and clapping from the crowd, or Harry's fashion narration over the music. But the physical separation helped. And I could see as I wended my way through the booths that I wasn't the only one who'd opted out of the show.

The tattooed bleached blonde whose sign advertised *Nails by Norma* was chugging down a canned energy drink while frantically knitting something very long and spider-webby in fluffy black yarn. A few booths from her, Duwane Douglass, the baby-faced African American guy who owned Douglass Photography, was kicked back in his chair indulging in a power nap. And the next row over in the Travel Exotica booth, a gray-haired woman wearing oversized eyeglasses was hunched over her laptop playing what sounded like an alien warfare computer game.

I left the gym and headed down the hall to the main exit door. The temperature outside had to be almost eighty despite the fact that it was late September. Still, it was breezy enough out and, save for the traffic sounds from the nearby two-lane highway, relatively quiet after the relentless hubbub of the expo.

I slumped onto a short concrete wall near the handicap ramp and let out a sigh.

Cam was getting married again. Logically, I knew I shouldn't care, should have expected he would move on at some point. Divorcing the man had been my smartest move in years, and I didn't regret it. Yet still I sat here wallowing in self-pity and feeling like the only girl in school who hadn't been asked to the senior prom.

"You okay, Nina?" came a familiar voice beside me a few long moments later.

I looked over to see my friend Gemma Tanaka. She must have come straight from the diner, as she was dressed in khaki slacks topped by a navy Peaches and Java T-shirt that had a couple of stray flour streaks decorating one sleeve. No doubt she'd come to pick up Jasmine from the show.

For the moment, however, she was giving me a worried frown.

"Really, Nina, is something wrong? You look like you just lost your best friend."

"I kind of did. I just found out that my ex-husband is getting remarried."

"Ah."

Gemma gave a sober nod, her salt-and-pepper locks softly bouncing. "Yes, I saw that in the papers. I figured you already knew. Sorry, I guess it's a little hard, especially when he's engaged to someone like Rue McFadden."

Rue McFadden?

I stared at Gemma in stunned surprise. Harry had said something about Cam's new fiancée being a sportscaster, though at the time it hadn't clicked. But even I knew who Rue was.

Tall, blonde, and at least ten years younger than me, Rue McFadden possessed the enhanced lips and boobs that were practically de rigueur for every media female. A fixture on one of the major networks, she had gone from token female interviewer to broadcasting celebrity within months of her first appearance. Currently, she was as famous for her TikTok videos showing her yukking it up with various male athletes as she was for her actual on-air work. Why she'd decided to settle down now, and with Cam especially, I couldn't guess.

Gemma, meanwhile, was pointedly glancing at her watch. "Sorry, Nina, I don't mean to be unsympathetic, but I've gotta go. I couldn't break away from the lunch rush before now, and I'd really like to see Jasmine all dressed up if it's not too late. She's supposed to be in the fashion show finale."

"Right, the big cake finish." Nodding, I jumped down from my wall seat. "I'll go with you. I've only been out here for a couple of minutes, so that should mean there's still time before the final dress is modeled."

We hurried back inside. Faint music from the fashion show greeted us as we headed down the hall toward the gym's double doors. As we reached that entry, I noticed at the far end of the hallway a tall male figure wearing a purple shirt.

John Klingel?

He was too distant for me to be certain, particularly since I couldn't see his face. But if it was indeed the florist wandering the halls, then he was violating our exhibitor agreement. The waiver we'd all signed had explicitly stated that, save for the gym and accompanying restrooms, the school was off-limits to everyone except district employees.

By now the man had disappeared down a side hall. Figuring it was none of my business either way, I promptly forgot about him as Gemma pulled open the gym door and we headed inside toward the stage area.

The audience had grown even in the few minutes I'd been gone, so that the only seats remaining were far to the side and back. I glanced over to where I'd been sitting earlier and was relieved to see that none of Harry's posse had claimed my empty spot.

"There," I told Gemma as I pointed in that direction. "Why don't you go sit next to Harry so you have a better view. I'll grab a chair somewhere here."

Gemma nodded her thanks and hurried that way. I found a seat near the back next to a glasses-wearing brunette about my age with a preteen girl who was practically her mini-me. Each wore the same black-framed plastic glasses and had the same mousy hair in a tight bun, and both were wearing jeans and a lightweight sweater set—the mom's beige and the daughter's pink. We gave each other a smiling nod of acknowledgment and then settled back again to watch the rest of the show.

The wedding dress styles had apparently grown more modern as the show progressed. A dramatic number in black lace was just now leaving the stage, replaced by a pair of models wearing more gender-neutral garb—one a trendy skirted tuxedo in white satin, the other a traditional black tuxedo, the trousers and jacket cut for a female figure. While Katy Perry's "I Kissed a Girl" played, the two women linked arms and paraded down the catwalk. I heard a few surprised murmurs around me, but judging by the applause, the younger audience seemed to approve the unconventional attire.

Once the couple left the stage, Tina Turner took over the PA. While the music icon belted out the age-old question about what love had to do anything, another of Harry's prerecorded spiels began. This one described a gown as "our final offering today, straight from London's Mount Street fashion district."

A willowy red-haired model came through the parted stage curtains. Her gown was an ankle-length, off-the-shoulder number in white silk with a plunging back and beaded mermaid hem that shimmered with every movement. As the model stepped and turned and stepped again along the catwalk, I joined in the applause. Given the opportunity to wear a dress like that, I told myself, I might consider getting married a second time.

Once the model finally left the stage, Harry's voice came back over the PA system. "Brides, friends, and relatives, we'd like to end our fashion show with a new trend for wedding receptions. Forget the ice sculptures and chocolate fountains and food boards. Why not surprise your guests with something even more fun?"

A fast-paced smooth jazz piece began to play as the stage curtain pulled open and the oversized faux wedding cake that had been on display earlier came rolling out. It was guided by Jasmine, still in her pretty bronze bridesmaid dress. Her partner was Ms. Saucy Hips, whom I finally recognized as the perky but definitely middle-aged Polly Hauer of PLH Mortgage. I glanced over to where Harry and Gemma sat. The latter waved excitedly to her daughter as Jasmine and Polly rolled the cake across the stage to enthusiastic applause from the audience.

They halted not far from the catwalk. While Jasmine stepped back a few paces, Polly fumbled with the cake's top layer. A moment later, a fountain of golden sparks erupted like something from the Fourth of July. The audience gasped and then oohed when Polly reached a hand into the sparks, demonstrating that the seeming pyrotechnics didn't burn like genuine fireworks. Jasmine, meanwhile, bent and did something behind the cake that promptly sent a cascade of pink LED lights chasing around the cake's tiers, drawing even more applause.

Smiling, Jasmine and Polly let the cake do its acrobatics for a few more moments. Then, looking like the letter turner on a television game show, Jasmine gave the old *voilà* gesture with one hand while Polly stepped forward again.

By now the fountain of sparks atop the cake had burned itself off. And with that, Polly smiled and tugged the top layer upward.

At least, that's what she attempted to do. Even from my distant seat I could see that the cake lid appeared stuck. Her smile broadening into a show of gritted teeth, Polly gave it another try. Jasmine jumped in to help, while someone in the audience began a rhythmic clap of encouragement that several others swiftly picked up.

Just when I feared they'd have to give up the effort, the top cake layer went flying backward on its hinges, hanging behind the main cake like an empty hatbox. As for the rest of the faux cake structure, it apparently was hinged from the back, for it abruptly split open like an apple that had been cleaved from top to bottom.

For a confused instant, all I registered was the fact that someone had tumbled out of the cake and sprawled faceup on the catwalk. *A stripper?* For a bachelor party, maybe—but that didn't make sense for a wedding reception. And hadn't Harry said something about flowers?

The momentary ripple of surprised laughter that had accompanied the woman's unexpected appearance faded to silence as she lay there unmoving. I half rose in my chair, focused now on the fact that the figure was a blonde dressed in a dark-blue suited skirt. Even from where I was, I could see the long strip of purple-and-blue cloth wrapped high around her throat.

"Roxanna!" I gasped out.

I doubted anyone heard me, however, for at the same instant Polly shrieked, "She . . . she's dead!"

And with that, Jasmine slapped her hands to her cheeks in an unconscious parody of that iconic scene from *Home Alone* and began to scream.

Chapter Four

The gymnasium promptly exploded into answering shrieks. The sound echoed despite the damping effects of curtains and booths, so that the atmosphere was like that of the final seconds in a home championship basketball game. Except that rather than standing and clapping, a good half of the spectators sent chairs tumbling as they rushed away in panic from the stage. The remainder stood where they were, some climbing on their seats for a better look. For my part, I started pushing forward through the melee, intent on reaching Roxanna.

"Wait!"

The glasses-wearing brunette who'd been sitting beside me grabbed my arm and gave it a shake. Shorter and thinner than me, she was a heck of a lot stronger than she appeared.

"I'm a doctor," she said over the hubbub. "What's your name?"

"Nina Fleet," I managed to choke out through the rush of adrenaline now surging through me.

The woman nodded, grip tightening. "Nina, look at me. I need you to stop and pull out your phone and dial nine-one-one while I go help that woman. Can you do that?"

I nodded back, understanding. I'd read once that, in an emergency, everyone yells about calling for help but no one actually does, because they assume someone else is already making the call. So one person has to be officially delegated to carry out the task. Apparently, today that someone was me.

"Calling right now," I assured her.

I was already punching in numbers as the woman dug out her car keys from her purse. She shoved the key ring into her daughter's waiting hands. "Buddy, go get my bag from the car, stat!"

Buddy appeared remarkably self-possessed in the midst of this crisis for a girl no more than twelve years old. She nodded.

"On it, Mom," she snapped back, and turned and ran.

Meanwhile, the police dispatcher was answering my call with the usual "Nine-one-one, what's your emergency?"

Barely had I gotten out the words "Cymbeline High School" when she cut me short.

"Thank you, ma'am, we've already been advised of the situation. We have paramedics on the way."

Shoving my phone back in my pocket, I hurried through what remained of the crowd, dodging tumbled chairs as I made my way toward the stage. I could see that Gemma—a former ER nurse—had already rushed forward and, after a quick word of encouragement to Jasmine, climbed onto the catwalk to help. The short brunette reached the stage a few steps ahead of me.

"I'm a doctor. Clear away, folks," she barked at a cluster of young women who hadn't fled but were leaning in eagerly for a look. Glancing over at me, she snapped, "Paramedics called?"

"On the way."

She nodded. Then, with a sharp look at Gemma, who'd already started checking vitals, she clipped out, "Nurse?"

"Ex."

"Perfect. I'll take over here while we wait on the paramedics. You take care of the woman who's about to faint."

She gestured toward the rear of the stage, where Virgie had burst through the curtained backdrop a moment earlier. Now, with a shriek, the older woman teetered dramatically on her high heels. Before Gemma could reach her, she went limp and would have hit the stage floor had Harry not suddenly leaped onto the platform and caught her.

Buddy, meanwhile, had made her way back inside the gym. Still huffing and puffing from what obviously had been a double-time sprint, she reached the stage hauling a medical bag almost as large as she.

Her mother gave her a swift smile and took the satchel from her.

"Good job. Now, you and this woman—Nina, wasn't it?—go see what you can do to calm those two down," she hurriedly instructed, pointing toward a weeping Jasmine and Polly. "And you, sir"—she stabbed a finger at Harry, who'd laid Virgie down and stepped back to let Gemma do her thing—"you keep all these looky-loos back and out of the way."

While the doctor began chest compressions, we all leaped to our assignments. Harry assumed what must have been his ex-military persona and cleared the immediate area of spectators. Buddy jumped up and took a sobbing Jasmine's hand. I climbed onto the stage and threw an arm around a shaking Polly.

Trying not to break down myself, I helped her off the platform and settled her on a chair so that the cake blocked her view of the catwalk. Not that it mattered, for she had squinted her eyes shut as she repeated, "So terrible, so terrible." I could only agree; still, I did my best to come up with some sort of reassurances.

"I'm sure she's only fainted. The doctor will bring her around, you'll see."

But even as I said it, I was pretty certain Roxanna would require miraculous intervention from someone much farther up the chain than a mere doctor. I'd gotten a good look at her when I'd reached the stage. The color had leached from her face, leaving her already-pale features almost white, while the stillness of her tangled limbs had been profound. Whatever stunt she had planned for the finale had obviously gone terribly wrong.

Needing better news, I glanced over at Virgie. Gemma had removed the woman's stiletto shoes and propped her legs on a couple of pillows that someone must have left behind in the audience. Virgie, at least, seemed to be reviving, because I heard her moan and saw her lift a weak arm. Then I looked for Jasmine.

She and Buddy were sitting on the edge of the stage, tightly holding hands. Jasmine seemed to be agreeing with something the younger girl was saying. I gave the pair a mental nod of approval. With Gemma having been a nurse, Jasmine would know the "hold it together while Mom helps" drill almost as well as Buddy. Despite her shock, the teen had rallied sufficiently after those first moments not to need one of the adults looking after her.

"Paramedics are here!" I heard Harry abruptly call.

The next few minutes were a blur of activity, with the EMT team rushing in and taking over for the doctor and Gemma. Three of the local sheriff department's deputies followed almost immediately, slowly moving the rest of us from the stage area and over to the vendor booths. Which made sense, I reasoned, as the situation had become an accident investigation.

Because my booth had both chairs and truffles, I herded Jasmine and Buddy in that direction. Harry escorted Polly over to John's booth next to me and got her seated. But where was the florist? Surely he'd heard all the commotion. I couldn't imagine that he'd abandon his booth.

On the other hand, maybe that had been the smarter move. From what I gathered, the few dozen brides and friends and exhibitors who hadn't rushed out of the building in the beginning were now on lockdown. More specifically, we'd been asked to do a variation on the old "shelter in place" until we'd been talked to by a deputy. But that wasn't sitting well with the pink-haired woman I'd earlier seen with Harry. After a few minutes of impatient toe tapping near my booth, she marched over to one of the deputies, who had just finished interviewing the alien-battle woman and was coming our way.

"Officer, I didn't see anything. Can't I just go home?" I heard her demand as they both halted in front of the florist booth.

The deputy shook his bald head. "Not yet, ma'am. We need to record everyone's name and contact information first. I was just about to talk to this gentleman here"—he nodded in Harry's direction—"and then I'll take your information next."

Tall and broad and dressed in a crisp tan uniform shirt and dark-brown trousers and tie, the African American officer was one of the same LEOs I'd dealt with as an unwitting bystander to a murder several months earlier. Deputy Jackson was his name, I recalled after a moment. The fact that he and his colleagues were assembling what seemed like a witness list wasn't a good sign. Neither was the fact that the paramedics hadn't loaded up Roxanna and rushed her to the hospital.

Pink Lady harrumphed her impatience but stuck around. Meanwhile, Buddy, who was sitting next to Jasmine with elbows on the table and fists to her cheeks, voiced my fear aloud.

"You know they don't take the person away—at least not right away—if they're already dead, don't you?" she informed me, eyes unblinking behind her glasses.

Before I could make a reply, Jasmine heatedly countered, "Don't say that! Ms. Roxanna is going to be fine. Right, Ms. Nina?"

Both girls whipped their gazes to me, looking for a ruling. I hesitated, then told the best truth I could.

"I don't know. Maybe they're trying to stabilize her before they take her to Cymbeline General and that's why it's taking so long. All I do know is it won't do us much good sitting here and guessing. Let's talk about something else."

Then, when neither girl responded, I continued, "Okay, I'll go first. Jasmine, that dress you're wearing is gorgeous. How did you get to be one of the fashion show models?"

"Ms. Virgie knows my mom. She called and asked if I'd do it. She said she wanted some *fresh faces*." Jasmine rolled her eyes a bit as she quoted the older woman, but I could tell she was pleased to have been asked. "Ms. Virgie even said that as payment for modeling, I could buy the dress for half off if I wanted to. I'm thinking about getting it for the winter dance."

"My mom said they were too cheap to pay for real models," Buddy interjected, straightening in her chair and kicking her sneakered feet against the table's white cloth. "That's why they asked you. Who wants to get all dressed up and go to weddings and dances anyhow? It's dumb."

Jasmine and I exchanged looks, though I wasn't surprised at such a response. After all, the younger girl's hairstyle and wardrobe were those of a forty-year-old woman. I answered, "It's okay to be smart and also to be pretty too. Besides, you'll be wearing a fancy dress at your mom's wedding, won't you?"

"Nope, she's not getting married."

Jasmine frowned. "She's not? Then why did you come to a bridal expo?"

" 'Cause Mom says sometimes we should do girly stuff together so that I can be *well-rounded*," the girl explained, and I heard her mother's voice in those last two words. "I didn't really want to come, but it's been okay. Except for the part where the lady fell out of the cake."

Great. Back to the subject we were trying to avoid. Hastily I said, "Buddy, your nickname is really cute. What's it short for?"

"Ooh, I can guess," Jasmine broke in before the girl could answer. "Bernadette."

"Nope!"

"How about Brenda?" I asked.

Buddy shook her head. "Still nope."

Jasmine shrugged. "Bethany. Bonnie. Barbara," she said in quick succession, getting a headshake each time. Then, with a sly grin, she added, "Bertha?"

"Bertha!" Buddy gave the older girl an appalled look. "Do you think I'm a grandma or something?"

I grinned back at Jasmine, then addressed the younger girl. "I guess we're both pretty bad at guessing. Why don't you tell us?"

"Fine, it's Roberta. That's an old-lady name too. Mom told me once that Buddy is a nickname for Robert. I hate being called Roberta, so when I was little I decided to change my name to Buddy even though I'm a girl. My mom said I am an autonomous being and can call myself whatever I want, so I did."

Autonomous being? Jasmine mouthed at me. I gave her a little headshake to warn her, *Let it go.*

But Buddy seemed to have already lost interest in the subject of her name and instead was now flipping through my binder of B&B photos. After a few moments, she stopped on one page and gasped. "Is that your dog?"

"That's Matilda," I told her, smiling. "She's an Australian Shepherd. *Her* nickname is Mattie."

"She's beautiful," Buddy said with a sigh. "All those colors. Black and gray and white and even brown. I always wanted a dog, but Mom won't let me have one. Is Mattie fierce? She looks it."

"No, not fierce," I assured the girl, "but she is a good protection dog."

In fact, in recent months the clever canine had helped solve a couple of murders, but I wasn't going to explain all that to Buddy.

Instead, I went on, "Her coat color is called blue merle. And you probably can't tell from the pictures, but like lots of Aussies, she has two-different-colored eyes. One is blue and one is brown."

"Wow!"

"That's called heterochromia," Jasmine interjected, sounding just a bit smug for being able to share that factoid.

Buddy, however, was less than impressed. "Everyone knows that. But I bet you don't know what they call those cats that have six toes," she said. Referring, I knew, to the so-called Hemingway cats found at the late author's historical estate-turned-museum in Key West, Florida.

Jasmine grinned, her golden eyes abruptly blazing with the intensity of a true competitor. Apparently, we were about to see the battle of the smart girls. "They're polydactyl cats. It's a genetic mutation."

Buddy huffed a little, her own spirit of competition obviously fired up as well. "Fine. What's the only animal that can't jump?"

"An elephant. How many eyes does a bee have?"

The younger girl frowned a moment, then triumphantly replied, "Five. So, what do you call the fear of the number thirteen?"

Jasmine rolled her eyes. "Way too easy. It's triskaidekaphobia."

"Wait, I have one for you both," I interjected, remembering John and Virgie's argument from this morning. "What do you call someone who has a phobia about things with patterns of holes or dots on them?"

Both girls frowned in thought, then traded baffled looks. It seemed I'd stumped the smartest girls in their respective classes, which wasn't surprising. Even assuming that Virgie's fear was an actual thing and not simply a personal quirk, I had no clue as to the answer myself.

"Trypophobia," came a voice behind me.

I turned to see Deputy Jackson, notebook in hand. Evidently he had finished questioning Harry, Polly, and the pink woman and it was my turn. When I gave him a surprised look, he shrugged.

"My sister has it. She freaks out if she sees honeycombs or coral or things like that. She won't even cut up a bell pepper because of the little seeds inside."

"Seriously?" Jasmine asked in disbelief.

He nodded. "Personally, I think it's just some weird thing in her head, but I looked it up online and lots of folks have it." He cracked just a suggestion of a smile. "Sure made it fun messing with her when we were kids."

Then, resuming his LEO demeanor, he said, "Ma'am, I need to get your contact information."

Forgetting about phobias, I gave the deputy my name, phone number, and address. He took it all down, then asked, "And what was your business here at the expo today?"

"This is my booth. I'm an exhibitor," I replied, waving my neck badge for proof.

He glanced at the pictures on my backdrop, and a look of recognition flashed across his face. "You're that B&B lady, aren't you? The one from that whole penguin thing a few months ago? And that Shakespeare play for the festival back in August?"

I nodded, trying not to wince in dismay. *Not* the reputation I wanted preceding me—"the B&B lady who stumbles across dead people."

He frowned and went on. "Did you witness what happened onstage with Ms. Quarry?"

"Only from a distance. I was sitting near the back, so I didn't see much."

"And do you have any personal relationship with the vic— with Ms. Quarry besides being an exhibitor here?"

I didn't miss the fact that he'd almost called Roxanna a victim—which did not bode well for her recovery. I felt my chest tighten. Doing my best to keep my voice from shaking, I told him, "I know Roxanna from the Chamber. We're not terribly close, but we're friends. We've done some doggy play-dates with her dog and mine."

Gustopher!

I'd forgotten about her Goldendoodle. He'd have been at Roxanna's place alone since morning, unless she'd had one of her neighbors looking in on him. If Roxanna didn't make it home tonight—I wasn't going to consider any worse option yet—I'd have to go check on him, maybe bring him back to the B&B.

The deputy finished making his notes, then glanced over at Jasmine and Buddy. The girls had lapsed into silence as soon as Jackson started questioning me, expressions wary as they huddled together, listening.

"Either of these young ladies related to you?"

I shook my head. "Their moms are the doctor and the nurse who were helping Roxanna before the paramedics got here. Buddy"—I indicated the younger girl—"was sitting on the same row as me, so she didn't see anything that could help you either. But Jasmine was one of the models onstage when Roxanna . . . when everything happened."

Which made the teen a prime witness to the accident.

A bit of mama bear that I didn't know lived within me stirred. Jasmine was a minor, so no way was I going to let the deputy question her without Gemma present.

Fortunately, I didn't have to tap into my latent grizzly, as all the deputy said was, "I may need to talk with her later, with her parents' approval. But if she's Gemma and Daniel Tanaka's girl, I know how to get hold of them. Peaches and Java makes the best coffee and cobbler in town."

Jackson made a final quick note and then gave me a crisp nod. "Thank you for your cooperation. If we have any questions later, we'll give you a call." He reached into his shirt pocket and pulled out a business card, which he handed to me. "Don't hesitate to call me if you think of something else that could be important. For now, you're free to go."

I nodded and slipped the card into my purse. "Thanks. But I think I'll wait here with the girls until their moms come back."

Then, as Jackson tucked away his notebook and started off, I called after him, "Deputy, can you tell us anything about Roxanna? Is she . . . all right? I mean, the paramedics haven't taken her away yet, have they?"

The man paused and glanced at the girls before turning to me, expression neutral. "I'm sorry, ma'am, I'm not at liberty to release any information. But I *am* sorry."

Which meant he was telling me, without actually telling me, that Roxanna and I weren't going to be sharing Chamber gossip again or planning more doggy playdates together. Roxanna was dead . . . and yet again I was a grim witness to tragedy.

Chapter Five

I bit my lip and nodded my understanding.

"Thank you," I managed. Then, as the deputy strode off, I summoned a weak smile and turned my attention back to the girls. "Buddy, there are lots more pictures of Mattie in that second binder. Why don't you and Jasmine look at them while I go over and talk to Harry for a minute."

"Can I have another truffle too?" Buddy asked in a small voice, her somber expression matching Jasmine's abrupt look of gloom.

Obviously, like me, the girls had understood the deputy's meaning all too clearly. Though, as if by unspoken agreement, none of us was going to say that one terrible word aloud—at least not yet. As long as we didn't, we could tell ourselves the deputy was wrong.

And so all I said was, "Sure, have as many truffles as you want."

I found a surprisingly subdued Harry tucked away on a folding chair behind all the greenery. I saw with mingled concern and surprise that John still had not returned to his booth. Polly was missing as well.

"Polly left a couple of minutes ago. I called her an Uber as soon as the deputy gave us the all-clear," Harry told me, answering one of my unspoken questions. "I made sure someone was going to be at her house when she got there. She'd mostly pulled herself together, but I didn't think she should be alone."

"She was pretty shaken up," I agreed. "It was good of you to take care of her."

"Not a problem." Glancing back toward my booth, he added, "How are the girls?"

"They're putting on brave faces, but they're shook up too. I'll stay with them until their moms break free. If you want to wait with me instead of calling an Uber for yourself, I'll give you a ride back to the house."

"Sounds good. Oh, I almost forgot, did the deputy tell you anything about how Roxanna was doing?"

His tone was deliberately casual, but his handsome features were drawn in concern. I belatedly realized that he'd probably spent time with her while recording the voice-overs. I didn't want to speculate if things had gone any further—with her flashy looks, Roxanna would be Harry's kind of woman—but at the very least, she wasn't a stranger to him.

Given that, I didn't want to tell him I was certain that the worst had happened, not until someone officially made the call. We'd all find out for sure soon enough. So I shook my head and went with the literal truth.

"Deputy Jackson told me he wasn't at liberty to reveal any details."

"Yeah, that's the line I got too." He pushed back the chair and stood. "Let me get my stuff from my booth, and I'll be right back."

While Harry went to collect his binders and signs, I did the same with my exhibit, packing everything into the pink plastic milk crate I'd attached to an old luggage cart so I could haul my display more easily. By the time I'd retrieved the binder from Jasmine and Buddy and added it to the cart, Harry had returned. He was wheeling *his* binders and signs in one of those sleek black rolling crates the professional trade show people used.

Feeling rather like a hick with my hillbilly version, I stashed my stuff behind the clothed table.

"Harry, do you mind waiting with the girls a minute?" I asked him. "I'm going to try getting back to the stage area and see if Buddy's mom and Gemma are about finished."

But before I had a chance to do so, both women came striding toward us. Gemma's expression was grim, the doctor's neutral.

Jasmine leaped from her chair and rushed to Gemma, her earlier hard-won composure crumbling as she silently wept in her mother's arms. As for Buddy, she walked over to her parent and calmly asked, "Can we go now?"

The woman gave the girl a perfunctory pat atop her bun. "In a moment. Let me talk to Ms. Fleet first."

Handing the medical bag to Buddy, she strode over to me and put out a hand. "We never were formally introduced. I'm

Dr. Meredith Garvin. Thank you for watching out for Buddy while I was otherwise occupied. I trust she was no trouble."

"Not at all," I told her as we briefly shook. "I'm just sorry she had to witness this . . . situation."

Dr. Garvin shrugged. "As a physician's daughter, Buddy is well aware that life is tenuous. Though, of course, we will discuss today's events on our way home, and I'll answer any questions she has."

Turning back to the girl, she finished, "Buddy, make your good-byes to your new friends."

Obediently, Buddy said, "Good-bye, Ms. Nina. Thank you for the truffles." And then, less formally, she added, "Maybe I can come see Mattie someday?"

"If that's all right with your mother, absolutely."

Then, going over to Jasmine, whose tears had subsided though she still clung to Gemma, Buddy say, "Good-bye, Jasmine. I'm sorry I made fun of your dress. I think you look like a princess."

Swiping the tears from her eyes, Jasmine extracted herself from Gemma's grasp and gave the younger girl a soggy smile.

"Thanks. Come see me at Peaches and Java sometime, and I'll make you one of our famous grilled peaches-and-peanut-butter sandwiches."

"Yum!"

With that, Buddy hoisted the medical bag again and stolidly made her way down the row toward the exit. Dr. Garvin followed after, though she paused as she reached Harry, who was posed casually with his wheeled crate.

"I'll pick you up at eleven AM tomorrow, Mr. Westcott," she told him. Frowning slightly, she added, "But on second thought, a tennis racket would be too much, so let's scratch that. Besides which, it would require that you wear shorts. I would rather see you in trousers. I trust you can make that adjustment. Good day."

I waited until the doctor and Buddy were out of earshot before I turned an inquiring look on Harry. "Tennis racket? Trousers?"

A fleeting look of embarrassment washed over his handsome features. Still, his tone was nonchalant as he made his reply.

"I already told you I'd booked my first customer for my Plus One business. Dr. Garvin has a family event tomorrow and needs a 'date' "—he gave the word finger quotes—"so she doesn't have to put up with her mother and sisters playing matchmaker all day. She calls me, and I quote, a godsend."

"Can't wait to hear how it goes." I smiled a little, picturing Harry hobbing with the nobs who apparently picnicked around tennis courts. But recalling the current situation, I sobered and turned to Gemma.

"Tell me, how is Virgie?"

"Better. Of course, she's still overwrought with everything that's happened—I mean, she and Roxanna were partners for years—but it was just a faint."

"She's fine," Harry confirmed, in case I wasn't taking Gemma's answer for granted. He paused and with a jerk of his thumb toward the floral booth added, "I don't know if you know, but John Klingel is her ex-husband. Actually, number one of two, from what I heard, but that's neither here nor there. He showed up at the stage right after the deputies ran the rest of you off, and he volunteered to stick around and drive her home."

I nodded. So that's where John had been. Though, considering the callousness of the argument I'd heard between the two earlier, I was a bit surprised he'd stepped up to help. But I had already pegged him as a decent guy, so his offering a ride didn't seem out of character under the circumstances. Actually, it was a positive that in the face of tragedy the pair had been able to put aside their mutual grudge for a while.

Which left the most important question—the one I really didn't want answered. Turning to Gemma again, I asked, "And Roxanna?"

Gemma shook her head. "We all tried, but there wasn't anything anyone could do. She was already gone when she fell out of that cake."

Jasmine gasped, and I heard a muttered oath from Harry. As for me, I felt my chest clench and my stomach shrink into a hard knot. I'd pretty well known all along that this would be the outcome; still, a flicker of hope that all might turn out well had burned within me. But with her words, Gemma had effectively blown out that tiny flame.

"Connie's already here talking to Virgie," Gemma went on. "I'm sure she'll be interviewing the rest of us at some point. And Reverend Bishop is on the way now to pronounce Roxanna," she soberly finished.

Reverend Bishop being the Reverend Dr. Thaddeus Bishop. He was a true renaissance man, serving as both Cymbeline's coroner and one of its two funeral home directors as well as pastor of the Heavenly Host Baptist Church. I'd met him a few weeks earlier when he'd had to perform a similar duty by pronouncing a man dead at my B&B. His manner could best be described as flamboyantly refined. Despite lapses into pomposity and his tendency to lecture, I quite liked the man.

As for Connie, Gemma had meant Sheriff Connie Lamb. I'd come to know the town's top-ranking law officer as an unfortunate result of being *that* B&B owner. About my age and possessed of a no-nonsense manner, Sheriff Lamb blasted away every existing cliché about small-town cops and lady sheriffs. I also knew that if she was on the scene, something was off about Roxanna's death other than the obvious bizarreness of the entire situation.

Beside me, Harry sighed. "What do they think happened?"

A few stragglers from the show still milled around the booths within earshot. Gemma gestured me and Harry closer, then lowered her voice.

"Right now, the talk is that it was an accident. They're guessing that when Roxanna climbed into the cake, somehow the scarf she was wearing got caught on something inside the cake's framework. She couldn't get it loose, and she ended up accidentally strangled."

I nodded. Terrible, but it made sense.

"That doesn't make sense," Harry broke in, contradicting my thought. "Last I heard, that cake was supposed to dump a huge load of flowers onto the stage. No one was supposed to be inside it. Unless maybe Roxanna changed plans at the last minute."

I stared at him in dismay, abruptly recalling how before the show he'd mentioned something about the cake and flowers and blackbirds. With the chasing lights and the gold sparkler display, the prop had been designed to be something that was both pretty and dramatic for a wedding reception, a step up from a plain old ice sculpture. No bride in her right mind was going to come bursting out of it like a hired stripper, so why would Roxanna have wanted to advertise it like that?

"Did you tell Deputy Jackson this?"

Harry gave a grim nod. "He said he'd look into it. But I guess it's possible she might have changed the plan at the last minute and decided to do the cake-jumping thing instead."

Which would make that the decision from hell, I thought as the knot in my stomach turned stone-cold. "What about Polly and Jasmine?" I ventured with a glance at the latter. "Wouldn't they have known what was supposed to happen when the cake was opened?"

"No," the girl choked out with a vigorous shake of her copper curls, while Gemma wrapped an arm around her for support. "Ms. Roxanna, she . . . she said it was a surprise."

On that note, the four of us abandoned the booth for the exit, making a doleful parade as we started off. The whirring from the wheels of Harry's and my carts was damped by the carpet and only grew into a buzz-saw-like sound once we reached the hallway outside the gym. While the others made their way to the door, I paused and reflexively glanced in the direction where I'd earlier seen a man in a purple shirt disappear around a corner.

If that had indeed been John, what had he been doing wandering elsewhere in the high school? And why had he only reappeared again in the gym after chaos had broken out at the fashion show?

You don't even know for sure it was John, I reminded myself as I turned away and followed after the others to the exit. After all, purple wasn't that uncommon a color for a man's shirt.

Once outside in the warm afternoon air again, Harry and I made our good-byes to the Tanakas and started toward my car. The dark-green Mini Cooper convertible had been surrounded by cars this morning, but now it stood out in the nearly empty parking lot. We loaded our carts into the back seat, and then I climbed into the driver's seat while Harry silently belted himself in on the passenger's side.

"Do you mind if we make a quick detour?" I asked him as I pulled the Mini out of the parking lot and out onto the highway. "I need to run by Roxanna's place and check on Gustopher.

"And this Gustopher is—?"

Surprised that Harry didn't know about Roxanna's pet, I quickly explained about the Goldendoodle, a mix between a golden retriever and poodle. Gus was a little taller and more streamlined than Mattie. He had a crazy pelt of apricot-colored curls like a poodle, though his overall build was retriever-like. In fact, he looked more like a giant stuffed toy than an actual dog. From what Roxanna had told me, she'd gotten him from a rescue organization after his original owners decided he was too much for them to handle.

I glanced his way. "So I guess that means you've never been to Roxanna's house before? I figured maybe you had, working on all those voice-overs for the expo."

Harry shook his head.

"She and Virgie and I met at Peaches and Java a couple of times to work out the details. And like I told you, Virgie's son has a studio, which is where we did the recording work for the expo."

I nodded. "Roxanna lives—lived—alone, and from what she indicated, the only family she has left here in Cymbeline are an elderly aunt and uncle in assisted living. I think her parents are in South Florida, and she has an older brother out in California, or maybe Oregon. Who knows how long it would take anyone else besides me to remember Gus was abandoned there inside her house?"

"Good point," he agreed. "Are you planning on taking him back to the B&B with us?"

I nodded. "He and Mattie get along great, so he won't be any trouble. And if none of her relatives want to take him, I'll keep him as long as I need to until I can turn him over to a rescue that will find him a new home."

And then Harry, being Harry, focused on the practicalities. "Do you have a key to her place?"

"No, but I had to check on Gus once before when she had to go out of town last minute. I know where she keeps—kept—her spare key."

"That's good," Harry said, before lapsing into silence, seemingly not inclined to say anything more.

Which was just as well. Surreptitiously, I swiped a tear from my eye as I drove on. Roxanna's death hadn't really sunk in yet; probably wouldn't until the funeral.

The only silver lining to this terrible, dark cloud now over me was the fact that I suddenly wasn't that concerned about my ex-husband's pending nuptials anymore.

A few minutes later we'd reached Roxanna's place. Her small home was in the older part of town only a few blocks from the Heavenly Host Baptist Church. Like other houses in the neighborhood, it was a cute cottage-style dwelling with a covered porch along the front and topped by a windowed gable.

Originally, the house had been painted white with white trim. Soon after she bought the place, however, Roxanna had repainted. Now the cottage boasted a pale-coral exterior with gray trim and a glossy black door. The waist-high picket fence that enclosed the pocket-sized front yard was painted the same gray as the house trim. That, along with the wooden rocking chairs on the porch with their glossy black frames and bright floral cushions, gave the residence a modern, almost beachy look. Certainly, the place stood out—but in a good way—from the rest of the neighborhood homes that still sported the white-on-white look.

Barely had I pulled the Mini to a stop at the curb when I heard barking from within Roxanna's house.

"That must be Gustopher," Harry said as he unfastened his seat belt and opened his door. "He sounds rather . . . large."

"You'll see," I replied with a faint smile as I got out. "Though usually he's pretty low-key about people coming over. I just hope he'll load into the car without Roxanna being here."

With Harry trailing, I started toward the porch, stopping at the circular garden to the right of the sidewalk. A knee-high rendition of Uga—the white English bulldog mascot of the University of Georgia, aka UGA—sat atop a flat sand-colored rock in a patch of mixed yellow, pink, and lilac pansies. Given that this outdoor resin Uga wore a painted red jersey with a large varsity letter *G* in black, he clashed more than a little with the recently planted blooms.

I glanced around to make sure no one was watching, then knelt and tipped the statue to retrieved Roxanna's emergency door key. Settling the pup back into place, I rose and climbed the three steps up onto the porch.

I hesitated there a moment beside the requisite big tin bucket holding a wilted tomato plant—every porch in South Georgia seemed to sport one—to which clung a few end-of-season cherry tomatoes. Abruptly, I felt like I was intruding on Roxanna's privacy.

Don't be silly, I tried to reassure myself. After all, I'd been to her house a couple of times before. This was different, however, going into her space after she'd left it for what had been a final time. But knowing how much Gustopher had meant to her, I was certain that from whatever plane she was currently on, she had given me her blessing to rescue her baby.

"Hey, Gus," I called through the closed front door as I brushed off a bit of dirt clinging to the key and inserted it into the lock. "It's me, Nina. I'm here to take you on a playdate with Mattie."

To Harry, who was practically on my heels, I said, "Why don't you step back for a minute so I can say hi to Gustopher and then introduce you properly?"

"Works for me," he agreed. Harry had made friends with Mattie but wasn't exactly what one would call a crazy dog person.

I turned the knob and opened the door a crack. Gustopher had a bad tendency to barrel into a person in his excitement to greet his human friends, and I wanted him to get over his initial jumpies before I walked in. As I expected, an apricot-colored snout promptly stuck its way between the door and the jamb.

"Hey, Gus," I told him. "It's me, your buddy, Nina. You mind if I come in?"

The pup gave a bark of what I took as assent, so I pushed the door open all the way and slipped inside.

Typical of the cottage-style houses, no separate foyer served as a transition between door and living space. Instead, when I stepped inside, it was directly into the living room. Roxanna had remodeled by tearing out the wall separating the living and dining rooms to make a single open space that served both purposes.

I smiled a bit as I scratched Gus behind the ears and glanced about. The room had a beachy feel similar to that of the house's exterior, the frames of the living area's couch and chairs having been chalk-painted white and artfully distressed to reveal a bit of chippy pale-blue paint beneath. The dining set and china cabinet had similar paint jobs, though the color scheme was reversed, with pale blue atop white. The only non-shabby item—though, technically, it should have been the shabbiest of all—was a small antique drop-front desk that still sported its original cherry finish.

A series of flat baskets in various sizes and weaves—some natural, others with ombre paint jobs in blues and pinks— hung on one wall. The other three walls featured watercolors or photographs with watery themes, the frames of which resembled planks salvaged from the curb on bulk-trash day. The remainder of the house, I knew, was similarly decorated.

Fine, so I read too many of those upcycle, chalk-paint blogs, Roxanna had admitted with a grin the first time I set foot inside her place.

I turned back to Gus.

"You ready to make a new friend?" I asked him, then pulled opened the front door again and peeked out to where Harry still waited on the porch. "You ready?"

"As ever."

"Good. Why don't you stick a hand in first so he can sniff it, then come in real slowly," I suggested, stepping back from the door to give the actor plenty of room.

But the Goldendoodle had other plans. His curly-haired snout nudged the door open the rest of the way before he zipped back around behind me.

"I thought we were doing the hand thing," I heard Harry say, just before an apricot blur flew past me and knocked the actor flat on his back.

Chapter Six

"Uh, Nina," Harry wheezed from where he lay supine on the porch, sixty pounds of Goldendoodle standing on his chest and vigorously licking his face. "Do you think you can persuade Gustopher to let me up?"

But I was already rushing toward the pair, torn between laughter and dismay. "Gustopher! Off, boy! Let's be polite, okay?"

Fortunately, the dog's black mesh collar and leash were hanging near the door. "Come on, boy, hop off," I told him again, once I'd hastily fastened on his collar and hooked the lead to it.

Gus let me drag him away, though his tongue still lolled happily and he danced in place as he watched Harry scramble back to his feet.

"Nice puppy," was the latter's ironic comment as he brushed himself off.

I gave Gus a pat before replying, "It's not his fault. He just wants to be friends." I had the dog sit and then continued,

"Here, let's try it again. Hold out your hand so he can sniff you. Gus, meet Harry. Harry, meet Gus."

Both man and dog complied with the hand-and-sniff thing. I nodded and smiled. "See, he's a good boy. And smart too. Look at all the tricks he can do."

Dropping the leash, I told the dog *shake*, then *down*, then *up* and *high five*, all of which he performed in rapid succession. My smile broadened.

"That's just the basics," I bragged to Harry. "He knows a lot more commands than that. Here's a really cute one that Roxanna showed me." Turning back to the Goldendoodle, I said, "Gus, hop like a bunny!"

The pup promptly rose on his hind legs, front paws tucked close to his chest as he bounced in place, tongue happily lolling.

"What a good boy!" I told him, giving him a hug. Then, handing over the leash to Harry, I added, "Now that *that's* settled, follow me. You can take Gus out back for a potty break while I get his things."

I marched the pair inside again and ushered them down the short hall off the living room. To the right, a door opened to a small kitchen. Beyond that lay a small guest bedroom. To the left was a straight staircase to the second floor. A tiny powder bath was tucked into the space under the steps. At the hall's end was a windowed door leading to the backyard.

Harry peered past the curtain, then unlocked the dead bolt.

"The whole backyard is fenced," I reassured him as he opened the door, "so it's okay to let Gus off the leash. Give me a couple of minutes, okay?"

Leaving the pair to bond, I made my way to the combination pantry and laundry room just off the kitchen. A couple of empty plastic laundry baskets (also chalk-paint blue) were stacked atop the dryer. I seized one and started loading up.

A partial bag of kibble and a new case of canned dog food went in first. An extra leash and a mesh harness were hanging from a wall hook, so I tossed those in with the food. On a high shelf alongside boxes of pasta I spied a cute red ceramic container about the size of a coffee can, with a clamp-style top. The canister was decorated with white paw prints and the words *Dog Treats* in white letters.

Harry could have reached the treat jar with ease. For me, who couldn't, a chalk-painted stool was stored under one shelf. I pulled down the canister and added it to the basket. Gus's bright-red ceramic food and water bowls were in the kitchen, so I emptied those and packed them as well. I'd seen some of his toys in the living room. I would grab a couple of those for him before we left.

I carried the basket back to the living room and was gathering up stuffies when Harry and Gus returned from the latter's pit stop. "Mission accomplished," the actor confirmed. "I think we're ready to go."

We might have been, but Gustopher seemingly was not. After that first leap-and-tackle, he had followed obediently alongside both me and Harry. But now the Goldendoodle had begun to whine. And as Harry reached over to hand me the leash, Gus abruptly pulled free. Leash dangling and sniffing loudly, he circled about the sofa and trotted into the dining area, the whining growing louder.

"What's the matter, does he need to go out again?" Harry asked.

I started to shake my head; then, suddenly understanding, I turned a stricken look on Harry. "He's searching for Roxanna. What do we do?"

Harry gave a helpless shrug. By now, Gus had determined that his human wasn't hiding in any nook or cranny. He rushed back to me and began anxiously sniffing at my shirt.

"Oh no," I choked out, remembering that last friendly hug Roxanna and I had shared and for which I was now very grateful. "He must smell her scent on me."

I dropped to my knees beside the pup and snuffled into his reddish-gold curls for several moments while he licked my damp cheeks. Finally, I raised my head and wiped my eyes on my sleeve, glad that my mascara was the waterproof kind.

Getting to my feet, I glanced back at Harry and said, "Sorry."

"Understood," he replied, looking a bit misty-eyed himself. He gave me an awkward pat on the shoulder. Then, clearing his throat, he continued, "So, are we ready to go now?"

I shook my head. "I just thought of something. Give me a second to run upstairs to Roxanna's room."

"Sure. While you do that, I'll give Connie a call and let her know we have the dog, in case she locates a next of kin who is worried about him."

Harry being also on a first-name basis with the sheriff—at least when she was off the clock—because they'd gone to high school together. Not that Sheriff Lamb cut him any sort of slack. In fact, she hadn't hesitated to haul him in for questioning the first time he and I were involved in a murder.

While Harry scrolled through the contacts in his cell for a number, Gus and I went upstairs. The stairway opened onto an upper hallway that paralleled the one below. Because the second floor had originally been an attic, all the rooms off the corridor had slightly pitched ceilings. To my right was a door to a small second bedroom that Roxanna had turned into an office. To the left was a full bath accessible from both the corridor and the third bedroom at the hall's end. That room Roxanna had designated as her master suite, which was where I was headed.

Once again, I found myself hesitating as I reached a closed door. This was Roxanna's most personal space in the house, and being there without her felt like an intrusion. But I was doing it for Gus, and because of that I knew she wouldn't mind. I took a steadying breath and let myself in.

The shabby beach theme continued here. The queen-sized bed beneath the dormer window overlooking the street was neatly made, white cotton comforter pulled tight to a simple whitewashed headboard. The latter was almost hidden by a proliferation of decorative pillows in shades of blue and green, one with a starfish pattern that complemented the crocheted blanket folded neatly across the foot of the bed. A whitewashed nightstand and mirrored dresser completed the furnishings.

Several of the ubiquitous flat woven baskets decorated one wall. However, all this beachy-ness was offset by a bright-pink braided rag rug in front of the bed and a whimsical mobile of equally pink wooden stars hanging from the corner ceiling.

Gus hurried in after me, once again doing his sniff-and-search routine. "Sorry, boy," I gently told him, "she's not coming home. But I'm going to get you something to remember her by."

Once, when Mattie had stayed at the vet clinic overnight following minor surgery, I had left one of my worn T-shirts behind, hoping the scent would comfort her while she was locked in a kennel. Mattie and I would do our best to substitute for Gus's missing human, but maybe having something of hers to sleep with for a few nights would help him settle in better.

Her laundry hamper was yet another basket, this one lidded and tall and in ombre shades ranging from sand to chocolate. I reached inside and plucked out the pale-pink T-shirt on top. Printed on its front in curly rainbow-colored letters was the phrase *In A World Where You Can Be Anything, Be Kind.*

I carefully folded the shirt into a tiny square and sighed. Today would likely be the last time I'd ever be in Roxanna's house, and I couldn't leave without a personal good-bye. Clutching the shirt to me, I whispered the words *Safe travels, my friend* and then closed my eyes.

83

I wasn't expecting a message back, exactly—wasn't waiting for those pink stars to go wildly spinning like something from a movie. All I really wanted was a feeling, some sense that whatever had happened to Roxanna, she was okay now.

And then Gustopher let out a single ominous-sounding woof.

I jumped. I might have let out a muffled shriek too. Definitely, goose bumps raced up both arms as my eyelids flew open. I saw the Goldendoodle standing on the bed, front paws propped on the headboard as he peered out the dormer window. I rushed to look myself, half expecting to see a spectral Roxanna standing in her front lawn.

Thankfully, no ghosts were wandering the yard. However, I saw what must have caught Gus's attention—a two-door silver coupe idling at the curb behind my green Mini Cooper. The car was distant enough, and its windows sufficiently tinted, that I couldn't make out who was inside.

A client looking for Roxanna?

Or simply someone parked for a moment to send a text or check their GPS?

Curious, I waited for the driver to exit. Instead, the car abruptly zipped back a few feet. Then, with a crunch of gears, it leaped forward and whipped around the Mini, barely missing clipping my car's rear bumper as it sped off.

Momentarily forgetting the *Be Kind* motto, I muttered a few uncomplimentary things about drivers of small silver sports cars. I earned a bark of agreement from Gus, however, which made me smile.

"Come on, boy," I told him, picking up his leash again. "I have a feeling your mom had a rule about no paws on the nice white bedspread. Let's go downstairs and finish your packing."

I found Harry in the living room perched on the arm of the cushionless couch, cell phone to his ear. I heard a couple of *uh-huh, uh-huh*s before he hung up just as I approached.

"Was that Sheriff Lamb?"

He shook his head. "She didn't pick up her cell, so I left her a message to let her know we'd been here and we were taking Gustopher. Did you find what you were looking for?"

I noticed that he didn't volunteer who he'd been talking to when I'd walked up. And, of course, it was none of my business. So I simply added the shirt to the basket and said, "I wanted something of Roxanna's for Gus to snuggle with tonight. I think we have everything now."

I eyed the kennel but knew that between me and Harry and our expo crates, we'd have just room enough left to stuff Gus and his basket in the Mini. Depending on what happened with Gus, maybe I could come back another time for it.

"I'm going to put this on Gus so I can seat belt him in for the ride," I added, retrieving his harness from the basket. Once I'd finished snapping and buckling, I gave the dog a quick pat. "All right, Gussie," I said, "we're off to a playdate with your buddy Mattie. You're going to have fun."

Letting Harry, who carried the overflowing basket, go first, I held tight to Gus's lead as I locked the front door behind me. Then, after checking again for curious eyes, I returned the spare key to its hiding spot beneath the Uga statue. Harry was already waiting by the Mini, so I unlocked it with my key fob.

While he rearranged our rolling crates to one side so Gus and his basket had sufficient room, I went around to the other door. Mattie often rode with me on errands that allowed for dogs, and so I permanently kept in the car one of those straps that clicked into the seat belt on one end and fastened to a harness on the other. I secured Gustopher for the ride, and then Harry and I climbed in front.

Neither of us said anything for a couple of minutes as I drove to the B&B. Even Gus was quiet from his spot in the back. But while idle chitchat seemed a bit out of place under the circumstances, I wasn't ready to be alone with my thoughts. Thus, when the silence grew too uncomfortable, I abruptly spoke up.

"So, tell me about your Plus One character for your date with Dr. Garvin. Since she's a physician, I assume her BF has to be some rich and connected businessman?"

That seemed a safe enough subject—and besides, I was genuinely curious to know how Harry planned to handle his role. But when he replied, the actor sounded less enthusiastic about the topic than I'd expected.

"Actually, she went with ex–pro athlete—Major League Baseball, to be exact."

I smiled a little, picturing Harry on his own trading card. Then another thought hit me. I'd never cared much about the sport, but even I knew that an awful lot of baseball fans were obsessed with stats. "Aren't you worried someone at the party might try to look up the fake you?"

"Believe me, no one is going to put out that kind of effort for a guy they met once. Even if they do, I'm covered. The full MLB roster in any given year is somewhere between eight hundred and nine hundred players. Quite a few of them just this season have the last name Anderson, which I've chosen as my *nom de guerre*. And since I plan to be vague on the year and team, that's a lot of players to sort through. Plus, I played first base on CHS's varsity team my junior and senior years, so I know the lingo."

"Oh yeah, what's that old expression?" I asked. "If you can't dazzle them with brilliance, baffle them with BS."

Harry, however, wasn't being particularly dazzling at the moment, making no response to my friendly jibe. "You okay?" I asked him in concern. "I mean, besides . . . well, you know . . . the whole situation?"

"I'm good. I'm just rethinking this whole Plus One gig," he confessed. "My first client, and she's trying to micromanage things before the party even starts. She actually called me after I left the message for Connie and told me what colors I need to wear tomorrow."

So *she* was the mystery caller. I slanted Harry a look. "Seriously, now she's costuming you?"

" 'Navy trousers would be best, or perhaps khaki,' " he quoted in a snooty tone that was a credible imitation of the doctor's voice. " 'But please, not black, and absolutely not brown. I'll leave the choice of shirt up to you, as long as it is collared with long sleeves. But nothing pink.' "

I allowed myself a snicker. "If I were you, I'd go all retro *Urban Cowboy* on her and wear something plaid with fringe." Then, summoning a more serious attitude, I asked, "If it's really that bad, can't you get out of going?"

He shook his head. "We signed a contract, and she's already put down a deposit. Besides, since this family picnic of hers will last most of the day, I'll be making a nice chunk of change."

He named a figure that made my eyes open wide.

"Wow! For that much money, she could tell me to dress like Little Bo Peep and I'd do it. I'd even bring my own sheep!

"And think about it," I added as I rounded a corner near the town square. "When you're in a movie or play, you can't show up in street clothes. Someone else tells you what to wear in that situation. So I'm changing my mind. My advice is to shut up and go with navy blue."

Harry laughed, the first truly cheerful sound I'd heard out of anyone since the ill-fated fashion show.

"I can always count on you to tell it like it is, Nina Fleet. Navy blue, then, and a nice pale-blue button-down to go with it."

What else he had planned, I didn't find out, for by then we were home again. Harry hopped out to open the driveway gate, and I pulled up to the small detached garage to the rear of the main house.

Even after all these months, I still shivered a little in anticipation every time I drove up and reminded myself that this gorgeous Queen Anne was my very own place. The house is three stories high, if you count the tower room that gives a 360-degree view of the surrounding neighborhood. It dates from the 1890s, built not long after Cymbeline was founded, and sits on a half-acre lot in Cymbeline's historic district. The property is separated from the somewhat busy street by a head-high wrought-iron fence, the gate of which Harry had just opened. A few months ago I'd installed a burnished metal sign on the fence—*Fleet House Bed and Breakfast*—making it official.

A sprawling century-old magnolia shades the far side of the lawn, looking like something out of *Gone With the Wind*. On the opposite side of the yard is the requisite peach tree— this variety being Belle of Georgia—which had just now finished yielding its latest crop.

I've already talked about the backyard, where my future outdoor weddings will be held. And I've already mentioned the home's "painted lady" color scheme: green and yellow for the main house and trim, the gingerbread detailing a clean bright white. A wraparound porch, partially screened in, makes for the perfect place to hang out on all but the hottest days.

I remained parked in the driveway so we could unload Gus and all our gear. As soon as I let him loose from his harness, the Goldendoodle bounded across the front yard, pausing at the peach tree to water it. I could hear Mattie's excited barking from the screened porch. That was where she'd been lounging all day—that is, when she hadn't been using her doggy door to access her personal fenced run area along the far side of the house.

Leaving Harry to do the heavy lifting, I hurried up the walk and climbed the steps to the front porch. "Mattie, guess what?" I called to her. "Gustopher has come for a visit."

I opened the screened door, and a gray and black and white furry rocket launched from the porch steps and landed in the yard. Gus came running to greet his friend, and the pair went chasing and tumbling through the grass. I leaned on the porch railing and laughed as I watched their antics.

Harry, meanwhile, had hauled the laundry basket that was Gustopher's luggage out of the Mini and joined me at the porch. "Where do you want this?"

"Kitchen is fine," I told him, and entered the access code to unlock the front door's electronic lock.

I'd recently added that feature so I could give my guests a temporary entry code when they checked in, allowing them to could come and go as they wished. That way I didn't have to hand out an actual front-door key or else be available to answer the door 24/7. Not only was this system far more convenient for all concerned, it was more secure. Though, once everyone was already in for the night, I did back up the electronic locks with the original dead bolts that required an actual key.

Harry and the basket trailing, I led the way down the main hall. With its floor-to-ceiling dark paneling, the corridor was always gloomy, no matter how many lights were on.

Doubling down on the gloom, it also served as a gallery of sorts, hung with vintage photographs and daguerreotypes of Mrs. Lathrop's long-dead relatives.

Since day one living here, I'd contemplated replacing the collection with modern prints. I'd even thought of painting the paneling some frivolous shade of yellow or coral to lighten things up. But my B&B guests always seemed fascinated with Ye Olde Hall o' Ancestors, so I had left the portraits there as a curiosity.

Besides which, by default Mrs. Lathrop's relatives were also Harry's. Slightly creepy as I found the lot of them, I'd feel guilty consigning his family members' images to a hall closet while he still lived in the house.

We passed the open doors of the formal parlor to the left and the dining room to the right. The hall opened into a larger corridor that I privately called the great hall, mostly because this was where the L-shaped staircase with its elaborately carved newel post and neatly turned balusters led upstairs. Beneath the staircase was a tidy powder bath, and at the end of the hall a windowed door leading to the gardens and lawn beyond.

At the opposite side of the corridor, pocket doors led to the house's oversized kitchen, which neatly married late-nine-teenth-century architecture with early-twenty-first-century technology. The counter-to-ceiling glass-front cabinets, painted a crisp white, were original to the home, as was the whitewashed floor with its scattering of rag rugs. And the farm-style stone sink that was big enough to bathe in had been around for a good hundred years.

The appliances, however, were strictly modern, thanks to Harry's great-aunt. She hadn't scrimped when it came to her top-of-the-line refrigerator, hooded cooktop, and built-in double oven. A narrow but long marble-topped island with a quartet of barstools served double duty as informal dining space and extra prep area.

"Drop everything back there," I told Harry, gesturing to my laundry room–slash–pantry, which, like Roxanna's, lay just off the kitchen, "and I'll sort it out. Do you mind getting my rolling crate out of the Mini when you get yours?"

"No problem."

He left through the kitchen's exterior door that opened onto a covered stoop leading out to the driveway. While he saw to our trade show gear, I parked the half-full bag of Gus's food atop Mattie's sealed plastic tub of chow. The case of canned dog food along with the bowls went next to that, and Gus's harness and leashes went on a hook next to hers. Momentarily setting aside the doggy treats, I carefully stowed the basket with Roxanna's shirt atop my washer. Later, when I settled the dogs for the night, I'd tuck it around Gus for him to snuggle in.

I carried the treat canister back into the kitchen. With its bright-red glaze and paw-print design, it was definitely cute enough to display on the counter. Tempting as it was to keep it, I'd give the canister to the Goldendoodle's eventual new owner when that day came.

Deciding that the pups probably needed snacks after all their running, I popped open the top and reached inside. But instead of grabbing little treat bones, my fingers closed on a small white bag—the thin plastic kind that takeout orders sometimes come in. Frowning, I pulled it out of the jar and set it on the kitchen island behind me.

The bundle was wrapped and knotted around itself to form a packet about the size and shape of a baseball. As the treat jar was otherwise empty, it was apparent that Roxanna had deliberately put the packet in there. And when I thought about it, the fact that the canister had been stored on a high shelf that most people couldn't easily reach was even more telling.

Torn between curiosity and unease, I started undoing the plastic. Once I'd unwrapped the bundle, it took me a moment to realize just what I had found. That is, until I removed the thick pink rubber band holding it together and dozens of hundred-dollar bills spilled across the counter top.

Chapter Seven

A few moments later, I heard the outside door open. I looked up from my barstool seat at the counter to see Harry steering our wheeled crates into the kitchen. Well, at least, he was steering his. My pink crate minus its luggage cart was awkwardly tucked beneath his arm. He closed the door behind him, parked his crate, and then set mine down with a *whoosh*.

"Sorry it took so long, but we had a slight malfunction," he explained, expression rueful. "I was pulling everything out of the car when the wheel came off your luggage cart. While I was trying to fix that, the whole thing separated from the crate. I left the cart outside by the steps, if you want to try to salvage it. But I really think you should consider investing in—"

He broke off all at once as he finally focused on what was piled up before me on the kitchen island—ten stacks of slightly curly currency.

Staring from me to the cash and then back again, he finally managed to choke out, "Is this what I think it is?"

"If you're thinking it's a buttload of Benjamins," I replied, using the slang for hundred-dollar bills, "then you're right."

"What did you do, rob a Brink's truck while I was outside?"

"Not even close. I found the money in there," I said, pointing to Gus's treat canister. "It was all rolled together and rubber-banded the way gangsters carry around their cash in the movies. Harry, I counted it. It's ten thousand dollars."

And then, as we gaped at each other, I added, "Ten thousand dollars is the exact same amount of money that Virgie accused Roxanna of embezzling from her!"

"Wait." Harry frowned and held up a hand for emphasis. "You're telling me that Roxanna stole all that money from Virgie?"

"I . . . I don't know."

I swiftly related the argument between the two women that I'd unwittingly eavesdropped on while in the girls' room at the high school. I explained as well that neither woman had known I'd overheard them.

"Roxanna swore to Virgie that she didn't do it," I finished, "and at the time she sounded truthful. But now I don't know what to think. I mean, it's pretty coincidental that the exact amount of money Virgie says was skimmed off the account was hidden in Roxanna's pantry."

"True," Harry conceded, "but I can think of other perfectly legit reasons she might have that much cash lying around."

"Such as?"

"Maybe it's an emergency stash—you know, in case a tornado or freak snowstorm comes through and the ATMs are down," he suggested. "Maybe she was saving up for a new car and figured if she hid the down payment from herself, she wouldn't be tempted to spend it on something else."

"Maybe," I echoed doubtfully. "The question is, what do I do with the money now? I mean, I can't just keep it. Should I call Sheriff Lamb and tell her what I found?"

Harry slanted me a look. "And what's *she* going to do with it? You ask me, unless the place has crime scene tape wrapped around it, any reasonable person would say the money's part of the house's contents. If it were me, I'd stick the cash back in that jar and carry it back to Roxanna's place for her family to find."

I hated to admit it, but Harry probably was right. By opening that dog treat canister, I'd also opened the proverbial can of worms. The smartest thing would be to put those figurative red wigglers back where they'd come from and concentrate on fostering Gus for as long as necessary.

I glanced at my watch. It was already after five, meaning it would be dark in a little more than an hour. But though I could easily make the trip up and back in that time, I wasn't up to returning to Roxanna's empty house so soon.

"I'll take this all back first thing tomorrow morning," I agreed, and began stacking the bills together again. "Since it will be Sunday, things should be quiet. But can you imagine if whoever packs up her house donates the treat jar to charity without looking inside it first?"

Harry gave me a wry smile. "Kind of like when someone donates an ugly oil painting that turns out to be a Van Gogh, right? That's why I'll be haunting the local thrift stores for the next few weeks." He reached for the handle of his rolling crate. "Now, if you don't mind, I'm going to head up to my room and regroup. I've got a big day tomorrow, and I want to do some research on my character."

"I'm going to get Gus set up and then do a little regrouping myself. If I call in a pizza later, you feel like splitting it?"

"Text me when it's here. And it goes without saying my half should be veggie."

Fortunately for the sake of a tasty pizza, Harry was vegetarian and not vegan, meaning cheese was part of his menu. I nodded my agreement, and he rolled himself and his crate out of the kitchen.

I managed to return the wad of hundred-dollar bills to a credible semblance of its original shape and rewrapped it in the bag. I stuck the whole shebang back in the canister and locked down the lid. Not that I planned to leave the canister in the kitchen. Harry and I might be the only ones in the house, but no way was I going to leave that kind of cash sitting out. Not long ago I had finally ponied up for a fireproof home safe, which I'd had mounted in the back of my bedroom closet. The treat jar could stay locked in there overnight.

I carried the cash-filled container to my personal quarters, which lay beyond the door located just before the staircase. Marked *Private*, the space was actually the home's former billiards parlor converted into a large bedroom with en suite bathroom. I had set up my personal office there, too, and even installed a mini kitchen consisting of a microwave atop a small refrigerator. As the billiards parlor in turn led out to the screened portion of the porch, I had a convenient manager's retreat right there in the house. Even when the B&B was filled, I could hide from the guests but still be nearby to set up break-fast and snacks and handle any emergencies.

With the money safely stashed away until tomorrow, I carried my crate of expo stuff over to my office area and hopped online to order a new rolling cart like Harry's. That done, I went outside and tossed the broken luggage cart in the trash—maybe one of the local scrap-metal guys could salvage it—and then checked on Gus and Mattie.

The pair had finally run their excitement out and were sprawled together beneath the magnolia, pink tongues lolling. I made sure the water bowl I kept beside the porch steps was clean and full; then, because I'd forgotten to do so when I drove in, I grabbed the key hanging unobtrusively from one porch rail and went to check the mail.

All the homes in the historic district have identical flip-top brass mailboxes mounted to their gateposts. Each house number is affixed in contrasting silver for easy identification. While the boxes aren't large enough to hold shipments from various online retailers—those get tossed over the gate by the delivery person—they're still large enough to hold a month's worth of bills at one time. And they have a cool vintage vibe despite having been installed only about twenty years ago when the district was officially christened.

So as not to have to wrestle with the heavy driveway gate, I made my way down the front walk and out the smaller entry gate. Fortunately for me, my gardener, Hendricks, keeps the honeysuckle on the front fence in check so that I don't have to battle grasping tendrils going in and out.

I unlocked the mailbox to find that, as usual, the contents were mostly of the junk variety. I sorted through the stack while I made my way back to the house again. A couple of bills always managed to sneak in with the solicitations for life insurance and time-shares, and I didn't want to miss them.

But as I separated the postal wheat from the chaff—the latter of which I'd deposit directly in the recycle bin—I found a heavy square envelope addressed to me in dark-brown calligraphy. Given the envelope's expensive ecru paper and the gold wax stamped with a rose that sealed it, the letter had to be personal correspondence. However, I didn't recognize the Atlanta return address.

Curious, I added it to the "keep" pile while I called the dogs. "Mattie, Gus, come on in if you want a treat!"

Of course they did, and so we went in the kitchen side door. The pups knew the drill and both sat politely while I pulled out the box of snacks from the cabinet, offering a paw in return for a couple of cookies. While they crunched away, I tossed the recyclables and reached for a steak knife. Carefully, I slid the blade beneath the sealed flap of the mystery envelope—it was so pretty I hated to simply rip into it—and pulled out a fancy cardboard presentation jacket.

"*Save the Date,*" I read aloud, staring in confusion at the brown calligraphy on the jacket's front.

Then realization dawned, and I tugged at the protruding loop of gold ribbon. Out popped a matching card with an embossed border, its message in the same brown calligraphy. Feeling suddenly blindsided, I dropped onto the barstool where I'd earlier been counting cash and began reading, though I barely registered the words.

Please save the date . . . upcoming wedding . . . Ms. Rue McFadden and Mr. Cameron Fleet . . . Atlanta, Georgia.

A late-February date—deliberately chosen, I was sure, so as not to conflict with the Masters golf tournament typically played in mid-April—was spelled out in larger lettering than the rest. A final line, *Formal invitation to follow*, ended the notice.

The dogs gave a woof, and I looked up. Harry had chosen that minute to walk in, probably in search of hot water for his execrable rooibos tea. He looked my way.

"*Déjà vu,*" he declared; then, obviously noticing my distress, he frowned. "Nina, is something wrong? Does it have to do with Roxanna?"

Momentarily speechless, I shook my head and proffered the card. He read it, then handed it back to me with a lift of a wry brow.

"Well, that's pretty open-minded of them, inviting the ex to the wedding. You planning on going?"

"Are you kidding?" I burst out, earning another woof from the dogs.

Ripping the card in half in a dramatic gesture, I tossed the pieces onto the counter and added, "The only event starring Cameron Fleet that I'll ever attend is his funeral, and that's only to make sure he's actually inside the box."

"Ooooo-kay," Harry replied, and waited.

I waited too, taking a calming breath . . . or three, or four. My vehemence surprised even me. Thankfully, only Harry and the dogs had witnessed that regrettable display of high school–like angst.

Finally, I shook my head and summoned a weak smile.

"Sorry, I guess that was an overreaction. I think I'm just feeling the aftereffects of everything that happened today. Besides, I probably got on the invite list by mistake. Whoever did the mailing must have mixed up my name with his cousin Nita. They're pretty close."

Though, actually, Anita Fleet Hampton, youngest daughter of my ex-mother-in-law's baby brother, was another one whose funeral I'd go to only as a double check. But that was a whole other story.

Harry, meanwhile, gave me a sympathetic look. "Don't worry, I understand what you're going through. I remember what a shot to the gut it felt like when I found out my ex got remarried."

"Your ex!"

I nearly fell off my barstool, my momentary bout of self-pity forgotten as I stared at him in disbelief. "Since when were you ever married?"

"Since a couple of days after high school graduation."

Then, when I continued to stare, he gave an airy wave.

"Didn't I tell you that story before? Commencement was on a Saturday, and on Sunday my child bride and I drove to Savannah right after her graduation party. Which I wasn't invited to, thank you very much," he clarified with a self-deprecating smile.

Then, while I listened in growing disbelief, he continued, "We stayed in a cheap motel that night—separate rooms, mind you—and went to the courthouse first thing Monday morning. Once the deed was done, we drove right back here to Cymbeline to our respective parents' homes."

"Wait. So you didn't tell anyone you got married?"

Harry shook his head.

"Not a soul. It was all very *Romeo and Juliet*. The plan was that we'd get summer jobs and earn enough for a deposit for an apartment in Athens. She would be starting fall classes at the university"—the University of Georgia, I knew he meant—"and I intended to find acting work in Atlanta. Once we were ready to make the move, we were going to announce the *fait accompli* to our families and then hit the road as official man and wife."

"So what happened?" I asked in unwilling fascination.

He shrugged as he idly picked up the torn save-the-date card and pieced it together again.

"The usual. After a couple of weeks of wedded bliss, my blushing bride thought the better of what we'd done. She told her parents, who told my father, who arranged for an annulment. And everyone pretty much took blood oaths never to breathe a word of what had happened. On the bright side," he finished, tossing aside the cardboard pieces just as I had done, "I didn't have to pay alimony."

"Oh, Harry, I'm so sorry. I don't know what to say."

"You don't need to say anything. It's been twenty years, so I'm pretty much over it by now," was his wry response. "It's not like we ever lived together as a married couple. But when my dad made sure to mail me the clipping from the *Cymbeline Times* about her wedding a few years later, that did kind of sting."

My inner mama bear that had come to life earlier in the day abruptly reared her ursine head on teenage Harry's behalf. I'd heard a few stories from Harry before about his father. I had long since concluded that if I ever met the man in person, we probably were going to have a little come-to-Deity chat, just because I can't abide a jerk. This story hadn't changed my mind any.

I was also dying to know just who this mystery woman in Harry's life was. But as he hadn't volunteered the info and he'd already spilled quite a lot just by giving me this peek into his past, I wasn't going ask. At least, not today. Instead all I said was, "So, do you see her around anymore? Or did she leave town with the new guy?"

"They left town. I'm not sure exactly what happened after that, but when I ran into her again not too long ago, she'd long since ditched that guy for husband number two, who lived in Atlanta. Well, technically husband number three, if you count me. Anyhow, we decided we still could be friends even after all that history between us."

He hesitated, his expression momentary clouding, before he added in a softer tone, "And I'm glad we did."

The seeming wistfulness in those last words took me by surprise. The Harry I knew wasn't much for sentiment—though maybe he simply kept that side of him well hidden. He was, after all, an actor.

"You're a better man than I am, Harry Westcott," I said with a smile. "Maybe I'll be to that point with Cam someday, but not in time for his wedding."

I left him to his tea and carried the mail with me back to my room. As for the invitation, I taped it back together and tacked it and the fancy envelope to my bulletin board over my desk.

Exposure therapy, I told myself, recalling that technique from an article I'd read online once. Seeing the save-the-date notice on a constant basis between now and February should desensitize me to the whole Cam remarriage thing by the wedding. The "friends again" thing would likely take longer.

The remainder of the evening proved blessedly anticlimactic. I spent some time before supper playing with the dogs and arranging a spot where Gus could sleep. Though Mattie normally claimed the foot of my bed, I wasn't sure she would allow another dog to join her. But the spare pillows I'd wrapped in an old blanket and put in the corner of the bedroom looked pretty cozy. Maybe when I returned the treat jar with its hidden money, I would pick up Gus's kennel in exchange.

After a solo pizza dinner—Harry had declined my invitation to eat together, taking his half of the pie upstairs—I spent the remainder of the evening on my laptop. With Mattie and Gus quietly snoring on bed and pillows, respectively, I updated my B&B email list with the new names I'd collected at the expo before things went bad. I replied to a couple of requests for information and gladly booked a three-day stay for two for the upcoming weekend. Then, with official business done for the night, I sent a personal email to John Klingel.

I used the excuse of checking on Virgie, not that I wasn't legitimately concerned about how the woman was handling her partner's death. Which was why I also asked him to let Virgie know that I had Gus safely at the B&B. I saved my true reason for the email until the end, however, asking in a casual postscript if the floral-arranging workshop was still on for Monday night. I wouldn't blame John if he'd canceled, but I was looking forward to that mental break.

Not surprisingly, I didn't get an immediate response, though hopefully the florist would be checking his email sometime before morning.

I stayed up longer than usual watching television in bed. That was partly because, with no guests in the house, I could sleep in late and partly because every time I shut my eyes, I saw a lifeless Roxanna tumbling from the prop cake.

There was a third part, however, one I was reluctant to admit to but that had been very quietly nagging at me all day. Something about her accident didn't seem right—beyond the obvious, of course. At some point I'd figure out what that something was, but for now I had no choice but to let it percolate in my brain.

It was almost two in the morning when I finally fell asleep with the remote control in my hand and a house-flipping reality show marathon in progress. I woke up approximately seven hours later to the TV still on and an exercise infomercial playing. Two pairs of sad puppy eyes were staring at me from the edge of the bed, plainly expressing doleful canine wonder over why they hadn't been fed yet.

With a groan, I shut off the television. I let the dogs outside for their morning potty break while I took a quick shower. Afterward, I put up my hair in a messy bun, dashed on a touch of eye makeup, and threw on skinny black jeans topped with a boyfriend-style pink-and-gray plaid shirt. And then, because I couldn't help myself, I turned on my laptop and pulled up the neighborhood gossip site, looking for news about what had happened to Roxanna.

I wasn't shocked to find several threads in process, all started by different people apparently hoping to have been the first with the news. While most were relatively respectful and filled with crying emojis, one thread really set my hair on fire with its cringeworthy subject line: *OMG! Killer Cake*. Many of its individual postings were from people feverishly speculating on what they'd seen happen during the fashion show and spreading what could be classified as "fake news." The other half were from people offering condolences and a few who'd simply typed three dots, the non-internet-savvy way to make sure they would be notified of future comments. But I found no new facts about the accident, and so after a few minutes of appalled perusal, I shut down the screen and went to call the dogs.

It was a quarter to ten by the time I headed to the kitchen, Mattie and Gus trailing after me and all three of us in search of a late breakfast. Harry was seated at the kitchen island, an empty bowl that had held his normal breakfast of Greek yogurt with granola before him, drinking his usual tea. Though he still had an hour to go before Dr. Garvin was to pick him up, he was already dressed for their so-called date.

I took in the navy slacks and pale-blue dress shirt he wore, the sleeves of the latter rolled to display tanned forearms for a deliberately casual air. He'd shaved his fashionable stubble, leaving his lean cheeks uncustomarily smooth. His hair was combed differently too, neatly parted on one side and slicked down instead of the casually mussed style he favored. If he was going for the retired-sports-figure persona, he had nailed the look.

With a teasing smile I told him, "Well, look at who's dressed up all fancy."

"And look who's not," he replied with a pointed look at my admittedly casual ensemble. "I take it you're not going to church this morning wearing that."

I would have come back with a snarky response to his dis of my non-working wardrobe, but Harry's comment sparked an unexpected idea.

And so, as I pulled clean dog bowls out of the dishwasher, I told him, "Actually, I am. On the way to Roxanna's place,

I'm going to drop by the Heavenly Host Baptist Church and chat with Dr. Bishop about her death."

"You're what?" Harry slammed down his tea mug with a thump and fixed me with a hard look. "What possible reason do you have for doing that?"

The vehemence of his question surprised me. Chalking up his reaction to nerves over spending the day with the good doctor, I levelly met his gaze.

"Because Roxanna was my friend, and something's bothering me about her accident. I can't quite put a finger on what's wrong, but I can't let it rest. That's why I want to talk to Dr. Bishop. He's the coroner, so maybe he knows something that I'm missing."

"There's nothing else to know," Harry shot back. "Why can't you accept that it was a ridiculous stunt that went terribly wrong? I have."

His words hung between us for a moment, and I saw something raw flash across his face before he shuttered his features into an emotionless mask. But by then realization had dawned. Now I understood his sadness when he'd talked about his fleeting marriage the day before—why he'd not mentioned the mystery woman's name.

"Oh no, Harry," I managed, through the sudden catch in my throat. "I'm so sorry."

"I don't know what you mean" was his cool response as he rose and put his dishes in the sink. "And now, if you'll excuse me, I have things to do before Dr. Garvin picks me up at eleven."

He stalked out of the kitchen with his usual elegance. I stared after him, wanting to stop him, to make him talk about it, but knowing that doing so would only make the situation worse. At best, he'd deny it; at worst, he'd admit the truth. But something told me that, either way, trying to force a confession from him would leave an irreparable rift in our tentative friendship.

And so I let him go, though I was pretty certain I now knew the identity of the mysterious girl Harry had eloped with out of high school . . . knew that, for a few short weeks, my friend Roxanna Quarry had once been Mrs. Harry Westcott.

Chapter Eight

I hurriedly fed the dogs and myself, then cleaned the dishes and set up the pups on the screened-in porch. My errands wouldn't take long, but I didn't want the rambunctious canine pair stuck inside alone. Together, Mattie and Gus had a tendency to be mischievous, so the less opportunity they had to get into trouble, the better.

By dint of rushing, I was out the door and driving off by ten thirty. Dr. Bishop's second service started at eleven (it said so on the church's sign), and my plan was to catch him outside beforehand. But beyond that, I'd been in a hurry to be gone before Harry came downstairs again. After our ill-fated conversation, the best thing would be to avoid each other for a time, until the awkwardness passed.

Though, depending on what I learned from Dr. Bishop, I might have to keep my distance from Harry even longer.

A short drive later I was turning down the street not far from Roxanna's place where the Heavenly Host Baptist Church held down a prime bit of corner real estate. Both the church and Dr. Bishop's funeral parlor (located on the corner right across the same street) had been converted from neat cottage homes. Both were painted identically, bright white with matching white shutters and trim.

Parking was in the former homes' backyards, which had been paved over and striped to each hold probably fifteen cars the size of mine. But with a church service about to start, both lots were filled, as were any curb spots for a half block in all directions. Glad I'd thought to wear running shoes rather than heels, I parked the Mini on the next block and speed-walked my way to the church.

With ten minutes to spare before the service would be starting, I joined the line beneath the green awning that stretched from halfway down the walkway to the church's wooden double doors. Most of the congregants were African American, though I did spy a couple of white faces in the two dozen or so people ahead of me. Greeting everyone as they entered the church was a tall, thin man wearing a black suit and clerical collar, an oversized Bible tucked under one arm. This, of course, was the Reverend Dr. Thaddeus Bishop, church pastor.

He was of African American heritage with a brick-red complexion and a neatly trimmed Afro and beard, both of which had once been a deep rusty color but now were liberally streaked with gray. Given that I now knew he'd headed the church since Harry was a teen, I pegged him for being in his late fifties. Minus the gray he could have passed for at least a decade younger. As far as I knew, there was no Mrs. Dr.

Bishop. But from the way several women clung to his proffered hand for longer than necessary as he greeted them, I suspected there was significant interest in that job.

I joined the smiling crowd, aware that I stood out—not so much because of my pale complexion but because everyone else was dressed in their literal Sunday best. The men wore suits and ties; the women (even the younger ones) wore modest dresses or skirted suits, most of the latter in primary colors and almost all with coordinating feathered or lace-bedecked hats.

I made a mental note to break out one of my former business outfits should I ever decide to attend an actual service, which was not out of the question. I could hear gospel music—faint from outside the church, but a rousing chorus every time the double doors opened to admit another churchgoer. Used as I was to the staid Episcopal services of my childhood, the joyous air I felt here had more than a little appeal.

Dr. Bishop was obviously an efficiency expert in addition to his other talents, for the line moved with a swiftness that the Disney folks would have envied. Within a couple of minutes I'd reached the door and was standing face-to-face with the pastor.

He broke into a smile of recognition as he took my hand in a warm grip.

"Ms. Fleet, it is a pleasure to see you again," he declared as we shook. "What brings you to my humble church this morning? Are you in need of the Lord's guidance?"

"Good morning, Reverend," I replied, meeting his smile with one of my own. "I probably could use a little divine assistance, but it's your help I'm actually here for. It's about my friend, Roxanna Quarry."

He promptly sobered. "Ah, yes, the unfortunate young woman from the bridal exposition yesterday. Such a tragedy. You say she was your friend?"

"Yes. We'd only met a couple of months ago, but I . . . I quite liked her," I told him, doing my best to keep the emotion from my voice. "I was there when the accident happened. So were some of my other friends, and their young daughters too. We're all shaken up by her death."

"A tragedy. One of my colleagues, Dr. Garvin, happened to be there and attempted to render aid."

"I was there watching her," I confirmed. "She sure jumped into action."

He nodded. "Not surprising. She is a skilled physician. Unfortunately, my understanding is that young woman was already past help. Perhaps if she had been found sooner . . ."

I hesitated, then forged on. "The thing is, something keeps nagging at me that there's more to the story than what I'm hearing from the police. It would really help me—would help all of us—to know that what happened to Roxanna was simply a terrible accident."

He gave my hand a final kind pat and released it. "Ms. Fleet, firstly, you know from our past interactions that I am not at liberty to speculate publicly on a deceased's cause of death. I can only call for an autopsy. The medical examiner must make the final ruling. And secondly, I must point out that I am about to be late for my own service."

"I understand," I replied in disappointment. "But I had to ask."

"However," he added, "I did make one pertinent observation. The manner in which the decedent's scarf was wrapped around her neck was not the way that one would normally wear such an accessory."

My hand went reflexively to my own throat. "Wait. You're saying—"

"I'm saying this is not the best time to chat," he said, smoothly cutting me short. "You must excuse me, Ms. Fleet. My congregation awaits."

He left me standing beneath the awning as he went inside. Echoes of gospel music continued to drift toward me as I mulled over what the pastor had said. I recalled Roxanna's outfit when she'd stopped by my booth, the way her pretty scarf had been slung untied beneath the lapels of her jacket. Yet when she tumbled from the cake, that expensive length of silk had been wrapped tightly about her throat.

Uneasiness settled over me. Now I realized it had been something about Roxanna's scarf that had pinged my subconscious. And it had taken the reverend's comment to thrust that incongruity to my brain's surface.

I thought back to what I'd seen of the prop cake itself. I'd not been close enough to study its construction—and, of course, my attention had been on Roxanna. But if I recalled correctly, the top layer that popped open had been made of what appeared to be little more than heavy pressboard stapled to a thin wood framework to make a circular box. Even if her scarf had somehow caught on a random splinter, the act of its being snagged would simply have pulled the cloth free. No way could the scarf have wrapped around her throat tightly enough to strangle her until she died—unless someone else's hands had done the actual wrapping.

And if that was the case, it meant Roxanna's death hadn't been an accident at all, but murder.

I made my dazed way back to my car, not daring to let my thoughts travel any further until I was sitting in the driver's seat, engine running. Only then did I ask myself that single, vital question: If Roxanna had been murdered, then who had killed her?

The obvious answer was Virgie. I'd overheard the women's fight that morning, had overheard Virgie's accusations of embezzlement that might have been true, given the wad of cash in the red canister in the car's passenger seat beside me. The last time I'd seen Roxanna alive had been perhaps thirty minutes before the fashion show began. That would have been plenty of time for her and Virgie to have gotten into another altercation somewhere behind the scenes. Maybe the argument had turned physical and Roxanna had ended up dead. And then, panicking, Virgie had hidden Roxanna's body in the most convenient spot, which happened to be the prop cake.

Though, of course, Virgie would have known the display was to be rolled out and opened onstage later, which would hardly have made it an ideal place for hiding a dead body. Which maybe poked a hole in my theory. But then, panic made one do odd things. So now the follow-up question was, what to do next?

Borrowing trouble.

That old saying of my grandmother's drifted into my mind. Could that be what I was doing? Maybe Roxanna had deliberately tied her scarf up high on her neck and out of the way before impulsively climbing inside the cake, planning a light-hearted gag and not knowing that she had unwittingly set herself up for tragedy. Maybe both the pastor and I had misinterpreted what we'd seen. So perhaps it was time for me to back away. Last thing I needed—that Roxanna needed—was for me to stir a pot that didn't require stirring.

Accidents did happen, after all.

I put the car into gear and made the short drive to Roxanna's house. By the time I got there, I'd come to a decision. As Dr. Bishop had implied, unless the medical examiner made the formal determination of homicide, Sheriff Lamb would have no need to investigate further. I had already given my statement to Deputy Jackson, and I knew that the sheriff knew where to find me.

I also knew that, should Roxanna's death turn out to be no accident, the highly capable Sheriff Lamb always got her man—or woman.

Given that it was Sunday morning, Roxanna's neighborhood was quiet. I parked at the curb as I had last time. Canister tucked beneath one arm, I got out and, first checking to make sure I wasn't observed, went to retrieve the door key from Uga. But when I lifted the statue, only the faintest key-shaped silhouette remained on flat sand-colored rock beneath the resin dog.

I blinked and looked a second time. When it was apparent that no key was there, I searched the mulch around the statue base. Still no key.

I frowned. When Harry and I had left the place yesterday, I'd been more than a bit distracted with Gus and dealing with all that had gone on. Had I only thought I'd returned the key to its hiding place?

I stood and dug through my purse twice and checked my jeans pockets, though I wasn't wearing yesterday's clothes. I even went back to the Mini and searched the seats and floorboard. But it seemed the key had vanished, just like in a shell game.

"Great," I muttered.

As far as I knew, I was the only one Roxanna had told about the Uga hiding spot, and she'd sworn me to secrecy. Which meant that I must have absent-mindedly carried off the key myself and left it somewhere at the B&B. And which also meant that if I wanted to unload the ten thousand dollars I was carting around, I'd need to find another way into Roxanna's house.

Treat jar still in hand, I headed back to the porch. The small-town mindset in Cymbeline extended to most folks being lax about locking up their houses. Maybe I'd get lucky and Roxanna had left one of the double-hung windows unlatched.

Setting down the canister behind the tomato bucket, I tried the windows on either side of the front door. Neither was unlocked. I made my way around the house, unhooking the lower portion of each window screen just enough to test the sash. It wasn't until I was almost back to where I'd started that a window—the one looking out from the dining area—slid upward as I pushed.

Relieved, I pulled off the screen the rest of the way and propped it against the outer wall, then pushed open the window as high as it would go. Plenty of room to fit through, I determined. Getting a leg up over the waist-high sill so I could straddle it and climb in, rather like getting on and off a horse, would take a more effort. Thinking longingly of the stool that I'd used in the pantry, I decided I'd have to go with option B—lean over the sill and shimmy my way in. Not the most efficient manner of entry, but I had no other choice.

I went back to the porch for the canister and then hurried back to the open window. It occurred to me as I leaned over the sill to put the treat jar inside that what I was about to do was technically breaking and entering. But I was putting something back into the house, not taking it out. And I planned to be inside only long enough to go from window to pantry and back again.

With more speed than grace, I wriggled my way through the window and landed in a heap on the hardwood floor. Dusting myself off, I picked up the treat jar and started forward, only to stop short again at the sight that greeted me.

The living area beyond looked like a South Georgia twister had come through it. Sofa and chair cushions and pillows were tumbled about on the floor, and the furniture itself was knocked askew. The credenza beneath the flat-screen television gaped open to display empty shelves, the DVR and cable boxes hanging out by their cords. A few dozen DVDs that must have been in with the equipment had been unceremoniously swept to the floor. The antique drop-front desk on the opposite wall was open, pens and stamps and stationery strewn about it. The desk's long drawer had been yanked out and lay upside down on the rug, its contents scattered as well. Even the blanket had been pulled from Gus's kennel.

I stood staring at the disarray for several shocked seconds, trying to reconcile the sight with how Harry and I had left the place just hours ago. Obviously, someone had been in Roxanna's house since yesterday afternoon in desperate search of something. And I had a bad feeling I knew what that something was.

I didn't bother to check if any other rooms had been torn apart. Hurriedly setting down the canister of hundred-dollar bills, I pulled my cell phone from my jeans pocket and for the second time in as many days dialed 911.

"Yes, I'd like to report a burglary," I breathlessly told the dispatcher who answered, then gave her my name and Roxanna's address.

To my shock, the woman replied, "We've had a report of this crime in process just a few minutes ago. Officers have already been dispatched to that address and should be arriving momentarily."

"Okay, thanks," I shot back, and hastily ended the call. How would anyone else know what had happened here? Unless they'd seen me checking windows and thought *I* was some sort of Sunday morning prowler?

My pulse, which had begun racing as soon as I'd seen the ransacking around me, now kicked up the pace to an all-out sprint. I grabbed the canister again. I needed to get rid of it and get out of the house before Sheriff Lamb's deputies showed up.

"Sheriff's Department! Don't move!" barked a man's voice from the open window behind me before I'd even taken a step.

I froze. So much for making an exit.

"Raise your hands where I can see them," the same voice demanded, "and turn around real slow."

I complied, lifting the treat jar skyward like an offering—or like I was about to cosh someone over the head with it. I turned slowly, halting once I was facing the window. A familiar figure holding a revolver pointed my way practically filled the window's frame.

"H-hello, Deputy Jackson," I managed. Then, in the words of every criminal ever, I added, "Th-this isn't what it looks like."

"Yeah?" was his ironic response, though to my immense relief he lowered his weapon and reholstered it. "You're Ms. Fleet, right? The B&B lady from the expo?"

I nodded, and he shook his bald head. "You mind telling me what you're holding there, ma'am?"

"Um, a dog treat jar filled with ten thousand dollars in cash."

His eyes narrowed, but all he said was, "All right, why don't you put the jar on the floor in front of you—real slow, now—and then take a couple of steps back from it and raise your hands again."

I did as instructed, relieved because the pottery canister, though it didn't weigh all that much, was starting to feel as heavy as a sack of concrete the way I was holding it.

Once I'd complied, he went on, "And can you tell me what you were doing with this jar of money?"

"Putting it back where I found it."

His expression went from quizzical to outright skeptical as he took in the disarray around me.

"Uh-huh. You should know, Ms. Fleet, that a neighbor reported someone of your description removing the screen from this window and climbing through it into the house. Was that person you?"

I nodded.

"And are you the owner of this house?"

"No, Deputy . . . but I can explain."

Which also was what every guilty party said right before the cuffs went on. Though I wasn't guilty of anything except, quite obviously, bad judgment. But just as I thought he'd allow me to defend myself, the deputy activated his shoulder mic.

"Dispatch, this is two-twenty-one. I need assistance with a ten-fifteen suspect needing transport."

I stared at him in dismay. I didn't know what 10-15 meant, but *suspect* and *transport* were pretty darned self-explanatory. Visions of my business going down the tubes flashed through my mind. Even if we cleared up everything once we got to the sheriff's department offices, being hauled off was not a good look. Who would want to stay in a B&B when the owner had been arrested for B&E?

"Sending the call now," came the dispatcher's voice I recognized from my 911 call, though it sounded far more tinny through the mic.

Jackson nodded and clicked on his mic again.

"Copy that," he replied, then added in a quieter voice, "Sorry, baby, looks like I'm going to be late for church. Can you get your sister to take the kids and I'll get there as soon as I can?"

"Already did that."

"Thanks. See you this afternoon. Out."

Looking a little rueful, the deputy said to me, "The dispatcher is my wife, Maureen. We try to work staggered shifts so one of us is home with the kids most of the time. Didn't quite work out that way this morning."

"I'm sorry," I told him, and meant it—for him and for me. "But I swear I wasn't trying to steal anything. The house was already trashed when I got here. I called nine-one-one to report it. Just ask Maureen."

He did just that, clicking his shoulder mic again. "Dispatch, this is two-twenty-one again. Can you confirm if more than one call came in about this B&E?"

To my relief, I heard Maureen reply back with my name and the time of my call just a few minutes earlier. With that, Jackson gave me a stern look.

"That part of your story checks out. But that still doesn't explain why you climbed through a window of an unoccupied house."

"That's because I couldn't find Roxanna's spare door key where I thought I left it." And then, as realization dawned, I exclaimed, "That's why it was missing! Whoever tore up the house must have known about the key, too, and used it to get in."

Jackson sighed. "All right. Maybe we can resolve this situation without a trip to the station. Why don't I come in and we'll chat a little more?"

For someone of his size and girth—not to mention the big belt o' police stuff strapped around his waist—the deputy managed to climb through the window with far more grace that I had, mostly because he was tall enough to easily swing a leg over.

Once inside, he took another look around, then said, "If you didn't tear the place up, then I'd better check to see if whoever did is still hanging around."

"Good idea," I managed, a small shudder abruptly racing through me. That possibility hadn't occurred to me, yet now I realized I could have been in danger this entire time from some unknown housebreaker.

He gave me a sharp look. "If I don't cuff you, do I have your word you'll wait here while I look?"

"Absolutely," I told him, and did the old *cross my heart* gesture from childhood for emphasis.

"Fine. Sit there"—he pointed to one of the dining chairs that looked undisturbed—"and don't touch anything or move a muscle until I come back downstairs."

I sat and didn't move while Jackson called Maureen back and canceled the backup. He pulled on a pair of latex gloves he'd had stashed in the utility belt; then, hand on pistol butt, he took off for the hallway. I waited, picturing each room he'd be checking: the kitchen, the guest bedroom, the powder bath, and then the rooms upstairs. When it seemed he'd been gone far too long—though logic told me that my nerves had probably skewed my sense of time—I started to worry. I'd seen enough slasher movies to know the drill.

Heroine waits while cop checks if crazed killer is still inside the empty house. Cop doesn't come back. Heroine searches for cop only to find him horrifically murdered. Crazed killer creeps up on heroine while audience screams for her to look behind her.

For I was pretty sure that whoever had torn apart Roxanna's house was no amateur burglar who'd happened on the unoccupied house by chance. He—she—had likely been in search of the cash I'd accidentally taken.

Then another thought occurred to me. Given that the cash matched the sum Virgie had claimed was taken, that person might also have been involved in the embezzling. And, taking *that* thought a step further, this person might also have had something to do with her death. And if they knew that I knew about the money—

"I had a feeling it might be you," came a sudden voice from beyond the window behind me, and I let out a shriek.

Chapter Nine

Deputy Jackson's instructions notwithstanding, I leapt to my feet and spun about. Leaning over the windowsill like a neighbor come to gossip was Sheriff Connie Lamb.

My height but with about fifty pounds more muscle than I had, the woman cut a no-nonsense figure in her tan uniform shirt and dark-brown trousers and tie. Her brassy blond hair—almost the same color as the big metal badge pinned to her chest—was twisted into a tight French braid. Her mirrored sunglasses reflected my shocked expression back at me, though I swiftly regained my composure.

"Sorry, Sheriff, I thought you were a serial killer."

"Yeah, I get that a lot," she replied, deadpan. "Where's Jackson?"

"Right here," the deputy replied, striding his way in from the hallway. "Don't worry, ma'am, everything's under control. I checked the rest of the house in case the suspect was still here. Whoever it was, he's long gone."

The sheriff slanted him a look. "He? Based on the witness description, I thought Ms. Fleet was the suspect, and it looks like she's still here—and left to her own devices. You want to tell me what's going on?"

Jackson looked as sheepish as a man of his size and appearance could. Still, I was impressed by his save as he replied, "Upon further questioning of Ms. Fleet, while technically she made an unauthorized entry, it turns out she was in the house for legitimate reasons not related to what appears to be a burglary. I asked her to remain here while I secured the scene first before I took her formal statement."

"Uh-huh."

Her expression was as skeptical as the deputy's earlier had been. She glanced about the room, taking in the disarray. "What about the rest of the house? Is it trashed too?"

He nodded his bald head. "It all looks pretty much like this. Stuff's thrown around, but nothing's destroyed, no graffiti, so I wouldn't say vandalism. And all the electronics are still in place, so I don't think it's a run-of-the-mill burglary. I'm guessing someone was searching for something specific, probably the cash Ms. Fleet was carrying around."

"Cash?" The mirrored-sunglasses gaze whipped my way.

I nodded. "Ten thousand dollars, all in hundreds."

The sheriff tugged off her sunglasses and hung them from her shirt pocket. Her icy-blue gaze regarded us both with restrained exasperation.

"Doug, why don't you sign out and join your girls at church, and I'll take it from here. If you'll unlock that front door on your way out, I'll come in and have a little chat with Ms. Fleet before I call in the crime scene boys."

A couple of minutes later the deputy had left and the sheriff had come in. Motioning me back to my seat at the dining table, she took the chair opposite me and pulled out a small notebook from her non-sunglasses pocket.

"Let's start from the top," she told me. "I received Mr. Westcott's voice message yesterday that you two took it upon yourselves to pick up Ms. Quarry's dog"—

"Gustopher," I helpfully supplied. "He's a Goldendoodle."

"—as a temporary foster situation until other arrangements could be made," she continued, ignoring my interruption, though I saw her write down the pup's name. "How did you access the house that time?"

I explained how Roxanna had previously told me about the key under the Uga statue—that and the fact that I was sure I'd put the key back again, only to find it missing on the return trip.

She held up a restraining hand before I could voice my theory that whoever had ransacked the house must have known about the key too. "We'll circle back around to that in a minute. Let's keep going in chronological order. What was the state of the house when you and Mr. Westcott entered to retrieve the dog?"

"You mean, was anything torn apart like it is now? No, everything looked the same as usual."

"So you've been in Ms. Quarry's house before?"

I nodded. "We went out for drinks once, and we had lunch over at Peaches and Java, and I picked her up here both times.

We did a couple of doggy playdates too, but she came over to the B&B for those."

The sheriff wrote for a moment, then flipped to a second page and said, "Tell me what went on once you and Mr. Westcott were inside."

"Not a lot. Harry took Gus out back to do his business while I went to the kitchen to load up his food and leashes and such. That's when I found the dog treat canister with the cash in it," I explained, pointing to the red ceramic jar still sitting on the floor. "Of course, I had no idea there was anything besides dog treats inside it until I got it home and looked inside."

"We'll circle back to that one in a minute too."

She made a couple of quick notes and then resumed her questioning. "What else did you do after you had gathered all the dog's supplies? Did you walk around the rest of the house, open any cabinets or drawers?"

I frowned and shook my head.

"You mean, did I snoop around in my dead friend's house?" I asked, more than a little offended. "No. Harry brought Gus back inside, and then—"

"Oh, wait," I interrupted myself. "Gus was upset because he couldn't find Roxanna anywhere, so I left Harry to call you while I ran upstairs with Gus to get one of her T-shirts. You know, so he'd have something of hers to comfort him at night while he slept."

My voice wavered a little, and for a moment I saw a flash of sympathy in the sheriff's pale eyes. But all she said was, "So you went upstairs. Was anything out of place there?"

"Not that I could see. I went into her bedroom, opened her clothes hamper, and pulled out the shirt."

I didn't tell the sheriff about my moment of silent contemplation, though I recalled something else. "One thing that was kind of unusual happened while I was upstairs. Gus started barking at the window, and when I looked out, there was a car parked at the curb right behind my Mini Cooper. It was only there for a few seconds before it took off down the street."

"Did you see a license plate? What about make, model, and color?"

I shrugged. "I couldn't see the tags from upstairs. But it was a silver two-door, kind of sporty looking. Sorry, I'm not good with car brands."

"Was the driver male or female?"

"I couldn't tell. Besides, the windows were tinted—but not the black aftermarket tint that will get you pulled over, just regular old factory standard gray," I clarified, earning a nod of approval from the sheriff with that detail. "Then Gus and I went back downstairs, and we all left the house. I locked the front door again, and I'm ninety-nine percent certain I put that key back where I found it."

The sheriff made a few more notes. Then her sharp blue gaze shifted to the red canister. "Since you've already been carrying it around, why don't you bring Gustopher's treat jar over here so we can discuss the money you found."

I did as requested, giving her a rundown on how I'd seen the canister on a high shelf in the pantry and how I'd used the step stool to pull it down before adding it to the rest of Gus's haul. I explained that, once back at the B&B, I'd opened the canister to give the dogs a late-afternoon treat, only to find something besides Scooby Snacks inside. I finished by describing how I'd counted out the wad of hundred-dollar bills before wrapping the cash up again so I could return the jar intact to Roxanna's house.

Once I'd ended my account, the sheriff slanted me a look. "Was there a reason you didn't call my office to report this find so we could secure the cash for Ms. Quarry's next of kin?"

"I was going to," I hurriedly defended myself, "but I talked to Harry. He convinced me it would be better to not say anything and just put it back where I found it. Not that we didn't trust your people to keep it safe, but, you know, red tape and all . . ."

I trailed off as Sheriff Lamb slowly shook her blond head, her free hand momentarily pinching the bridge of her nose.

"Word of advice, Ms. Fleet," was her dry response. "Next time you need legal advice, ask someone other than Harry Westcott. Now, would you please explain how you ended up climbing through a window instead of entering Ms. Quarry's residence via the door like you did the first time?"

I told her again about the missing key, emphasizing that I was very sure I'd put it back beneath Uga when Harry and I had left the house the previous day.

"Interesting," she replied, pursing her non-lipsticked lips. "You relocked the front door when you left yesterday, and it was locked today when you returned. And the rear door was locked as well?"

"It was today," I confirmed. "And I remember seeing Harry unlock it yesterday when he took Gus out back."

She nodded and made a note that I assumed was to ask that question of Harry later. But what she said aloud was, "You know, I've been a cop for almost twenty years, and I can't even guess how many burglaries I've investigated. But I can say that in all those cases, never once was the suspect considerate enough to lock the door after himself once he was finished ransacking the place."

She paused, the silence giving me a moment to realize that the whole locked-door thing *was* rather odd. I could see the burglar closing the door to avoid the attention that an open door would bring, but why take the extra step of locking it? And, presumably, taking the key with them afterward?

The sheriff, meanwhile, continued, "There's a good chance the person who broke in was looking for something very specific. Detective Jackson seemed to think it might have been the money you found. To your knowledge, did Ms. Quarry ever speak in public about keeping a lot of cash lying around the house?"

"No," I told her, "but there is something else you probably should know. At the bridal expo, I overheard an argument between Roxanna and Virgie Hamilton. Virgie accused Roxanna of embezzling money from their joint business account. She claimed Roxanna had taken ten thousand dollars."

The sheriff's already ice-blue gaze turned suddenly glacial. She set down her notebook and pen to lock eyes with me.

"Ten thousand dollars," she repeated. "The same amount as in the dog treat jar. And did you tell Deputy Jackson that little detail about Ms. Hamilton's accusations yesterday when you gave him your statement at the expo?"

I shook my head, refusing to feel guilty. "No. And at the time, I didn't think it mattered. I like Virgie well enough, but she's not the nicest person out there. A couple of hours before the fashion show, I overhead another fight she had with her ex-husband. That one got pretty nasty too. So as far as I knew, the whole embezzling thing was just Virgie being . . . well, Virgie."

"Right," the sheriff agreed. "Just Virgie being Virgie—until Ms. Quarry ended up dead under suspicious circumstances. And until you discovered ten thousand dollars stashed away in her house."

Now it was my turn to stare as the words *suspicious circumstances* sunk in. My previous doubts about Roxanna's death abruptly resurfaced. "Are you telling me that what happened to my friend wasn't an accident?"

"Not at all. Let's just say that since our friends at the ME's office don't work weekends, we won't officially know how Ms. Quarry died for another day or two."

"But unofficially . . . ?"

The sheriff gave me a tight smile. "Unofficially, I suggest you stick to innkeeping instead of burglary, and don't go gossiping around town about our discussion today. And unless you plan to go through Georgia peace officer training, I also officially suggest you leave the investigation of Ms. Quarry's death to my people. Agreed?"

I nodded.

"Now, do you have any other bombshells you'd like to drop on me?"

I shook my head.

"Then thank you for your cooperation, Ms. Fleet. You're free to go."

Maybe it was just me, but I heard an implied *for now* in her words. And as I was smart enough to know to get going while the getting was good, I hurriedly rose.

"Thanks, Sheriff."

Then, figuring I might as well ask, I added, "Any chance I can take Gus's crate with me? I didn't have room in the car yesterday, and if he ends up staying with me for a while, I'll need it."

"Sorry, nothing leaves the house until the scene is released," she replied, only to surprise me by adding, "but I'll see if one of us can drop it off to you later."

One of the perks of living in a small town, I told myself as I thanked her again and headed out. But once back in the Mini and on my way home again, the import of what I'd learned began to sink in. Though Sheriff Lamb hadn't said so in as many words, I could read between her law-enforcement lines well enough to know that my suspicions had proved correct.

Roxanna's death had been no tragic accident but a deliberate killing.

Blinking back tears, I again recalled seeing her pretty patterned scarf tied high and tight around her neck. Murdering someone in that way, up close and personal, was surely the most heinous act someone could commit on another person. But had her death been planned from the start, or had it been a crime fueled by blinding anger and opportunity? And was the murder tied to the ten thousand dollars I'd found—which sum might or might not be the same cash Virgie had claimed Roxanna had stolen? Or had she been killed for some totally unrelated reason?

But possibly the most important question was, now that I knew we were dealing with something other than an accident, what was I going to do about it?

"Stop it!" I shouted aloud, to the dismay of the elderly man in the lane beside me as we both waited at one of Cymbeline's few traffic lights.

Stop it, I silently repeated. Sheriff Lamb had explicitly warned me not to get involved. And, truth be told, I wasn't eager to play junior detective and go poking around looking for suspects. The smart thing would be to keep my head down and let Sheriff Lamb and her deputies do their jobs. Because, for all I knew, the medical examiner might come back with the determination that her death *had* been an accident.

The dogs enthusiastically greeted my return home by begging for a snack. I obliged, glad for their furry company in the otherwise empty house. It was almost one PM, meaning I had another three or four hours alone before Harry returned from his quote/unquote *date* with Dr. Garvin. Which was perfectly fine by me, given that we'd parted this morning under less-than-friendly circumstances. But I realized now how much I'd come to depend on the actor being my sounding board.

Which maybe meant I'd made a mistake in telling Harry he could stay past the thirty days we'd originally agree on. The longer he remained in my house, the more he became a permanent fixture in my life. And given that I apparently hadn't quite shaken off the last man in my life—why else would Cam's pending marriage have knocked me for a loop?—no way did I want to set myself up for that kind of failure with any other man.

Shoving aside the issue for now, I decided that keeping busy was my best bet. But after lunch and a little playtime with the pups, I found myself uncharacteristically at loose ends.

Since opening the B&B, I'd usually spent my Sunday afternoons cleaning after the weekend guests had departed. But as I'd deliberately not booked any guests for the past couple of days, everything was already in place. I'd done my wash the night before, and as always, the lawn and gardens were Hendricks's bailiwick. All of which meant I was chore-free for the day. While normally I would have relished the respite, suddenly that big chunk of free time seemed impossible to fill.

I could finish one of the three or four mystery novels that sat half-read on my bedside table, but I wasn't in the mood to try solving someone else's murder. I could haul my single-gear bicycle out of the garage and tool around the neighborhood, except that the tires were low and my hand pump had gone missing. I could even break out the cute bag of yarn I'd bought on impulse a few weeks back in hopes of teaching myself to crochet, but I knew I didn't have the patience for that today. And so, leaving the pups playing together in the fenced-in side yard, I made my way to my bedroom office and opted for the default of settling in front of my laptop.

I made a quick check of my email and typed a few replies. That done, I meant to browse social media, maybe scroll through a couple of those clickbait pages that showed glamorous celebrities sans makeup. But after a few minutes of idle surfing, I instead found myself on one of the popular car-ratings sites looking for silver two-door sedans.

Specifically, silver two-door sedans that looked like the one that had briefly parked behind me the day before at Roxanna's.

Remembering how I'd heard the grinding of transmission gears, I was able to narrow down my search to makes and models available in stick shift. Harder was recalling the vehicle's exact silhouette, since I'd seen it from above. After an hour of scrolling through what seemed like a dealer's lot worth of cars, I decided what I'd seen had been a Nissan . . . or maybe a BMW. Which meant the driver was either budget minded or rich, which left a significant pool of possible owners.

My eyes practically spinning in my head, I logged off the computer. While I wasn't confident that I'd actually ID'd the car in question, I was certain that should I see the vehicle again, I would recognize it. Whether its presence at Roxanna's house was coincidental or significant remained to be seen.

I stood, stretched, and then looked at the clock and groaned. Barely three PM, leaving a good chunk of the day still to get through. I went to the door leading out to the porch and let the dogs inside again. The pair trotted in together as if they'd been a team forever and simultaneously leaped onto my bed. Both circled a few times atop the comforter before flopping down for their pre-supper snooze.

I smile fondly at the pair, grateful that my Gus-fostering venture seemingly was working out well. As for myself, despite the weekend's turmoil, I still had the workshop at Midsummer Night's Flowers tomorrow as something fun to look forward to.

The florist's email had been among those I'd read earlier, since he had finally replied to my message from yesterday. His response had been surprisingly chatty given that he and I had only just met.

Yes, despite yesterday's tragedy, our seminar is still on—fourteen paid customers (including you!) are all ready and eager to learn. Besides, I've already ordered the supplies.

Yes, Virgie is holding up relatively well, though you can imagine she is not her usual self. And as her son is not exactly the nurturing type (millennials!), it has fallen to me to help her deal with the shock of her partner's death.

What interested me more, however, was a final comment at the end of his message. According to the florist, the infamous prop cake had been Virgie's idea, which was why she was taking Roxanna's death so hard.

I did a little bed-flopping myself, finding a spot between the two pups to sprawl with my head propped atop a bevy of fancy pillows while I mulled over that portion of his message again.

The prop cake was Virgie's idea, which was why she felt guilty.

Of course, that was what she'd told John. And since to this point everyone had been calling the death an accident, that could make sense. On the other hand, maybe Virgie's guilt actually stemmed from the argument she'd had with Roxanna a few hours earlier. Which was likely something she'd not tell her ex, but it made even more sense. The pair had been friends—at least at one time—and surely it would be painful to realize her last interaction with Roxanna had been an acrimonious one.

Or could it be that Virgie's feeling of culpability was far more telling—because she had strangled Roxanna herself?

"What do you think, puppers?" I murmured aloud, glancing from Mattie to Gus on either side of me. Both were happily snoring away, however, and so they made no response. I thought about it a while longer, then finally shook my head. A true southern woman, Virgie's weapon of choice was cutting words. I could see her wielding a pearl-handled pistol from a socially acceptable distance, but only in self-defense. Even at her angriest, I couldn't picture her brutally choking the life from someone.

In fact, such a killing seemed more the act of a man.

I sat up again so abruptly I dislodged the dogs, who scrambled not to tumble off the bed. While I didn't style myself as a true-crime buff, I'd read enough to know that murder by strangulation was predominantly a man's crime, and almost always perpetrated against a woman. In fact, it was as much an act of angry power as it was a convenient method of dispatching someone without resorting to a gun or knife.

Besides, whoever had killed Roxanna had to have been strong enough to lift her into the cake.

A scene from yesterday flashed through my mind—the sight of a tall man in a purple shirt disappearing down a corridor where none of the exhibitors were allowed. I'd not seen his face, but the color of his shirt was the same as the one John had been wearing. And the florist had been conspicuously absent from his booth before and during the fashion show, reappearing only after Roxanna's body had been discovered.

But if Roxanna's killer was John, what motive could he have had for such a heinous crime? Could he have been acting on some sort of misdirected defense of his ex-wife? Punishment, maybe, for the embezzlement—assuming that actually had occurred? Or had there been some darker relationship between the two?

Then I shook my head. No way could John have done something like that. True, I had only just met the man, but he had radiated a rare decency despite the obvious antipathy between him and Virgie. After she'd treated him with contempt, he still had rushed to her side when she collapsed and even seen her home again. People like that didn't commit cold-blooded murder.

Did they?

The dogs, who had settled back down again, abruptly sprang to attention, and Mattie gave the bark that meant someone was on the property. I glanced at the clock and saw it was almost four. It had to be Harry returning from his outing with the good doctor. For the moment, I let thoughts of murder slide in my curiosity to know how the actor had fared in his first attempt as male escort.

"C'mon, you two," I told the pups as I jumped up from the bed. "We need to catch our friend Mr. Westcott before he can hide in the tower room."

The pair eagerly trotted after me as we hurried from my bedroom into the main foyer. My plan was to lie in wait there at the stairway so I could "accidentally" run into him returning from his so-called date just as I was headed to the kitchen to fix myself and the dogs a pre-supper snack. As I'd closed the driveway gate after me earlier, Meredith (might as well think of her in more familiar terms now) would have dropped him off at the curb. And so I waited for as long as I judged it would take him to walk from the pedestrian gate to the front door.

And kept waiting.

After a good minute had passed and the front door still hadn't opened, I grew concerned. Already the dogs were bored with the wait and had flopped to the wooden floor, sprawling into dual tripping hazards. I frowned. Even if Harry had forgotten his house key, he knew the code to get inside.

I gave him a few more seconds; then, sidestepping the pups, I hurried down the corridor to the front door and threw it open. At first glance, I didn't see Harry. That is, until I looked down to find him lying faceup on the porch, eyes closed and limbs sprawled in a pose that looked uncannily like the way Roxanna had lain after falling from the ill-fated cake.

Chapter Ten

I stifled a gasp. Only yesterday, someone I knew had unexpectedly died. Surely it wasn't about to be two for two!

"Harry, what happened? Are you okay?" I choked out, dropping to my knees beside him and shaking his shoulder when he didn't immediately reply. "Harry, open your eyes and talk to me. Do I need to call an ambulance?"

He blinked a few times and squinted his baby blues open, then gave me a lopsided grin. "Nope, don't need no amblua— ambula—whatever you said. I'm just having . . . a little trouble . . . with your door."

His grin broadened as he held up his key, narrowly missing stabbing me in the eye with it.

I snatched the key from his hand, my fear evaporating as I sank back onto my heels and fixed him with a stern look. Sounding like every clichéd housewife from every ancient sitcom I'd ever seen, I demanded, "Harry Westcott, are you drunk?"

"As a skunk, Nina Fleet, as a skunk," he cheerfully agreed. He floundered a moment like a turtle flipped over on its shell, then subsided and stuck out a hand again. "Be a lamb and help me up, won't you?"

I muttered a few choice words beneath my breath as I grabbed his arm and sharply tugged him up into a seated position. He sat there a moment, presumably to regain whatever equilibrium he had left.

"Please tell me that Dr. Garvin wasn't this snockered when she drove you home," I said, when it looked like he'd recovered his bearings somewhat.

He shook his head, the gesture sending him swaying where he sat.

"Snockered?" he echoed with a sloppy grin, though he drew out the word so that it sounded more like *schnockered*. "Really, Nina, you need to . . . update your slang. And don't worry . . . I took an Uber."

So at least he hadn't pickled every single brain cell. "You think you can stand now?" I sourly asked him, getting to my own feet. "I'm not about to let you lie out here for the whole neighborhood to see."

"I can stand just fine," he assured me, and then promptly proved himself wrong when he tried but miserably failed to rise.

Still muttering, I grabbed his arm again. After a great deal of pushing and pulling, Harry was finally upright.

"Told you," he said with a triumphant grin, only to have to grab the porch railing to keep his balance.

I frowned back. I could tell he'd definitely had a drink . . . or five or six. And not just because he wouldn't pass one of those side-of-the-highway sobriety tests that required walking in a straight line. As an actor, he had long since modulated his native Georgia accent to more neutral midwestern tones. But under the influence, he had reverted to his original speech pattern, far softer and drawlier than my own East Texas twang. Which was too bad for him, since the accent reminded me of my ex-husband when he'd tied one on.

Meaning I wasn't predisposed to be sympathetic.

"All right, get inside," I told him, holding open the door. "You'd better go sit in the parlor, because you'll break your neck if you try the stairs."

I referred, of course, to the main staircase. I didn't even want to imagine him attempting to climb the ladderlike steps going up to the tower room. For sure I'd be calling the EMTs then!

Fortunately, he was amenable to my suggestion. With me holding him steady on one side and a curious Gus and Mattie following after us, he obediently made his way to the parlor. That room was, as the name implied, the formal space where visitors sat a spell, as the old-timers put it. As far as B&B guests were concerned, the parlor and dining room were the designated public areas in addition to the lawn and gardens outside.

The parlor lay behind a pair of chestnut pocket doors, which fortunately were already slid open, revealing the working fireplace with an intricately carved mahogany surround that was the centerpiece of the room. Harry collapsed on one of two antique blue velvet sofas that had been there even before his great-aunt's time. I settled on one of the matching slipper chairs—low-slung, armless seats upon which well-bred nine-teenth-century ladies had situated themselves to pull on their shoes. These days, they made for a comfy perch for those of us more vertically challenged.

"All right, Harry," I told him as he slumped sideways against the sofa arm, pretty well melting into the threadbare fabric, "you're stuck here in the parlor until I'm convinced it's safe for you to try the stairs. Understood?"

" 'Stood," he agreed, using his hands at either temple to manually shake his head in the affirmative.

With anyone else, I might have been tempted to laugh; that, or else simply leave them to sleep off the booze. Instead, my original pique was fading, replaced by concern. For in all the months I'd known him, I'd rarely seen Harry drink any-thing stronger than his rooibos tea. And I'd certainly never pegged him as a day drinker, particularly not while on the job—which he had technically been while at the party. Some-thing must have happened to send him off on such a spree.

"Stay right there," I told him, though there was likely little chance he could leave the room under his own steam. "I'll be back in a minute."

He lifted his arm in an exaggerated pantomime of check-ing a nonexistent watch. "I'll . . . time you."

I rolled my eyes but made no comment as, leaving Gus and Mattie to stand guard, I headed to the kitchen. I had some experience sobering up intoxicated men after being married to Cam. Unfortunately, I knew that the usual advice of coffee and a cold shower did nothing more than leave one tending to a wide-awake, chilly drunk. But I did have a couple of tricks up my sleeve that always seemed to work.

I returned to the parlor a few minutes later hauling a tray filled with a small pitcher of cool water and a cup—both plastic, since I didn't trust Harry with glassware in his current state— along with a couple of sports drinks and a bottle of aspirin. Setting down the tray on the delicate wooden coffee table between the two sofas, I poured the water and handed it to him.

"Drink that," I directed. "The water will help flush the alcohol out of your system a bit faster and counteract your being dehydrated. And that's velvet—try not to soak the sofa while you're at it!" I hurriedly added as he sloshed a good portion of the liquid while two-handedly aiming for his mouth.

Once he'd finished the glass, I poured him seconds, which he managed to finish with only a few drops spilled that time.

"Good," I told him. "Give that a few minutes to settle, and then start drinking the sports drinks to get some electrolytes back in your system. That and taking a couple of aspirin will help with the hangover you're going to have."

"You are a true . . . Florence Nightingale," he replied, struggling with the childproof cap on the aspirin bottle. When it was obvious he wasn't going to master that particular challenge, I took it from him, opened the top, and shook out two pills.

"Stick with the liquids for now," I instructed. "I'll be fixing supper in another hour or so. I'll make you a toasted PB&J sandwich. Simple protein and carbs. It'll help with the hangover."

"Sounds delish. Maybe after a little nap." He swallowed the aspirins, leaned back against the sofa, and shut his eyes. A moment later he was snoring.

So much for finding out what had happened at the party. "C'mon, pups," I told the dogs, who'd been watching the whole episode with interest. "We'll let Harry sleep it off for a while. You can help me write up a welcome newsletter to email to all the women who signed up at the expo yesterday."

But barely was I back at my laptop starting on that project when my cell phone rang. I didn't recognize the incoming phone number; however, as my cell phone was also my business line, I answered in my best professional innkeeper's voice.

"Fleet House Bed and Breakfast. This is Nina Fleet; how may I help you?"

"Uh, yeah, hi," came a man's voice. "My name's Ryan. My fiancée was at that bridal thing yesterday, and she, uh, picked up your brochure?"

He sounded young and tentative. I smiled a little.

"Hi, Ryan. Are you interested in booking a weekend honeymoon stay, or would you like to talk about holding a rehearsal dinner here, or maybe even your wedding?"

"Yeah. I mean, maybe. She really liked your place. I thought maybe I could come by and take a look in person. You know, to see if I like it too."

"Of course. Are you free tomorrow morning? Say, around ten?"

He was silent a moment and then replied. "Yeah, that would be good. Can you tell me your address?"

I told him, then added, "If you give me your email address, I can send you some rate sheets and additional information so you have a better idea of the services we can provide."

We being me and Mattie, though he didn't have to know that.

"No, no email!"

I frowned a bit at this sudden vehemence, but then he quickly added, "I mean, she might see it on my computer, and I kind of want this to be a surprise. My fiancée thinks I hate the idea of a B&B."

"Got it," I replied, smiling again. "So I'll see you tomorrow at ten, Ryan. Thanks so much. Oh," I hurriedly added, "I'm sorry, I didn't get your last name."

But Ryan had already hung up.

I shrugged. Hopefully this wouldn't be an exercise in futility. While I hadn't been in the wedding venue biz for long, I knew in general that grooms—especially young ones—rarely had much input in any wedding arrangements. But since Ryan's fiancée had specifically mentioned my B&B to him, things might work out favorably for me.

Setting down the phone, I finished composing my *Thanks for visiting Fleet House B&B's booth at the Bridal Expo* email and forwarded it to my new listings. With that checked off the business to-do list, I shut down my email for the day.

But rather than immediately logging off, I hesitated as my gaze inexorably settled on the taped-together *Save the Date* card I had tacked to my bulletin board over my desk. Then, knowing I'd regret it, I pulled up the Google search engine and typed in *Cameron Fleet Rue McFadden engagement*.

I'd expected to get several hits, but what came up in my search were pages and pages of Cam and Rue. From Twitter comments to magazine profiles to YouTube clips of interviews, everything I wanted to know about this latest sports power couple was there for the viewing. Of course, there were the inevitable paparazzi shots of the pair kissing at this exclusive restaurant, holding hands in that stadium box, flashing Rue's boulder-sized ring in front of those people.

I clicked through a few more images, recalling as I did so how my picture had been taken with Cam at various charity events over the years. Back then he'd still been an up-and-comer with only a couple of major wins, and so the coverage had never been as . . . overwhelming as this media blitz. Too, I'd been a lowly civilian without a penchant for dresses cut up to here and down to there.

Rue, on the other hand, was a nationally known broadcaster whose outfits invariably looked a few sizes too small for her—and not in a bad way. Of course, it made sense that the sports and entertainment media were all over their engagement. It didn't hurt that they were a perfectly matched pair appearance-wise, both being equally blond and beautiful.

A real-life Ken and Barbie, I thought sourly. *I wonder if Vegas is already making book on how long the marriage will last and which one of them will get stuck paying alimony when they split.*

Before I could sink deeper into snarkiness—or, worse, give way to temptation and do a second Google search for *Cameron Fleet's ex-wife* just to see if anyone had mentioned me—I wisely shut down the computer. I followed that by pulling down the accidental invite from my bulletin board and sticking it in the trash can beneath my desk.

So much for exposure therapy, I decided. With that one bit of online surfing, I'd reached my limit.

Needing a distraction, I spent the next hour lounging on my bed catching up on a sitcom I had DVR'd for future binge watching. By the time I had watched a couple of episodes, it was almost six PM, meaning suppertime. Feeling slightly less stressed, I got up off the bed and headed to the kitchen. I paused first at the parlor door, however, to check in on Harry.

He was still snoozing—or was still passed out, depending on how you defined his current state of unconsciousness. In complete defiance of the "no dogs on any furniture except my bed" rule, Mattie lay sprawled beside him with her head across his lap, sound asleep herself. The Goldendoodle lay twisted in a half circle, all four paws skyward as he snored away too.

I smiled a little at the tableau and took a quick picture with my cell phone, mentally titling the shot *A Boy and His Dogs*—and then, with a muffled snort, changing it to *Let Sleeping Dogs Lie*. Given how Harry always claimed not to be much of a pet person, I'd use the photo to later to give him a hard time.

Then, temporarily leaving the trio of sleeping beauties to their dreams, I went to rustle up food for both humans and critters.

Of course, within 2.5 seconds of when I opened the dog food bag and started pouring, the pups magically appeared at my feet, their supersonic canine hearing having picked up the familiar rustling even in their sleep.

"Hold your horses," I admonished them with a smile as they bounced and circled in anticipation. "Let me get you fresh water, and then you can chow down."

Once the dogs were happily scarfing their kibble, I pulled out the ingredients for Harry's PB&J and then returned to the parlor. This time the actor was awake, though he was huddled with elbows on knees and face in hands and looking more than a little like something the proverbial cat had hauled inside.

"So you've decided to rejoin the living?" I coolly asked from the doorway.

He looked up at me through bleary eyes. "Maybe. I haven't quite decided yet. I think I'll go splash some cold water on my face."

"You do that. I'll go put together that sandwich for you."

I returned a few minutes later, plate in hand, to find him back on the sofa, though this time sitting upright as he cradled a half-empty cup of water. He looked a bit more bright-eyed now, if not exactly bushy-tailed.

"Looks like you'll pull through," I told him as I marched toward him.

He shuddered. "That's still up for debate. Do me a favor, Nina . . . don't ever let me do that again."

"Sorry, that's all on you. I'm not my Harry's keeper," I sternly told him, then immediately contradicted myself by handing him the plate. "Now, eat."

He doubtfully eyed the toasted sandwich—Harry being the sort to go all healthy and organic in his food choices—but obediently took a bite, and then another.

"Thanks, I think this helps," he admitted, sounding more like his old self again. "Where did you learn that cure?"

"Trial and error. And much as I'd like to trash-talk Cameron Fleet, we're talking about you now," I told him. "So what happened? I thought you were supposed to be earning a big fat paycheck pretending to be Dr. Garvin's boyfriend. Were they serving super-potent Jell-O shots with the barbecue or something?"

"I don't do Jell-O shots *or* barbecue," he informed me, and I recalled that gelatin was technically ground-up cow bones and thus something vegetarian Harry didn't eat. "We were drinking celebratory champagne. The bottles kept coming, and it seemed rude to refuse."

"Celebratory?" I echoed in confusion while he paused to take another bite of PB&J. "Weren't you at a family reunion? What was everyone celebrating?"

"Oh, didn't I already tell you?" He set down his sandwich and raised the cup of water in a mock-toasting gesture. "Apparently, congratulations are in order. As of this afternoon, Dr. Meredith Garvin and I are officially engaged."

Chapter Eleven

"Engaged?" I squeaked in a voice high enough that it should have brought Mattie running. "As in, the two of you are getting married?"

"That's usually how it goes," Harry replied. "Fortunately, as her new fiancé is some washed-up ballplayer named Harold Anderson, I'm pretty sure the wedding will never happen."

Now it was my turn to hold my head in my hands. In the short time I'd known the man, I'd seen him accused of murder, threatened by a knife-wielding stalker, and even cast in a rewritten version of *Hamlet* to help catch a murderer. But impulsive marriage proposals were a whole other level of bizarre, even for him.

Well, except for his original lapse into matrimony back when he was eighteen.

I sunk onto the sofa opposite him and asked, "Do you want to talk about it?"

Harry shrugged. "There's not much to tell. I played my role as doting boyfriend to perfection, and I found sufficient non-meat products on the buffet to make a tolerable meal. Best of all, none of the family knew anything about baseball, but all of them were thrilled to meet a former professional athlete. Bottom line, the reunion went swimmingly for the first hour or so."

"Until . . . ?" I prompted.

"Until the slew of family good news." He raised a hand and started ticking off fingers. "First, cousin Bobby and his wife Glenda announced they were expecting baby number three. Then sister Jen and husband Phil started showing pictures of the new mansion they'd just bought in Savannah. Uncle Lester had to brag about his son Pembroke's making partner at some law firm in Atlanta. Oh, Meredith's father and her Aunt Miranda got into dueling photos of their respective Galapagos Islands vacations last spring."

"Sounds pretty grim," I agreed, feeling a little sorry for the good doctor having to compete against a family of one-uppers. "I guess having a new boyfriend"—I gave the word finger quotes—"wasn't enough to win her the 'Best in Family' competition."

"Exactly. I suggested she try a brag or two about her daughter, but apparently Buddy's accomplishments can't trump giant tortoises and law partnerships. No, she needed something that would put the spotlight solely on her. So she offered me a nice bonus if I would propose to her during the family's annual croquet tournament."

I gave him a hard look. "Really, Harry, you'd stoop to fake-asking a woman to marry her for cash? I thought the whole escort thing was kind of smarmy already, but this bogus engagement is really beyond the pale, even for you."

"For your information, the only stooping was when I got down on one knee in the center of the croquet court," he loftily replied, brushing imaginary grass from his trouser leg. "Don't worry, I gave Meredith her money's worth when I pledged my undying love."

While I waited expectantly, he continued, "I stole the paper ring off Uncle Lester's cigar and used that instead of a diamond. The proposal was a mash-up of *Romeo and Juliet* meets *The Wedding Singer* meets *Little Women*—the Winona Ryder version, of course. There wasn't a dry eye in the house when I was finished."

"I'll bet there wasn't," was my wry response, not that I doubted him. I'd seen Harry onstage, and he was pretty memorable.

He continued, "As soon as Merry—that's what I call her, by the way—said yes, her father broke out the case of champagne they were saving for dessert. Everyone started offering toasts and congratulating her for landing such a great guy. After about an hour of guzzling Dom and being slapped on the back by every man there, I decided it was time to exit stage right."

Exit, pursued by a bear, I wryly thought, recalling that memorable, tragicomic stage direction from *The Winter's Tale* (hey, Harry wasn't the only one who read Shakespeare). The sentiment seemed appropriate. I had a suspicion that Harry had released a figurative grizzly with his little stunt . . . not that it was my problem.

155

Aloud, I merely asked, "So how are you going to get out of the engagement?"

"The usual way. When a decent enough amount of time has passed, she'll let her family know I did something outrageous—probably cheated on her with another woman—and that she called it off."

Then something else occurred to me. "Wait, what about Buddy? She was at the reunion, right? She knows who you are from the expo. How did she not blow your cover?"

Harry gave a sheepish shrug. "Actually, Meredith bribed her with a new smartphone if she kept her mouth shut. But I've still got burn spots on my back from where she glared lasers at me the whole time."

I suppressed a snort. "That takes care of Buddy, then, but you'd better hope none of her male relatives are the vengeful sorts. They might come after you with shotguns once they hear you're a low-down dog."

I grinned a little. Any family that played croquet and featured cases of Dom Pérignon at their family reunions probably didn't track down cheating fiancés with loaded firearms. That wouldn't stop me from ribbing Harry about it, however.

And he did look a bit alarmed as he replied, "I didn't think about that. Maybe it will look better if I do the breaking up, not her."

Then, holding up his now-empty plate up, he added, "Nina, would you be a lamb and make me another toasted PB&J?"

After a second sandwich—which I grudgingly made for him, but only because I decided I wanted one for myself—Harry rallied enough to take himself upstairs. I told him I had a potential guest coming in the morning at ten, and he agreed to make himself scarce during the tour. So I wouldn't have to rush in the morning, I did a little final tweaking of the rooms and made sure I refilled my little rack of brochures and business cards at the front door. That accomplished, the pups and I made an early night of it too.

*   *   *

I was up later than usual in the morning, as I didn't have breakfast to lay out for guests. Mattie and Gus were content to sleep in as well, and so it was almost eight when, still dressed in gray sweats, I finally made my way with the pups to the kitchen. To my surprise, Harry was already there, sitting at the kitchen island drinking his tea. Like me, he was wearing sweats. Unlike me, he looked less like he'd just crawled from bed and more like he'd stepped from a sportswear catalog.

"Feeling better?" I asked as, leaving the pups to pester him for some head scritches, I pulled down their bowls from an upper cabinet and then retrieved the dog food bag from the pantry.

"Much improved," he confirmed, "despite the fact that you force-fed me peanut-butter-and-jelly sandwiches."

"Toasted PB&Js," I clarified. "Not only are they guaranteed to help sober you up, they take the edge off any hangover.

And you couldn't have hated them that much or you wouldn't have eaten two of them."

I poured the dog kibble, which Mattie and Gus polished off in a few gulps once I'd set down their bowls.

Harry, meanwhile, gave an exaggerated shudder. "I must have been drunker than I thought." And then, tone turning contrite, he added, "Sorry for all the trouble I put you through."

"That's okay," I told him, and realized I meant it. "It's been a difficult couple of days. But on the bright side, at least you made a nice chunk of change with this whole escort thing yesterday."

"Yeah, well, about that . . ."

He stared down for a moment at his teacup. When he looked up again, his expression was sober.

"I suppose it's confession time," he told me. "I've been mulling over the whole proposal thing this morning. And much as it pains me to say this, even though the fake engagement was Meredith's idea, I think you were right. Proposing to her like that was pretty smarmy. So I'm going to call her later this morning and make arrangements to return her checks. Both of them."

I stared at him, uncertain which shocked me more—Harry Westcott admitting that I was right, or Harry Westcott giving back hard-earned cash. Definitely not in character for the man. Maybe he was feeling more charitable because he'd been mulling over his ill-fated marriage to Roxanna . . . which bit of history I was still going to confront him with at some point.

But what I said was, "If it helps, I think you're doing the right thing. And I'm proud of you too."

He rolled his eyes. "Well, that certainly makes up for losing first and last months' rent on a new apartment," was his ironic reply.

I smiled a little. "What are you going to do if someone else calls you to be a plus one?"

"I'll cross that bridge when I come to it. For now, I plan to revise my terms of contract to include no wedding proposals." Then, switching subjects, he asked, "What about your day yesterday? Did you put Roxanna's cash back where you found it?"

I grimaced. "That's right, I didn't get to tell you what happened when I went back to her place with the money."

While Harry huddled over his rooibos and I made myself a cup of coffee, I related my unfortunate encounter with the local sheriff's department, along with my discovery that Roxanna's house had apparently been broken into before I'd done my own B&E. And though the sheriff had dismissed it, I told him my theory that the burglar had likely used the same spare key I'd left under the Uga statue, meaning he—or she—probably knew Roxanna more than casually.

One thing I didn't mention was my visit to Dr. Bishop's church and his comments about the oddly-tied scarf. Neither did I tell Harry about Sheriff Lamb's unspoken message that, in her opinion, Roxanna's death had been something other than an accident. For one thing, I didn't want to plant painful images in his brain about the final minutes of a woman I was certain had once been his wife. For another, willingly or not,

I'd promised the sheriff to keep my mouth shut. I was pretty sure that if she found out I had I broken my word, she wouldn't hesitate to toss me in the clink—oops, more outdated slang!—for obstruction or something.

By the time I finished my tale, Harry's expression had gone from mildly surprised to intensely concerned. And not only because I'd made sure to repeat Lamb's acerbic jab about not taking legal advice from an actor.

"Sure, your burglar didn't find the cash," he agreed, "but that doesn't mean they aren't still looking for it. Think about it. If they're the same person in that silver car you saw the other day, chances are they'll figure out you took more than Gus when we left the place. And since they'd have no reason to know you gave the money to Connie for safekeeping, they might come here looking for it."

I set down my coffee mug with an unintended bang. True, the thought had already crossed my mind on a hypothetical basis, but having Harry say it out loud made it suddenly and frighteningly an actual possibility.

"But how would they know I was the one who took the canister?" I demanded, hoping to poke holes in both our arguments. "I doubt they could recognize me through the upstairs window."

He gave me a pitying look. "Every other car on the streets these days is silver, but you're the only one I've seen in Cymbeline driving a green Mini Cooper. If the burglar knew Roxanna, chances are they know you—or at least know *of* you. You won't be hard to track down."

So much for holes. My hands were trembling just a bit as I picked up my mug again and took a steadying sip. "What are you saying? Do I need police protection or something?"

"Probably not . . . but I'd definitely watch your back for a while. What do you have planned for today?"

"Not much. I already told you about that kid named Ryan stopping by at ten to decide if he and his fiancée want to book their wedding here. And I'm attending a flower-arranging seminar at John Klingel's florist shop tonight at seven."

"Maybe I should go with you."

"No need for that," I assured him. "Including John, there should be fifteen of us crammed into his shop. No crazy guy in a silver car is going to come after me with that sort of crowd. It's probably better if you stay here and keep an eye on the house. I know I have a security system, but—"

"But security systems can be breeched," he said, finishing my thought. "All right, Mattie and Gus and I will stand guard while you get all artistic with flowers. And I'll give Connie a call too. You know, see if she can have her deputies step up their patrols around here."

"Thanks, I appreciate that," I told him, feeling marginally better about the situation. But only marginally.

Much as I wanted to talk things through with Harry, I couldn't, not knowing what I did about him and Roxanna. And particularly not after our argument over Dr. Bishop yesterday, when I'd seen the pain her death had caused him. True, things had seemingly been patched up between us without any discussion—taking care of someone when they're drunk and vulnerable tends to do that—but my peace of mind now wasn't worth ruining his again. All I could do for the moment was take his advice and watch my back.

That, or break my promise to Sheriff Lamb and do a little investigating of my own.

I left Harry and the pups to hang together while I grabbed a quick shower. Time to take off my Secret Squirrel hat—that being Harry's sardonic nickname for me when I theorized about murder. I wanted to be at my innkeeper best when I talked to Ryan.

I focused my thoughts on business while I let the hot water beat down on me. If Ryan and his fiancée agreed to hold their wedding at my B&B, it would open whole new horizons for me. I'd have actual wedding pictures to post on my website and add to my brochure, which hopefully would attract other future brides and grooms.

Tourist town that it was, the B&B game in Cymbeline was competitive, particularly in these uncertain times. I had no illusions I could make a significant living as an innkeeper without stepping up my game. And while I wouldn't be hurting for cash anytime soon—my divorce settlement had made sure of that—I truly wanted this venture to be a success. Even one wedding party a month would make a huge difference to my bottom line.

Mentally and physically refreshed after the shower, I pulled on black jeans and one of my logoed oxfords, this one pale pink with the logo in black. I made a quick email check, glad to see an automated notice from my website booking tool showing another three-day reservation for the coming weekend.

A little before ten, Harry departed via Uber for Dr. Garvin's office, where he had confirmed she would be on a Monday morning. I put Mattie and Gus in my room—while my promo clearly stated we had an official B&B dog, some guests weren't too keen on that—and then killed time playing word games on my phone. I'd already opened the gate so Ryan could drive right in.

At ten past ten, I finally heard a car outside and peeked out the front window. But rather than seeing my expected potential customer, I glimpsed Sheriff Connie Lamb climbing out of her patrol car.

Forgetting about Ryan, I hurried out to meet her. She wasn't heading up the walk to the porch, however; instead, she had popped her trunk and was leaning into it.

"Hello, Sheriff," I called. "Is everything all right?"

The woman straightened and turned toward me, mirrored sunglasses flashing in the morning sun.

"Good morning," she greeted me. "I've brought you the dog crate from Ms. Quarry's place."

"Right, thanks so much," I exclaimed, having forgotten that she had promised to send it over. I would have expected one of the deputies to be handling the task, however, and not the sheriff herself. Which meant she was either big on customer service or had an ulterior motive for stopping by.

With luck, it would be the first.

I suspected it might be the second.

By now, she had pulled the crate from the trunk. Like the one I had for Mattie, it collapsed into a nice flat package. But since Gus was quite a bit taller than the Aussie, his crate was larger and a heck of a lot heavier. Not that one would guess that from the way the sheriff hefted it with one hand and set it beside her car.

"Would you like me to carry it inside for you?" she asked, closing the trunk.

I shook my head. I might throw out my back carting the darned thing to the house, but no way was I going to play helpless female and let her do the lifting for me.

"I've got it," I told her, hoisting the crate just enough to drag it away from the patrol car and lean it against my knee. "Could I offer you a cup of coffee for your trouble?"

"Thanks, but I'm actually on my way to the ME's office. I want to light a fire under them about your friend."

"I see."

I paused, meeting her mirrored gaze and waiting for the other shoe to drop. And, after a moment, it did.

"I know you gave Deputy Jackson your statement at the bridal expo, and you and I chatted at Ms. Quarry's house yesterday, but I was wondering if you'd mind answering a couple of more questions concerning Ms. Quarry's death."

I frowned a little—as far as I knew, I'd given all the answers I could—but nodded. "Sure. I'm not sure what more I can tell you, but I'll help if I can."

"Excellent." She pulled the ever-present notebook and pencil from her shirt pocket and immediately caught me off guard. "Did Ms. Quarry ever mention anything about an ex-husband to you?"

"You mean, Harry Westcott?" I exclaimed without thinking, then slapped my free hand over my mouth. But, of course, it was too late to call back the words.

And apparently that wasn't the answer Sheriff Lamb was expecting. She lowered her sunglasses so that I could see her pale-blue eyes.

"Excuse me? Would you mind repeating that?"

"Actually, I'd rather take the Fifth," I replied with a weak smile.

The sheriff didn't smile back.

"You're not on trial, Ms. Fleet, so the Fifth Amendment doesn't apply here," was her dry response. "We're just having a little friendly conversation. You don't have to answer if you don't want to, but I'd really appreciate it if you could help me out. Now, are you telling me that Mr. Westcott and Ms. Quarry used to be married?"

"Maybe. I think so. I mean, I'm not one hundred percent certain."

I hesitated. I'd already spilled the tea, so I might as well justify my theory. And so I continued, "Harry told me the other day that he got married right out of high school and that the marriage was annulled a few weeks later. But he never actually admitted that it was Roxanna he married. I put two and two together later on from a few other comments he made."

"I see. So we're talking an annulled marriage from two decades ago, but no actual corroboration from Mr. Westcott as to who the woman he married was."

"Exactly. And I really hope you won't ask him about it. He's having a hard time right now, and Roxanna's death hit him pretty hard."

"Yeah, well, it hit me too. Roxie and I were friends back in high school."

I stared at her in dismay. "Oh no, I'm so sorry. I didn't know."

Though I really should have put two and two together on this one as well. I knew that Harry and the sheriff had gone to high school together. If Roxanna had been in the same class, it made sense that she'd also have known Connie Lamb, and vice versa.

Lamb, meanwhile, slid her sunglasses back into place and scratched out something on her notepad. She went on, "While that's an interesting bit of trivia for our next reunion, for the moment I don't think it has any bearing on this case. Unless that changes, how about we pretend that the subject never came up?"

I sighed in relief. "I'd appreciate that."

"Fine. Now, let's try this again. My info says that Ms. Quarry was married and divorced twice. The phone number I have is for the second ex-husband, who's out of Atlanta. They split right before she moved back to Cymbeline a couple of years ago."

I shook my head. "Roxanna told me that she had an ex, but that's about it. She didn't mention there were two of them. And she never said anything about the most recent guy, good or bad. I don't even know his name."

"Maybe you'd recognize it if you heard it. It's Slater. First name Bryan. No, wait."

The sheriff pursed her pale lips and flipped back a couple of pages in her notebook, then gave a satisfied nod. "Sorry, it's not Bryan . . . it's Ryan. Ryan Slater."

Chapter Twelve

R^{yan?} Those little alarm bells went off in my head again. Was it coincidence that Roxanna's ex-husband—the man Sheriff Lamb was trying to track down—had the same first name as the young man who'd called to schedule a look at the B&B?

And who should have been here by now.

I glanced at my watch. It was almost ten thirty, well past time for the guy to be merely running late. Normally I would have assumed he'd simply changed his mind about coming by and hadn't been polite enough to call back and cancel. But with this sudden new information, another scenario occurred to me.

Maybe Ryan had spied the sheriff's department car parked in my driveway and kept on driving—because his true intent in touring the house had nothing to do with booking the place for a wedding.

Then I gave myself a mental shake. These days, seemingly every male under the age of forty was named Ryan. My first instinct was likely right. The name thing had to be a coincidence.

"No, I never heard Roxanna mention that name," I told the sheriff. Then, recalling what else she'd said about him, I asked, "Why are you looking for this Ryan guy if he doesn't even live in Cymbeline?"

She didn't answer, simply gave me a look over her sunglasses and flipped her notebook closed.

"I appreciate your cooperation, Ms. Fleet. Once we connect with Ms. Quarry's next of kin, I'll let them know you're temporarily fostering her dog in case one of them wants to claim him."

I waited until she had pulled out of the drive and disappeared down the street; then, with only a small amount of huffing and puffing, I hauled the crate up the porch steps and inside. The pups watched with interest while I set up the wire cage in my room alongside Mattie's little den. I lined the bottom with a spare blanket and added both the T-shirt I'd borrowed from Roxanna's hamper and Gus's favorite stuffed bunny toy. Once I'd finished, the Goldendoodle promptly trotted inside and flopped down in the familiar space with a contented little woof.

"Good boy," I told him, while Mattie gave her friend's new digs a curious sniff before retreating to her own crate.

Just as with Mattie, I'd leave the crate door open so Gus could go in and out as he wanted. As soon as my weekend guests arrived, he and Mattie would be confined to my room and their outside exercise area, but until then they could wander freely about the downstairs.

By now it was almost eleven. As my morning's tour had apparently fallen through, I decided to treat myself to lunch at Peaches and Java. Not that I didn't indulge in Daniel's cooking on a regular basis, given that I always made a plate for myself when the diner catered breakfast for my guests. But it had been a while since I'd had time to stop in for one of their equally delicious noon specials. Besides, I needed to run by Weary Bones Antiques down the block from them.

I smiled to myself. A week earlier, I had dropped off a painting for the shop's owner, Mason Denman, to do an appraisal. The modest-sized oil had come with the house, hanging in what would become my bedroom. A bit creeped out by the subject matter—it appeared to be a bucolic country landscape until you noticed screaming figures and slaughtered livestock in the distant background—I'd promptly hidden the artwork in a closet. Running across it again a few months later, I had given in to curiosity and showed it to Harry, who recalled it from his childhood.

"Gave me nightmares," he'd admitted.

He also remembered that, like me, Mrs. Lathrop and her late husband apparently had "inherited" the painting from the house's previous owner. That meant it was at least a century old, though Mason had cautioned me that age didn't necessarily mean it had any particular value. Thus, my hopes were modest, especially as I'd struck out with the last artwork I'd had Mason appraise.

Making sure Mattie and Gus had food and an unlocked doggy door to the porch and run beyond, I grabbed my purse and keys. The outside temperature was mild enough that I decided to walk the few blocks to the town square. I closed the driveway gate on my way out against any errant weekday tourists who decided to take a gander at the place in my absence and strode off.

Weary Bones was one of my favorite places to shop in Cymbeline, and not just because I had a small passion for antiques and collectibles. Besides being an expert in eighteenth- and nineteenth-century art and accoutrements, Mason was one of those people who truly enjoyed sharing his knowledge. Beyond that, he was something of a character—from his trademark dyed-black pompadour to his ever-present vintage pocket square (a different one every day).

It also didn't hurt that Mason always had his pudgy fingers on the pulse of town happenings. While Sheriff Lamb had been noncommittal about any updates regarding Roxanna's death, chances were the antiques shop owner would know the latest.

I heard the familiar jingle of bells as I entered the shop. The place always had a restful vibe about it, partly from the faint scents of old wood and beeswax that hung in the air and partly from the soft strains of classical music playing over the sound system. Mason stood behind the old-style wood-and-glass counter along the wall to my right. He looked up at my entry, and a smile split his face as he gave an enthusiastic wave. Today's pocket square, I noted, was a muted orange tie-dye.

"Nina, what perfect timing," he called. "I'm just now examining your painting."

"So, you think this one will make it to Christie's?" I asked with a smile as I headed his way, referring to the famous auction house. "We didn't do so well on the last painting I brought you."

The first oil was one I'd found in an upstairs closet, left behind by Harry's great-aunt. Painted in the cubist tradition, it was a typical portrait of a woman whose image had been deconstructed by the artist and then put back together haphazardly on the canvas, hands here and eyes there. Not my preference, style-wise—that is, until I spied the first few letters of a painted signature, *P-I-C*, the rest hidden beneath the amateur framing job. And so, visions of millions dancing in my head, I'd taken the painting to Mason for a look.

The man gave a commiserating chuckle. "It just wasn't your time to find an unknown Picasso in your closet. But this painting shows a bit more promise. I was just about to have Lowell take it out of the frame for me. You remember Lowell, don't you? Ah, here he is now," he added, indicating the tall, thin, and very blond man headed from the back room toward us.

I'd met Lowell briefly at the Shakespeare festival the month before, where he'd attended the opening-night performance of *Hamlet* as Mason's date. With a startling tan, courtesy of a spray booth rather than the sun, he was probably half Mason's sixty-something years. But his smile was gentle and his manner quiet, and what I had seen of him so far, I'd liked.

"Lowell has decided to learn the antiques business," Mason said with pride, giving the man an approving pat on the arm. "He has an MBA, so he's already taken over the store's books. And now I'm teaching him how we go about verifying and appraising."

"Good for you, Lowell," I told him, plopping onto the stool in front of the counter. "I have to say, it's pretty tough running the whole show by yourself. I think Mason was smart to take on an assistant. So, are you having fun?"

"I am," he agreed with a soft smile. "Well, except that Mason gave me this huge stack of books I have to study every night on every subject you can imagine. Right now I'm working on nineteenth-century porcelain. And believe me, he quizzes me on *everything*."

"You're learning from the best," I replied, smiling back. "So, speaking of quizzes, what do you think of my painting?"

"Not a clue if it's worth a thing," was his cheerful response as he took the picture back from his boss. "Artwork is next week's lesson. But I have to say, I totally adore this landscape. If you want to throw out a price right now, I'll probably buy it."

"Appraisal first, offers later," Mason admonished the man. "Now get back to work, Lowell, while I chat a minute with Nina."

He waited until the younger man, my painting in hand, had returned to the storeroom. Then he turned to me, cheerful expression promptly sobering.

"Tell me what happened with Roxanna. Word is you were there at the expo when she was killed."

While I knew full well Mason's penchant for gossip, I hadn't expected him to launch so bluntly into the subject. But given that one reason I'd stopped by the shop was to learn what *he* knew, I could hardly fault him for wanting news from me. Besides, I'd seen him and Roxanna chatting at the Chamber meetings many times. It stood to reason he was concerned about someone he must have considered a friend.

"If you read the papers and the local Listserv, you know basically everything I know," I told him. "I have to say, it was all pretty horrifying. Everyone did what they could to help, but it was too late when we found her. I think Sheriff Lamb is supposed to hear today from the medical examiner about how she really died."

"Well, I have my theories about that."

He lowered his voice, though the bells on the door would have warned us had anyone else come in.

"You're right, I've been reading every single post on the Cymbeline online group. You ask me, what happened at the expo wasn't an accident."

"Exactly," I agreed, keeping my own voice quiet now. "I can't say anything too specific because I promised Sheriff Lamb I wouldn't, but it looked like someone tied that scarf around her neck. The problem is, I can't think of anyone who hated her enough to want to murder her."

Mason gave an inelegant snort. "Really? Let's just say Karma finally caught up with our dear Roxie—Karma being one of those people she'd screwed over since she came back to town."

"Wait, what?"

I stared at Mason in shock, glad I was sitting, as my knees—heck, all of me—suddenly felt weak.

"Are we talking about the same Roxanna Quarry?" I choked out, once I found my voice again. "She was one of the nicest people I knew here in Cymbeline. That's why I couldn't think of anyone who could possibly have held a grudge against her."

"Bless your heart, Nina Fleet," Mason replied, pompadour quivering in sympathy as he leaned across the counter and patted my hand. "I could name six or seven people right off the top of my head who probably danced a jig when they heard what happened to her."

I gave my head a vigorous shake. "No. I don't believe it."

"How long did you know Roxanna?" he persisted. "A month, maybe two? You were just a casual friend, so there wasn't any reason for you to see that side of her. And she and I got along great. But some of the folks she did business with . . ."

He paused and then added, "Let's just say that when it came to the almighty dollar, our Roxie wasn't above pulling a few dirty tricks."

I blinked. And then, as suspicion niggled at me, I ventured, "You mean . . . like embezzling from a partner?"

He gave me a keen look. "I could see her doing that. I know she took a couple of ex-husbands for every cent she could. She even bragged to me about how she'd pretty much bankrupted the company she owned with ex number two and then walked out with a huge bonus before she divorced him. That was right before she came back to Cymbeline."

"But I never heard her talk about money like that," I protested. "She lived in that cute little house. And she drove a Ford."

And she hid a wad of hundred-dollar bills big enough to choke a horse in a dog treat jar.

Mason gave me a regretful look. "Nina, I'm sorry. I might be trash-talking her now, but I really did like her. And you know, maybe I'm wrong. I hope I am. She was smart and had wonderful taste. A real go-getter."

"I hope you're wrong too," I said, and managed a weak smile as I rose from the stool. "Speaking of go-getting, I'd better take off. Let me know about the painting, okay?"

Still in a daze, I made my way out of the shop and crossed the square, heading for Peaches and Java. Of all the things Mason could have told me about Roxanna, I wouldn't have expected this. It was like suddenly I was mourning someone who hadn't truly existed.

Except that Harry had seemed broken up by Roxanna's death, and he'd parted from her on unhappy terms. Even Sheriff Lamb—an actual classmate of hers—had appeared dismayed on a personal level. And while I'd never known Mason to be untruthful, maybe he had an exaggerated view of Roxanna's faults. But Gemma was the one person I knew I could trust to see through any bull and give it to me straight.

A couple of minutes later I was pulling open the door of the combination small-town diner and funky coffee shop. The food and the friendliness of both customers and owners definitely fit the first category, as did the diner counter and pastry case backed by a double-stacked commercial oven and an open grill. The artisan coffee and mismatched tables and fixtures fit the coffeehouse vibe.

Of course, there were a few Georgia-specific touches, like the anthropomorphic male and female peaches painted on the restroom door, indicating it was a unisex facility. But unique to Peaches and Java was the collection of ukuleles in various colors and sizes hanging on the far wall. Not only were the small stringed instruments a tribute to the Hawaiian portion of Daniel Tanaka's mixed heritage, but he also occasionally pulled one down and played it.

In fact, because Mondays were traditionally slow days for the diner and the place was currently empty of customers, Daniel had taken a musical break. As I walked inside, I saw him kicked back in a bar chair beside the diner counter. One of the larger ukes was clutched to his chest as he strummed a plaintive version of what sounded like an old Rolling Stones tune. But once he caught sight of me, the man grinned and abruptly switched lanes, launching into a vibrato-heavy version of the familiar beauty pageant theme song "There She Is."

Despite my doleful mood, I couldn't help smiling.

"Thanks, Daniel," I said as I wandered over to my usual table—two vintage school desks situated face-to-face so that their flat work surfaces formed a tabletop—and set down my purse. "You sure know how to make a girl feel special."

"Hey, we aim to please."

He ended the song on a flourish and went to hang the instrument back on the wall with its fellows.

"It's your lucky day, Nina," he continued, going back around the counter. "It so happens I whipped up a batch of your favorite tomato basil soup this morning. You want a bowl along with your usual?"

That currently being a BLT with avocado on toasted white.

"Perfect," I told him as I settled in my chair and looked around. Given that it was a school day, Jasmine was in class instead of helping at the diner. As for Gemma, unless she was hiding out in the storeroom, she'd apparently left her husband to run the place by himself.

"So where's your better half?" I asked Daniel as he brought over the soup and a glass of unsweet tea to get me started. I added with another smile, "Not that I don't adore spending time with you, but I kind of needed to talk to her."

"Since it was slow, she ran off to do a few quick errands. But she should be back around noon."

Which, according to the peach-shaped clock on the far wall, was about twenty minutes away. I nodded and started on my soup while Daniel returned to the counter to make my sandwich. By the time I'd finished the savory bowl, he was back with my BLT quartered into triangles and stacked into two columns held together with frilly toothpicks. A small dish of mayo-cado dip and a mound of homemade black-pepper potato chips filled the rest of the plate.

"Looks great," I told him as I enthusiastically reached for a chip. Then, gesturing at the empty chair across from me, I added, "If you're not busy, I'd love the company, as long as you don't mind watching me eat."

"Hey, watching customers eat is what I live for."

He squeezed his bulk into the student-sized seat and gave me a considering look. "What's bothering you, Nina?"

I paused midbite. "Is it that obvious?"

"It's that obvious," he replied. "And I'm guessing it had to do with the woman you saw die at the expo. Jasmine is still pretty shook up about the whole thing, but she insisted on going to school today anyhow. You know, climb back on the horse."

"Jasmine's a tough kid," I agreed. "The same with Dr. Garvin's little girl, Buddy. The two of them held up better than a lot of the adults."

I took another bite of my sandwich, which suddenly didn't taste quite as yummy as usual. Washing it down with tea, I continued, "The whole thing was pretty upsetting, but there's more than that. Have you ever thought you knew someone, and then you found out you didn't really know them at all— and in a really bad way?"

"A couple of times, yeah."

Remembered anger and sadness momentarily flashed across Daniel's normally cheery features. But all he said was, "The worst part when that happens is that you feel like a total idiot for believing in someone—and that only makes you more cynical the next time you meet someone new. So, who did you find out was a fake friend?"

I hesitated, staring at my last bite of sandwich. Then I sighed and said, "It's Roxanna, the woman who was killed at the expo.

"Not that she was ever awful to me," I hurried to clarify. "At least, not that I know of. But I heard rumors she basically screwed over a lot of other people. The problem is that, now that she's dead, I won't ever be able to confront her and hear her side of the story. So I'll never know if I was an idiot or not."

"That's a tough one," he agreed. "But here's another way to look at it. Would it make your loss easier if you accepted the rumors as truth?"

"No. It actually would make it harder."

He nodded and gave me a small smile. "I think Oscar Wilde said it best: *The truth is rarely pure and never simple.* So if you want my advice, I say forget what you've heard and go with the truth you actually know—that Roxanna was a good friend to you.

"And now," he added as the diner door opened and a young couple wandered in, "time for me to get back to work."

Before I could reply, he had eased himself out of the chair and headed to the counter, where the pair had taken a seat. By then, another two groups had walked in, which meant Daniel would be tied up for a while. I finished my sandwich and chips, then rose and tucked a couple of bills under my plate before giving Daniel a wave on the way out.

I headed across the square in the direction of home, feeling better now than I had when I'd left Mason's shop. Daniel was right. Roxanna had been a good friend to me, and nothing was going to change that. The only other truth I'd concern myself with would be uncovering the facts about her death.

As for my promise to Connie Lamb that I'd mind my own business and keep my mouth shut about what might be a murder—well, I'd simply have to make sure the good sheriff didn't catch me conducting my own investigation.

Chapter Thirteen

By the time I reached the house, I had the start of an action plan laid out in my head. Tonight's workshop at the florist shop would be the first milestone in my under-the-radar investigation of Roxanna's death. John could possibly have insight into Roxanna and Virgie's partnership that I could pry from him—and even if he didn't, he still might know something of value. Besides, I hadn't quite crossed John off my list of potential suspects. If nothing else, I needed to pin him down to learn if it had been he lurking in the high school's back hallway right before the fashion show.

Heading inside, I checked on the pups, who I found stretched out on my bed and snoring mightily. Mattie opened her blue eye long enough to see it was me; then, with a half-hearted woof of acknowledgment, she returned to her nap.

That was two out of three roomies. Harry wasn't lounging in any of the public spaces, so I called up the ladder to the tower room for him. I heard no response, meaning he wasn't yet back from his rendezvous with Dr. Garvin.

I checked my watch again. It was close to twelve thirty, and he'd left before ten. With maybe thirty minutes of that time spent traveling back and forth, that still would have given him two hours to settle a situation that theoretically should have taken maybe a quarter hour to resolve. On the other hand, maybe he *had* taken care of business in a few minutes and then decided while he was out to shop or do lunch or something.

But no matter. Harry could take care of himself.

I decided not to spend time worrying over his whereabouts, especially since I had things to do. Instead, I returned to my bedroom and booted up my laptop. Then, figuratively putting on my Secret Squirrel cap, I opened a blank spreadsheet, titled it "Suspects in the Roxanna Quarry Killing," and began typing.

Given that no official ruling had been made on her death—at least, not that I'd heard—my first entry in the *Suspect* column was the generic offender *Accident*. I was pretty sure I'd be crossing out that one by the end of the day, but to be thorough, I left it in. I didn't have a motive to attribute to the prop cake, so I left its line in the column titled *Why?* empty. But in the third column, headed *Why Not?*, I thought a moment about everything I'd seen when Roxanna tumbled from the cake, then made the note *Inner prop cake structure didn't appear to have a place where a scarf would catch.*

Then I went on to the next suspect.

On paper, Virgie Hamilton definitely looked like a guilty party. Under the *Why?* column for her, I listed *Embezzlement claim against R* and *Big secret fight between V and R*. I thought another moment and then remembered to add *Web domain poaching accusation*—though technically that would have been a motive for Roxanna. Then I frowned and added something John had mentioned.

The prop cake was Virgie's idea.

How that fit in, I wasn't certain, but since John had mentioned it, I didn't want to forget it.

Unfortunately for Virgie, the *Why Not?* listing was shorter. I put down *Age/strength* and then *Partners for several years* as my reasons why she wouldn't—or couldn't—do it. Then I moved to the next obvious suspect, John Klingel.

He was on the list mostly because of the hallway incident. That and the fact that he'd been MIA when Roxanna had likely died. I put those two entries into his *Why?* column and then added a third comment: *Virgie's ex-husband, possibly does her dirty work?*

Not that I actually believed the last. His entries in the *Why Not?* column were *No motive* and *Genuinely nice guy* along with *Likely not the only man in town who owned a purple shirt*. But to be scrupulously fair in compiling the list, I jumped back to John's *Why?* column and made another addition.

Likely strong enough to heft a dead body.

This made me pause a little, and I blinked away sudden tears that made it difficult to read the screen. Then, with a steadying breath, I continued the list with the man Sheriff Lamb had been looking for: Ryan Slater, Roxanna's ex-husband.

Somehow I suspected that the sheriff's reason for tracking him down went beyond simply locating a next of kin—which, if they were divorced, he technically wouldn't be. But if Mason were to be believed—and I had no reason to doubt him—Roxanna had once boasted that she'd bankrupted her most recent ex before divorcing him.

"Talk about motive," I muttered aloud.

Maybe Slater had been stewing over what she'd done for the past couple of years and finally decided to try to recoup some of his losses. Which could mean he was the one who'd trashed her house, looking for cash he'd somehow learned she had. Assuming, of course, that he had followed Roxanna back to Cymbeline.

But that didn't necessarily mean he had killed her . . . though it also didn't mean he hadn't.

I frowned. Statistically, a spouse—or an ex—was always the most likely suspect in their partner's suspicious death. And as the bridal expo had been open to the public, he could easily have slipped into and out of the place unnoticed.

I entered all those bullet points under his *Why?* column, though for the moment I left his *Why Not?* column blank. But I did add an asterisk to his name, and at the bottom of the spreadsheet I added the note *Possibly the same Ryan who wanted to tour the B&B?* And then, after another moment's thought, I added another asterisked comment.

Possibly the driver of the silver two-door?

My last entry was *Karma*—as in, one of the numerous people who, according to Mason, might have had a wish and a motive to do Roxanna harm. The trouble was that I had no clue who any of these people were. I'd have to pay another visit to the antiques shop and learn more.

I was racking my brain for anyone else who should be on the list—maybe Polly, since she'd known about the prop cake in advance?—when Mattie and Gus abruptly awakened. The pair let out synchronized barks before leaping off the bed and rushing out my open bedroom door and down the hall.

Harry, I told myself, realizing that the sudden feeling that swept over me was relief. Given Harry's past connection to Roxanna, and with her killer still at large and possibly driving a silver car, I wasn't comfortable not knowing where he was.

On the other hand, maybe the dogs were barking at Ryan, who perhaps had finally shown up.

Opting for caution, I quickly saved the document and closed my laptop. I grabbed my cell phone and shoved it into my jeans pocket, then joined the dogs at the front door. Rather than throwing it open, however, I instead first peeked out the curtained sidelight to see who was there.

As I'd pretty well assumed, it was the actor headed up the main walkway. But my heart stopped momentarily when, through the tangle of honeysuckle on the front fence beyond him, I caught a flash of a silver car.

False alarm, I reassured myself. What had Harry said previously about every other car on the streets these days being silver? Apparently, he wasn't far wrong in that. It had to have been his Uber pulling away from the curb.

But for the moment, I put aside thoughts of mystery drivers and burglars. What I wanted to know was how Harry's meeting with Dr. Garvin had turned out.

Not wanting to be too obvious about my curiosity, however, I refrained from waiting in the foyer to pounce as soon as he opened the door. Instead, I rushed off to the kitchen to start some coffee. Harry had lived here long enough that I knew his usual routine upon returning from somewhere was to brew up a cup of his infamous tea. "Accidentally" catching him in the kitchen would make for a good excuse to see how his errand had gone.

I hurriedly popped a pod into the coffeemaker and, sticking my favorite *I ♥ Aussies* mug under the brew head, pressed the start button. I had just pulled out my quart of whole milk from the fridge when I heard the front door open. Mattie and Gus proved excellent wing-dogs, guiding him with a few well-placed yaps down the hall and through the kitchen door.

"Oh, you're back," I said in feigned surprise. "I thought the dogs were playing around." Then, to be polite, I added, "I'm making myself a latte. Would you like one?"

This time, my surprise was real when he shrugged and said, "Sure," then dropped onto one of the kitchen island's bar chairs.

I surreptitiously eyed the actor while I heated the milk in a small pan. Normally he lectured me on the evils of caffeine and fat whenever I indulged in any sort of a coffee drink. The fact that he felt compelled to defile his personal body temple with a big foamy mug of milk and coffee meant that it was either the end of the world or things had not go well with Dr. Garvin.

Just before the liquid hit the boiling point, I pulled it off the heat. By then my coffee had finished brewing, so I grabbed a second mug—this one decorated with a tap-dancing cartoon frog—and started another cup, then whipped out my hand frother and got to work foaming up the hot milk. In a few minutes I had two mugs of coffee liberally laced with milk, with an extra dollop of foam on top of each. I gave Harry the frog mug, then took the seat opposite him at the counter and took a sip of my own latte.

We drank for a few moments in silence. But when Harry finally spoke up, it was to ask, "How did your tour with the reluctant bridegroom go?"

I glanced at him from over the top of my mug. The fact that he was interested in my morning obviously meant he was trying to avoid discussion of his own.

"It didn't go. He was a no-show. Either he found a venue he liked better or he changed his mind. It happens. Oh, and after you left, Sheriff Lamb dropped by with Gus's crate," I continued. "I thought that was pretty nice of her."

And then, since I recalled that Harry had already mentioned that his temporary teen wife—presumably Roxanna—had remarried, meaning that it wouldn't come as a shock to him, I added, "She's looking for Roxanna's ex-husband, some guy named Ryan Slater. Did she ever mention him to you?"

"Not a word," he replied.

"Me neither, but I'm sure Sheriff Lamb will track him down." And then, as casually as I could, I continued, "So, that was my morning. What about you? How did Dr. Garvin take it when you gave her back the checks?"

Harry took a sizable slug of his latte before fixing me with a melancholy look. "Not well," was his succinct reply.

Then, when I silently regarded him for several long moments, he gave an aggravated sigh.

"Fine, if it will make you happy, I'll tell you all the gory details. I got to her office, and everything was nice and cordial for the first fifteen seconds, until I handed back the checks. It pretty well went south after that."

"So she got mad," I replied with a shrug. "What's the big deal? At least you're finished with her now."

"Finished? Not by a long shot."

Harry's slight smile held no hint of humor as he continued. "Meredith took back the checks, no problem. But then she said that since she hadn't paid me, she considered my public proposal a voluntary offer and her public acceptance made it a valid verbal contract. She reminded me that there were more than fifty witnesses who saw me on bended knee pledging my troth. Bottom line, if I try to weasel out of our fake engagement, she's going to sue me for breach of contract."

"What? That's crazy."

"You think?" Harry asked with a snort. "She said the only way she's going let me out of the proposal is if I'll keep attending events as her fiancé through the holidays."

"You mean Thanksgiving?"

"*And* Christmas, *and* New Year's Eve. Plus any formal event on her calendar. Right now, she has me scheduled for this coming Saturday night. Some sort of gastroenterologists' annual awards banquet in Savannah. She's supposed to make a speech. I'm to sit in the audience and gaze admiringly at her.

"And no, there's no point in pulling some kind of public scene to make her want to dump me sooner," he added, anticipating what I was about to suggest. "She told me, and I quote, 'Do that, and your next role will be defendant in a court case.' "

"Harry, that's crazy," I repeated, righteous indignation rising in me on his behalf, even as I struggled not to burst out with a big old *I told you so*. "She can't make you do anything you don't want to do. This is a free country."

"Oh, did I leave out the part where she said she'd sue me?"

"No, you were quite clear on that, but it sounds pretty bogus to me. Why don't you call that attorney of yours—you know, the one you used to try to wrangle your great-aunt's house from me—and see what he has to say about it?"

Harry shot me a sour look—mostly, I'm sure, because I had reminded him about his previous legal woes. But all he said was, "I already thought about that. Unfortunately, he's not currently taking my calls, so I went to the library to look up precedents on that sort of suit. That's why I was gone for so long. My takeaway is that when it comes to civil law, anyone can sue anyone else for anything they want. And sometimes they win."

He took another sip of latte and added, "Nina, I don't have any choice but to play her game. I can't afford to fight her in court if she decides to file a suit."

We both mulled over the situation for another moment or two. Then I suggested, "How about I talk to her, woman-to-woman, and see if I can convince her to let it go? I already told Buddy she could come over sometime to play with Mattie. That would be a good excuse to invite her mom over."

"Over here?" Harry shot me a look of horror. "Are you kidding? Last thing I want is that woman inside my—well, your—house. She figures out the door code and bam, before you know it we're coming home to bunnies boiling on the stove."

Despite myself, I couldn't help but laugh at his reference to the 1980s movie with Glenn Close and Michael Douglas. Though I could understand why Harry was sensitive about the situation, given that he had been being pursued by a female stalker when I first met him. An experience like that was bound to make one a bit paranoid. But this was definitely different.

"All right, Harry, time to dial down the drama a bit," I told him. "I agree that Dr. Garvin is being totally unreasonable, but she's definitely not a whack-job. You saw how she took charge at the bridal expo, rendering aid and assigning tasks. And no one I've talked to about the, uh, incident, has anything bad to say about the woman. She's just an incredibly focused person . . . but I kind of think you have to be that way to be a good doctor. Besides, her daughter is a pretty cool little girl, and that doesn't happen by accident."

Then, when he still looked unconvinced, I added, "No offense, but I really doubt she's obsessed with you. I think the problem is that you played your boyfriend role too perfectly and she wants to keep that level of excellence going. Being a doctor, she's used to working with high-caliber staff. You know how it is—once you find a great employee, you don't want them ever to quit."

"I *was* pretty good," he conceded, sounding slightly mollified, "so maybe you're onto something. I guess the revised plan is to play things by ear. I'll go to that Savannah event with her and then try talking to her again after that."

"I think that's a good idea. Now, do you still feel brave enough to stay home with Gus and Mattie tonight while I go to John's workshop?"

"I think I can manage." And then, sounding less prickly, he added, "Thanks for being a sounding board. Who knows, maybe it'll turn out Meredith and I have more in common than her checkbook."

I laughed. "You never know. Just promise me that if your engagement turns into the real deal, you'll hold your wedding here."

"Deal," he agreed with a grin, raising his mug in a toasting gesture, which I reciprocated.

But barely had the clink of ceramic on ceramic died than my cell phone began to chime. Setting down my latte, I stood and pulled my phone from my jeans pocket, hurriedly checking the caller ID.

"It's Mason Denman. He was still examining your great-aunt's landscape when I stopped by his place earlier. Maybe he's finished with the appraisal and calling to tell me it's worth a fortune."

And on that hopeful note, I swiftly swiped to answer the call.

The conversation was brief, my end of it being mostly a series of *uh-huh*s and *yes*es as I listened. When Mason had finished, I replied with a subdued, "Not what I wanted to hear, but thanks for letting me know," before I ended the call.

It was only after Harry rather ostentatiously cleared his throat that I realized I had been staring at the blank phone screen for several seconds after I'd hung up. I glanced over at him and saw he was frowning now.

"What?" he asked in concern. "Is the painting worth a fortune and you're about to faint in shock? Or did Mason tell you we should donate it to the Museum of Bad Art and you're wondering how to break it to me?"

"Actually, he didn't have any updates on the painting yet. He was calling about Roxanna. You know how Mason is—he always manages to get the jump on everyone when it comes to gossip."

"That's his reputation." He paused; then, suddenly looking a little ghostly himself, he asked, "Has he heard something new about . . . you know?"

I nodded, hoping I could deliver the news without going all blubbery. And so I took a deep breath and prepared myself to power through.

"Apparently the medical examiner's report is out. I'm sorry, Harry, but the official word is that it wasn't an accident. Her death was ruled homicide by strangulation, with the weapon being a silk scarf."

He nodded, then muttered a few choice words that pretty much echoed what I was thinking. But he didn't appear surprised at this conclusion, despite having railed against that very possibility the day before.

I fleetingly wondered at his change of heart, but all I said aloud was, "And that's not all. According to Mason, Sheriff Lamb already has a suspect in custody as of thirty minutes ago."

This, apparently, was more surprising news, for Harry's gaze sharpened. "A suspect? Who?"

"Virgie Hamilton. She's been arrested on suspicion of murder."

Chapter Fourteen

With that, I dropped back onto my barstool. But watching Harry's reaction to what I thought would have been a bombshell, I was surprised to see his strained features suddenly relax. Almost as if he had expected me to name someone other than the dress shop owner.

But before I could give that unexpected notion further thought, he said, "You don't really think Virgie did it, do you? I mean, even though your official statement is probably why Connie arrested her."

"Wait, what? Are you saying it's my fault?"

Though, of course, it was. I was the only person besides Virgie who'd known about the argument she'd had with Roxanna at the bridal expo, the only one who'd overheard the accusation of embezzlement. And I'd given the sheriff an almost verbatim account of the women's brief but vicious fight. Beyond that, I was the one who had discovered the stash of money that, quite conveniently, was the exact figure Virgie claimed had been embezzled.

But now that Harry had stated it so baldly, I realized he was right. Compelling motive or not, I couldn't picture her stooping to that sort of violence. Which was why I answered, "No, I don't."

"Then we're in agreement. So who do you think actually *did* kill her?"

"I'm not sure," I told him. "But I'm going to do my best to clear her name. I already have a list of possible suspects."

*   *   *

Fifteen minutes later, Harry and I had reconvened in the dining room, my laptop with its "Suspects in the Roxanna Quarry Killing" document opened before us as we sat side by side at the table. The actor gave the spreadsheet a once-over, then slanted me a look.

"Secret Squirrel strikes again. Please don't tell me that if I go into your room, you'll have a bunch of head shots and maps and sticky notes taped to the wall."

"Funny," I told him, my tone saying just the opposite. "Besides, there's not been time for that. I only just started the list this afternoon so I could organize my thoughts."

"Well then, let's see what you have."

Borrowing my mouse, he scrolled through the listing a second time, stopping at the entry for Roxanna's most recent ex. "Bankruptcy?" he asked. "Where did you hear that?"

"From Mason, and he said he heard it directly from Roxanna."

Harry looked like he wanted to reply to that, but he apparently thought better of it and kept scrolling to the next entry. " 'Karma'? As in a person with that name, or the spiritual principal?"

"As in the spiritual principal. Cause and effect," I clarified. "According to Mason, he knew at least half a dozen people right here in Cymbeline who had a serious beef with Roxanna. I was hoping if I talked to him again, maybe he'd actually name those names."

Once again, I thought Harry was going to comment on Mason's theories, but all he said was, "Right. And speaking of names, you left off an important one: Virgie's son, Jason."

"Okay, I'll put him on the list."

I took the mouse back from him and added the name *Jason Hamilton* to the spreadsheet. "Now, why is he a suspect? I mean, other than the fact that he was handling the lights and sound for the expo, which puts him in the right place?"

"Because he and Roxanna were hooking up."

I stopped mid–mouse click to stare at him. "Seriously?"

He nodded, and I did some quick mental math. Virgie and John had married not long after high school and had been together for ten years before they divorced. And she'd apparently remarried almost immediately, with her son being born not long after that. So if Virgie was in her early sixties, that would make Jason thirty-one or thirty-two years old. A little young for Roxanna, who had been around Harry's age— thirty-eight, thirty-nine—but not creepily so.

The odder dynamic was the fact that he was her business partner's son.

"Did Virgie know about this?" I asked. "And how in the world did you find out?"

"He has an apartment over her dress shop, so probably. And Roxanna told me," he answered in swift succession.

Frowning, I tackled the second answer first. "That's kind of personal information to be sharing. She didn't say anything to me about him, not even while she was slugging down margaritas when we went out for happy hour the other week. Any reason she'd tell you about her personal life?"

"Because I went back to Jason's studio one afternoon a couple of weeks ago to do a pickup session for the expo announcements. You know, rerecord a few flubbed lines. Anyhow, I got there early and walked in on him and Roxanna doing a little pickup session of their own."

I grimaced. "Yikes, embarrassing."

"Yeah, pretty much."

I thought about it another moment and then said, "You ask me, that sounds more like another motive for Virgie. You know, going all mama bear over her innocent son being corrupted by an older woman. Unless Roxanna and Jason had a falling out before the expo?"

Harry shook his head. "I don't think that was it. After the session—mine, not theirs—she took me aside to apologize. She told me that their relationship had been going on for a while and that things were pretty great between them. But she didn't want to go public until they both agreed to move beyond booty calls to actual dating."

"But maybe actual dating wasn't what Jason wanted," I suggested. "Maybe he was fine with the status quo and he didn't like that she was pushing for a commitment."

"Possibly," he agreed. "For all we know, Roxanna wasn't the only one he was doing a little 'work' with at the studio."

Nodding, I typed in those motives for him, adding a final one that echoed John's list: *Virgie's son, possibly does her dirty work?* I moved over to the *Why Not?* column and thought a moment, then added, *They seemed happy together.*

That done, I turned back to Harry.

"I think we skipped over the ex-husband too quickly. I wish we knew for sure whether or not Ryan Slater is the same Ryan who was a no-show this morning."

"Well, that's easy enough to check out. Pull up the call history on your phone."

I showed him the unknown number listed. "And before you say anything, I know I could just hit redial and ask him for his last name. And if he's a different Ryan, it's no big deal. But if he *is* Ryan Slater, he'll know something is up."

"True. But if he thinks it's just another solicitation call coming through . . . here, let me." And before I could ask his plan, Harry was reading off the number on my screen and dialing it on his own cell phone.

"Hello," he said, when whichever Ryan was on the other end answered. Effortlessly lapsing into an old-time movie star transatlantic accent, he continued, "Is this Mr. Slater . . . Mr. Ryan Slater?"

He paused, listened, and then gave me an exaggerated nod and a thumbs-up.

"Excellent, thank you for confirming. Mr. Slater, this is Graham Winston of Wild Hare Tours out of Atlanta, Georgia. First, I must let you know that this call is being recorded for quality purposes. And now, I'm pleased to announce that you have won a free one-week vacation with Wild Hare . . . hello? Hello? Mr. Slater, are you there?"

He paused and gave me the patented Harry Westcott raised brow before showing me the screen with the call ended. "Hmm, apparently not."

Expression smug, he stuck the phone back into his pocket and said, "And *that* is how it's done. Unless there's more than one Ryan Slater running around Cymbeline, it looks like your mystery bridegroom is Roxanna's latest ex-husband."

As he was already patting himself on the back for his cleverness, I didn't think I needed to join in. Instead I asked, "What do you think? Was he just calling to confirm who I was? Or do you think he actually came by and was scared off when he saw Sheriff Lamb's patrol car parked in the drive?"

"Good questions. Maybe you should give him another chance." And then, when I stared quizzically at him, he added, "Call the man back, Nina, and see if he will reschedule."

"Oh, right."

Before I had time to talk myself out of it, I picked up my phone and pressed the redial button. Apparently, Ryan was now screening his calls, for almost immediately I was transferred to voice mail. A generic recording instructed me to leave a message at the tone.

"Hi, Ryan. This is Nina Fleet from Fleet House Bed and Breakfast. I think we missed each other this morning. If you'd like to reschedule your tour, I'm here this afternoon if you have time. Otherwise we can try again tomorrow, since I'll be out for most of the evening tonight, starting around seven. Let me know."

I left my phone number, then hung up and gave Harry a smug look of my own.

"And that *also* is how you do it. If he was the one who tore up Roxanna's place looking for the money, then he might take the opportunity to try to break in here while I'm gone. But little will he know that you'll be here to catch him in the act."

"Seriously, Nina, who writes your dialogue for you?" Harry replied with a snort. "And I hope all you mean by 'catching' is that I will call the proper authorities if I see anyone skulking about."

"That's all you need to do. That and keep Mattie and Gus safe."

"I think I can manage."

And then, abruptly, his demeanor sobered. "Just so you know, Nina, this isn't a game to me."

"It's not to me either," I gravely assured him. "I want to clear Virgie's name, but the main thing is learning the truth about Roxanna's death."

Harry nodded. "If there's anything I can do to help find Roxanna's killer, I'll do it, no questions asked. She might have had her flaws—all right, she did have flaws—but they weren't her sum total. And she didn't deserve what happened to her."

"I know," I said, and instinctively reached over to grasp his hand. "I miss her too."

We sat like that in silence for a few moments. And then, when it went from a gesture of friendship to feeling rather awkward, I let go and reached instead for my mouse and laptop.

"I need a mental break from all this," I told him, shoving back my chair and standing. "I'm going to take the dogs for a walk. Do you want to come with me?"

Harry shook his head. "I'm going to take my mental break upstairs in bed. Let me know when you're headed out to your flower thing so I can lie in wait on the off chance that your boy Ryan has anything nefarious up his sleeve."

I left him there contemplating the ornate plaster ceiling medallion above the table. By the time I'd swapped my work shirt for a casual T-shirt and changed into walking shoes, then headed back to the kitchen pantry to retrieve the dogs' leashes, the dining room was empty again.

"Come on, pups," I told them. I clipped leads to collars and then put on my version of a harness, which was a cross-body purse holding my phone, ID, and a few dollars for emergencies. That was another advantage of the keypad entry—as long as no one manually flipped the dead bolt lock after me, I didn't have to worry about hauling a door key around.

As it was a workday, most of the people I saw in and around the street were Cymbeliners rather than tourists. Though it was late September, summer was taking its time saying good-bye and the midafternoon temperature was a good eighty degrees. Fortunately, the mature oaks overhanging the streets kept things shady, meaning that if I strolled at a moderate pace, there was little danger of breaking a sweat.

Normally when Mattie and I went out together, we walked to the downtown square. I'd already made a trip there today, however, so I kept to the neighborhood. This was fine by Mattie and Gus, mostly because they could bark with impunity at the plump squirrels hanging out in the green canopy. The squirrels, in turn, seemed to take almost human pleasure in taunting passing canines with squeaks and chirps and flicks of their bushy tails. I knew that their country cousins wouldn't be as bold, given that we were well into squirrel-hunting season in Georgia.

But I decided to cut the pleasant walk short when I realized I was spending most of the time at high alert. Moderate as the afternoon traffic was, seemingly every other car that passed us was silver or gray, triggering a bit of anxiety. The turning point came when Gus lunged so unexpectedly at a passing vehicle that he almost pulled the leash from my hand. But as he began barking up a storm, ratcheting up my paranoia yet another notch, I fortunately noticed the squirrel clinging to a nearby tree trunk.

"So that's what has you all agitated," I gently chided him. "I think we've all had enough. Let's go home."

But by coincidence or unconscious design—thinking back on it later, I suspected the latter—the return trip took me a block off the main square. Along this particular street, the old homes were situated close to the sidewalk and thus ideally suited for conversion into retail establishments.

The ground floors housed the actual businesses, while those homes with a second story mostly retained that space as residential. A few owners lived above their shops. The majority, however, had transformed their second floors to full-blown apartments. These rentals were accessible either by an exterior stairway or else through the second "formal" front door common to many vintage homes in the South. This street was where Virgie had her dress shop, and another block down was Midsummer Night's Flowers.

I'd be back at the latter in a few hours, so I didn't bother wandering all the way to John's place. But I decided that a casual stroll past the bridal shop might be in order.

Virgie's Formals was housed in a modest two-story Queen Anne that called to mind a wedding cake—white, with porch railings and an exterior staircase painted pale pink, the curlicue trim and windowed front door a coordinating fuchsia. The original double-hung windows of the front bay window had been replaced with three single-glass panes, the better to show off the lace- and tulle-bedecked white wedding gown flanked by strapless bridesmaid dresses in various hues staged there.

I climbed the two steps to the covered front porch for a better look. The hand-painted sign—curly fuchsia letters on a white background—hanging in the display window had been flipped to assure me the shop was *Open*, though it was dark within. Just in case, I checked the front door. I found it locked, as I'd expected.

"We're closed," a gruff male voice abruptly called, making me jump and Mattie woof. "And no dogs allowed inside anyhow."

Feeling unduly guilty—after all, this was a retail business, so technically I was well within my rights to be rattling the door—I looked about for the speaker. I finally spied him half-way down the outside staircase. He was dressed in faded jeans cut off below the knee and a black-and-blue plaid flannel shirt with its sleeves rolled up high above his elbows.

Save for his outfit, I might have mistaken him for John at first glance, for he was tall and blond and stocky. But this man was a good thirty years younger than the florist, and his soft features were set in a scowl quite the opposite of John's usually cheery, florid demeanor.

I recalled Harry mentioning that Jason Hamilton lived over the dress shop, and a little flash of triumph made me inwardly smile. The perfect opportunity to question Roxanna's "sort of" boyfriend—the boyfriend who was near the top of our suspect list—had just dropped into my figurative lap.

I shushed the pups, who were softly growling, and waved.

"You must be Virgie's son, Jason. I'm Nina Fleet, owner of the B&B a few blocks that way," I said, and pointed in the general direction of my place.

Somewhat to my surprise, Jason clomped down the remaining stairs to join me on the porch. Mattie, meanwhile, nudged herself protectively in front of me while Gus merely raised an upper lip to display sharp canines. I gave both pups reassuring pats and went on, "I was hoping to find Virgie here. I'm a friend of hers."

"Yeah . . . and?"

He folded his arms over his chest, showing off tattooed biceps that could only come from hard work with weights and a few sessions at Mightier Than the Sword Tattoos right outside Cymbeline. While he wasn't my type, I could see what might have attracted Roxanna to him, despite his blustering manner. He was young and good-looking in a "Chris Pratt before he lost all the weight" way. He definitely gave off a masculine vibe that I wouldn't have expected from a guy who worked sound and light. Obviously, he had a few artistic bones within all the beef.

But I wasn't there to judge his date-worthiness, only to get information. And so I further explained, "I'm kind of worried about her after all that's happened. I wanted to check in with her and make sure she's okay."

"Then you came to the wrong place," was his curt reply. "You wanna see Ma, you're gonna have to visit county lockup. That's where they're holding her. They think she murdered her business partner."

"What?"

It wasn't hard to feign surprise, given that Jason's blunt description of the situation was hardly what one would expect of a loving son. Unless he actually believed Virgie had done it? If so, his anger would be understandable, assuming he'd actually had feelings for Roxanna.

Then I shook my head.

"No," I protested aloud. "I was at the expo when it happened. Virgie was so upset she collapsed and needed medical attention. No way did she do it."

Jason's scowl deepened. "Well, that's not what the cops say. And let's just say I believe them more than her. I could care less if she rots in jail for the rest of her life."

I stared at him a moment, unsure how to reply. But one thing was certain. Either both he and Virgie were innocent of any involvement in Roxanna's death or they were better actors than even Harry Westcott.

And so I simply said, "I'm sure things will work out, one way or the other. And, no offense, if I can help her in any way, I will."

Leaving out, of course, the part where I confessed feeling responsible for getting her arrested in the first place.

"Suit yourself. She's not getting a penny of bail money from me."

He waited silently, and I took the hint. Wrapping the dog leashes more tightly about my wrist—both Gus and Mattie continued to eye him suspiciously—I climbed down from the porch. But barely had I taken the few steps to the sidewalk when another thought hit me, bringing with it a theory that I couldn't let go untested.

"Jason," I called back to him, "you were at the expo on Saturday, so maybe I saw you there. Do you remember what you were wearing that day? You know, so I can try to remember if we crossed paths."

He shrugged and gave me a hard look that revealed nothing.

I met his hostile gaze with a cool look of my own. He might be young and burly, but that didn't mean I was going to let him run roughshod over me. And so, needing to prove or disprove my theory, I tossed the figurative dice.

"Wait, I remember now. You were wearing a long-sleeved purple shirt, right?"

When he still made no reply, I gave a shrug of my own and started down the sidewalk. I'd hoped to eliminate either John or Jason from my suspect list with his answer, but it looked like I was back to square one.

That is, until I heard a single word behind me. "Plum."

I halted and turned to stare at him. "Excuse me?"

"Plum," he repeated. "The shirt I was wearing was plum, not purple. And I didn't see you at the expo at all."

Chapter Fifteen

"I know gut feelings don't count," I heatedly protested, "but I'm almost one hundred percent certain. The man I saw in the back hallway of the high school had to be Jason Hamilton. I know that doesn't exactly prove anything about Roxanna's murder, but maybe it eliminates John from our suspect list."

"Or maybe it just means that purple—excuse me, plum— is a popular fashion choice for men this season," Harry countered. "I think I've got a shirt that color in my closet too."

It was a little after six PM, and we were once again sitting in the dining room. I'd already fed the dogs and finished a quick cold supper of my own so that I could be out the door again by half past the hour. I'd planned to have this conversation with Harry as soon as I'd returned from my walk. Unfortunately, he'd still been ensconced in the tower room, which meant I'd been impatiently waiting for the past couple of hours to share about my chance encounter with Virgie's son.

And all that built-up anticipation was why his pooh-poohing now was so deflating.

And then he added, "If nothing else, you've located another piece of our puzzle. I'll admit that was good detecting on your part."

"Well, *I* thought so," I agreed, not quite mollified. Then, to change the subject slightly, I asked, "Are you sure you'll be okay here all alone while I'm at the workshop?"

"I'll be fine. I'm going to leave all the inside and outside lights off so it'll be obvious you're not home. Since this Ryan person never called you back after that message you left him, he might be waiting for this opportunity. We'll make it as easy as possible for him."

Then he paused and gave me a considering look. "But I must admit, I'm a little worried about *you*. I know it's not exactly the mean streets of Cymbeline out there, but you'll probably have a bit of a walk to your car in the dark once that workshop is over. No, I'm not saying you can't take care of yourself"—he cut me short when I would have protested—"but under the circumstances, I'd feel better if you call me when you leave and stay on the line until you're safely driving off."

Now it was my turn to give him a look.

"Why, Harry Westcott!" I exclaimed in an exaggerated southern accent while I fluttered my eyelashes. "You really do care about me."

"I can't believe you ever doubted that," he replied with a slow smile that made me suddenly catch my breath in a most unexpected way.

And then, before I could wonder if I'd misjudged our contentious relationship all this time, he added, "Anything happens to you, I have to figure out a new place to live until I can afford my own place."

"Gee, thanks," I managed, reminding myself that the only relationship between me and Harry was that of tenant-landlord. It made for a tenuous friendship but nothing more. "I think I can get to my car on my own. Don't worry, I'll be fine."

"Suit yourself," he replied. "But if someone in a silver two-door drags you off the street and kidnaps you, don't say I didn't warn you."

*   *   *

"Welcome, everyone," John Klingel exclaimed as he ushered us into the workshop area at the rear of his flower shop. "I'm so excited to meet all you future floral designers. Now, find a seat, and we'll get started."

Like the other businesses on the block, Midsummer's Night Flowers was housed in a converted private dwelling. While Queen Anne homes predominated on the block where Virgie's Formals was located, the addresses here were primarily southern cottage-style architecture. John's place was a larger version of Roxanna's cute but modest house.

I'd arrived early enough before the class started that, once I'd grabbed my name tag, I had time to wander about the shop. The walls of what once had been separate living and parlor and dining spaces had been pulled down to create a single large retail area. Glass-fronted floral coolers lined the side wall closest to the shop's main entry, their shelves holding oversized buckets filled with a jungle's worth of greenery and blooms. A display of non-floral items—decorative vases, tiny gift book, stuffed animals, balloons, and even chocolates—took up the opposite wall.

Tables in the middle of the store held dried flora, everything from hydrangeas and pampas grasses to the obligatory baby's breath and eucalyptus. Next to them, a counter-height table with stools was piled with the same sample books I'd seen displayed at the expo. This consultation space was conveniently set up alongside the checkout area, the latter easily identifiable by a kitschy hanging sign in the shape of a vintage pointing hand that read *Check Out Here*.

The back room where we were gathered now was far more utilitarian. A long table staged with buckets of dried flowers as well as foliage and fresh blooms took up space along one wall. At right angles to the flower table was a worktable, above which hung an impressive selection of ribbon—satin, velvet, burlap, even twine—in myriad hues and conveniently stored on a series of dowels. While normally the table would likely have been littered with scraps of ribbon and bits of discarded foliage, tonight it held boxed cookies along with pitchers of tea and water that John warned us were for break time later.

The class area consisted of three worktables lined up end to end, with enough chairs for twenty people. A few basic supplies—bowls, foam, scissors, and utility knives—were already staged in the center of each table. John took the spot at the head of the tables while the rest of us grabbed seats along the sides.

He gave us a few moments to settle in and introduce ourselves to our tablemates. I greeted the people around me, though I kept an eye on John as I did so. As usual, he was smiling, but tonight lines of stress had thinned his plump cheeks. And when he thought no one was looking, his lips drooped into an expression one could only call melancholy. Obviously, the situation with Virgie had taken a toll on him. Hopefully I'd be able to pull him aside at some point in the evening to offer what support I could.

After a minute, he raised a hand, indicating silence. "Again, welcome. If you will look around, you'll see that we're a diverse group tonight. That tells you that floral design is something anyone and everyone can learn."

We all nodded as we surveyed our classmates. Roughly half were white ladies of retirement age who likely did fun classes like this on a regular basis. Another handful were women in their thirties—probably moms taking a night off. At the next table over, however, a college-aged Latino youth with a shaved head and the thinnest of moustaches sat next to a wizened white gentleman who had to be eighty. Across from me was a Black father-daughter duo, the shy little girl—Tisha, as her stick-on name tag proclaimed her—looking as if she could be in Buddy's grade. Her bearded dad, who had previously introduced himself as Titus, grinned at me and shrugged.

"This is actually our Daddy date night for this month," he explained. "We got tired of doing restaurants."

Everyone was smiling, including me, and I realized that flowers were indeed the universal language, as I'd often heard claimed.

"We're going to have fun and learn a lot tonight, so fasten your seat belts," John continued. "First off, we're going to review the five elements of design. They are line, space, form, color, and texture. Once I've explained those concepts, we'll put together a very simple floral arrangement so you can see a real-life example of how those elements work together. Sound good?"

When we murmured our agreement, he continued, "After that, we'll talk about the seven main design principles—accent, balance, composition, harmony, proportion, unity, and rhythm—and then work on a second arrangement that's a little more advanced. And don't worry, your work sheet has plenty of cheat notes so you don't have to memorize everything right this minute."

As promised, we spent the next hour on lecture and hands-on. Being someone who'd previously stuck grocery-store flowers in a clear glass vase and called it good—what John had smilingly told us was called the "chop and plop"—I was surprised at how much theory went into a professional arrangement. By the time we stopped for a brief break, my head was spinning with terms like *floral mechanics*, *surface structure*, and *mature foliage*. But I hadn't forgotten one of my goals for the evening. And so, while the rest of the students eagerly rushed the cookies and drinks table, I sought out John.

"I heard about Virgie," I told him as we move slightly away from the others. "I'm so sorry. How are you holding up?"

He shrugged. "Not too bad."

And then, smile slipping, he corrected himself. "Okay, it's pretty bad. Virgie's a mess, and so am I. Of course she didn't murder Roxanna, but apparently someone overheard the two of them fighting right before Roxanna was killed. That makes her a prime suspect."

"Oh, not good," I replied, praying that neither of them ever figured out that I was the *someone*. "But I have to say, that's a pretty big jump—to accuse someone of murder just because of an argument. Heck, I heard her fighting with *you* at the expo. I think that's kind of what she does."

"Yeah, yelling is definitely one of Virginia Ann's main forms of communication," was John's wry reply. "But there's also something about an embezzlement accusation, so things are even more complicated."

I gave a sympathetic nod, hoping he didn't notice my involuntary wince. But all he did was sigh and scrub a weary hand over his face.

"Anyhow, thanks for your concern, Nina. What I'm concentrating on right now is trying to raise the bail money and then finding a criminal attorney to represent her. And that's not easy when the two of us are both strapped for cash."

"Well, if things get too bad, I'd be happy to donate to the cause."

"Not necessary, but I appreciate the sentiment."

He looked at his watch and summoned a smile. "We've still got a few minutes of break time left. Why don't we grab some cookies and a drink?"

I smiled back as we joined the others, but my expression of pleasure was as false as his. A friend was dead and an innocent woman was accused of the crime—the latter most likely because of me. And here I was, munching sugar cookies and arranging flowers like life was good.

But I didn't want to be the one to cast a pall over what so far had been a fun learning experience. And so, when the lecture resumed a few minutes later, I did my best to keep up that smile as John launched into a quick demonstration of what he called the mechanics. He'd shown us earlier how to use green floral foam soaked in water as a base for the arrangement. Now he led us in forming a tape grid, which was exactly what it sounded like—a crisscross pattern of cellophane tape atop the mouth of a vase. As he did so, he explained how it was the simplest way to keep the flowers upright and separated.

Once we'd mastered that, we learned a similar technique using chicken wire. A flat piece could go over the vase's top, like a premade tape grid. But he also showed us how to shape the wire into a ball that was inserted in the vase just above where it began to narrow. Despite my earlier lapse into melancholy, I couldn't help but be buoyed by John's passion for his craft. I had regained much of my original enthusiasm by the time he demonstrated what he called the "cheats"—a chunk of Styrofoam at the bottom of a too-tall vase; an inverted bowl to fill space in a too-broad dish; a cheap plastic pail slipped inside a vintage wooden bucket.

"And now, students," he exclaimed, once he'd displayed the final bit of floristry magic, "it's time to turn you loose with your new knowledge. You each already have a vase with a tape grid sitting in front of you. You can choose what you like from the buckets of flowers and fillers and foliage to create your own original floral design to take home with you. You've got thirty minutes. And, go!"

We rushed to the table like we were taking part in a game show, laughing as we picked and chose, trying out colors and textures and exchanging advice.

"Give everyone a chance at all the buckets," John called over the hubbub. "Remember, you want at least three different selections for your design. Maggie"—he indicated one of the retirees, who already had an armful of pink carnations—"be a dear and put a few of those back for someone else. And, don't forget, people—line, space, form, color, and texture!"

I'd opted to go with an arrangement that was a bit more Zen-like. While the rest of the class was sorting through the usual carnations and tulips and baby's breath, I was drawn toward the foliage and what John had called the "form" flowers—iris, bird-of-paradise, anthurium. I moved over to one side of the table to avoid the worst of the crush. And that's when I noticed the small vase of dried lotus pods—some natural, others dyed—tucked behind a bucket of white daisies.

Instinctively, I reached for the lotus pod that was painted gold . . . and realization hit me so hard that for a moment I thought I'd been slapped.

But while I wanted to shout out my brainstorm to the entire class, I clamped my jaws shut. I finished making my choices, then concentrated on putting together my arrangement. John made the rounds while we labored, offering advice if asked but otherwise letting us do our own thing. And when it was nine o'clock, he used a paring knife to clink on a tall glass vase, signaling *time's up*.

"Good work, ladies and gentlemen," he praised us. "Every one of you did an excellent job with your original arrangements. You now are official floral apprentices. Please, give yourself a hand."

He led us in a round of applause, then added, "I have certificates of completion for all of you. And remember that because you've taken this class, you are eligible for a ten percent discount for all your future supply purchases here at Midsummer Night's Flowers."

With that, we rose and gathered our arrangements, then followed John out of the workshop and back into the main store. There we queued up beneath the pointing-finger sign while John handed out more kudos along with the parchment certificates. I smiled a little at the beaming expressions of Titus and his daughter standing in front of me. They held matching arrangements of red and yellow gladiolas, miniature carnations, lilies, and ferns, Tisha barely able to see over the top of hers.

"Great job," I told them. "Those look really professional."

"I was the designer," Tisha proudly spoke up, while Titus smiled through his beard. "Daddy just did what I told him."

While normally I'd be impatient to be on my way home after an event like this, I had deliberately lagged behind the rest of the class. And so I was the last in line for my certificate.

"I hope you enjoyed yourself tonight, Nina," John said with a tired smile. "Usually these classes perk me up, but I have to admit, it was hard staying focused tonight."

"Don't worry, I doubt anyone noticed. And I learned a lot, so thank you."

I paused, waiting until Titus and Tisha had left through the front door so that only John and I remained in the shop. And then, setting my arrangement on the checkout counter, I told him, "I know that Virgie didn't murder Roxanna, and now I can prove it."

John gave me stunned look. "What are you talking about? What could you know that the sheriff doesn't?"

"This."

I plucked the gold-painted lotus seed pod from my arrangement and held it so he could see it. "Remember at the expo when Virgie was yelling at you in her booth? And then she saw one of these painted lotus seed pods and freaked out. She has this phobia."

"Trypophobia," John confirmed. "She's had it ever since I've known her. It's not really a fear. It's more this visceral reaction to the sight of hole clusters and little dots. There's some theory about it being an evolutionary holdover . . . but what does that have to do with murder?"

"Roxanna was strangled with the scarf she was wearing. And her scarf had a pattern that looked like this," I said, indicating the lotus pod. "If Virgie reacted so violently to this flower thingy, I don't see how she'd be willing to put hands on a yard-long scarf all covered in tiny circles."

John frowned. "That's true. The problem is, you and I know it, but I doubt the sheriff would believe your theory."

"Maybe not. But Deputy Jackson knows all about trypophobia. He said his sister has it. If we talked to him, maybe he could convince Sheriff Lamb to dig deeper for another suspect."

"Maybe," he echoed, sounding uncertain. "I don't know, Nina. I really appreciate what you're trying to do, but for now I just want to get Virgie bailed out. But I'll be sure to mention this to the attorney when we find one."

I managed a smile. "Good. Thanks again for the class, John. It was fun."

Grabbing up my vase, I hurried out to the street while the florist locked the door behind me. I'd expected John to be more enthusiastic about my hypothesis, but best I could tell, the revelation had hardly resonated with him. Maybe I should do as I'd suggested to him and call Deputy Jackson myself. For now, I'd worry about getting my flower arrangement—and myself—safely home.

The street parking had already been full when I'd arrived around quarter to seven, meaning I had parked my Mini

Cooper the next block down. But with my fellow apprentice florists having already driven off into the night, the street was now empty. And with only a single streetlamp on the corner, the block was mostly bathed in darkness.

I glanced back at the florist shop in time to see the interior downstairs lights dim in quick succession, followed a moment later by a single upstairs light turning on. Apparently, John was one of the local merchants who lived above his business. Everyone else on the street had long since left for home elsewhere or else was already tucked in bed, for no other lights were evident.

Too late, I remembered Harry's flip comments about Cymbeline's mean streets and prowling silver cars. Not that I didn't think he was exaggerating—a lot. But needing both hands to manage my top-heavy floral design made it difficult to follow those familiar personal safety tips for walking alone after dark. You know, like having one's phone in one's hand ready to dial 911 at any instant or holding one's car keys' pointy ends out like a weapon. Though, on the bright side, the vase was sturdy enough to make a decent cudgel. And as I had only a block and a half to traverse and I didn't see any traffic about, I wasn't worried.

That is, until I reached the corner. I looked both ways, then stepped off the curb—only to see a flash of silver in the glow of the nearby streetlamp as a small sedan barreled toward me.

Chapter Sixteen

I think I screamed.

I probably managed a wordless prayer.

I know I leapt backward with an agility that I had no clue I possessed as, vase cradled in my arms, I stumbled and tumbled onto the sidewalk behind me.

Safe! Or was I? I had barely registered the sudden dagger-like pain in my left ankle resulting from my unintended acrobatics when the seemingly out-of-control vehicle skidded to a halt just a few feet from me.

The coupe idled there at the curb and revved its engine, high beams blinding me so that I couldn't make out who was at the wheel. I realized in terror that this was no careless mishap on the driver's part, that he was deliberately toying with me. With my injured ankle, I couldn't possibly scramble away in time if he decided to stomp on the accelerator.

And then, with an ear-jarring crunch of gears, the car screeched backward, whipped to one side, and took off into the night.

I'm not sure how long I huddled there on the sidewalk once the car had left. All I know is that I struggled for several moments not to pass out from the stomach-churning pain of my injured ankle. It was dark and quiet again, and the street was once again empty of cars. But more than a cool night breeze made me shiver.

I hadn't imagined what had just happened. Some unknown person had violently threatened me, had possibly tried to kill me. Whether the car was the same silver vehicle I'd seen at Roxanna's house the day of her murder, I wasn't certain. It seemed too great a coincidence for it not to be. And while the immediate danger appeared over, I still had almost a block to go before I reached the safety of my car. What if the driver came back again?

Somehow, I got to my feet. Then, vase once more clutched to my chest—most of the water it once held having been soaked up by my T-shirt—I painfully hopped and limped my way across the street and on down the sidewalk as quickly as I could.

After a seemingly interminable hike, I was standing beside my green Mini Cooper again. I sagged against the car in relief for a few moments before unlocking the passenger door and sticking my battered flower arrangement on the floorboard. Then, using the car hood for support, I hopped my way around the front of the Mini to the driver's side door and crawled inside.

The first thing I did was turn on the engine and auto-lock all the doors. Then I sunk back into my seat and tried to catch my breath while I waited for my racing heartbeat to return to a slightly more normal rate. Logically, I knew I should be calling the sheriff's department to report the attempt on my life. But for the moment all I wanted to do was go home and put my foot up and wait for the pain to subside.

Fortunately, it was my left ankle that was injured, meaning I was still able to drive. After several steadying breaths, I felt composed enough to put the car in gear and head off. But given the amount of pain I was in, the five-minute drive back to the B&B seemed to last a good hour. By the time I pulled into my darkened driveway and turned off the engine again, the last thing I felt capable of doing was wrangling the heavy wrought-iron gate closed behind me.

And so I pulled out my phone and dialed Harry's cell.

"Hey, how did it go tonight?" I asked, in as normal a tone as I could manage, when he answered on the first ring. "Did the mysterious Ryan come prowling around in the dark while I was gone?"

"Not a peep from anyone named Ryan—or anyone else." Then, tone sharpening, he asked, "Where are you, anyway?"

"I'm parked in the driveway. Be a lamb, would you, and get the front gate for me?"

I'd given up trying to sound normal; in fact, my voice trembled outright. And apparently Harry could hear the distress in my words—or perhaps it was the co-opting of his "lamb" expression that set off his radar—for he demanded, "Nina, are you all right?"

"Not really. Can you come out here now?"

The call abruptly ended. A moment later the porch lights blazed on, illuminating the yard and driveway. The same glare silhouetted Harry so that he resembled someone out of a B movie as he came striding from the house toward me. And frankly, I'd never been so happy to see him before.

By the time he reached the car, I had already rolled down the driver's window.

"What's wrong?" he clipped out. "Did someone follow you back here?"

I shook my head. "No, I hurt my ankle. I don't think it's broken. It's probably just a bad sprain, but it's hard to walk on it. Maybe you can help me into the house after you catch the gate?"

He opened the door and reached out an arm. "Let's see how you're doing."

While he steadied me, I managed to unfold myself from the driver's seat and stand up beside the car. But when I took a tentative step, I shrieked a little despite myself and would have collapsed had he not caught me.

"Forget it," he clipped out. "We're taking you to the emergency clinic."

I didn't bother to protest as he literally swept me off my feet and carried me around to the passenger side. Pulling open the door, he settled me in.

"Buckle up while I run back inside and get my wallet."

"No, wait," I blearily said, and grabbed his arm before he could shut me in. "My flower arrangement is in the back. Can you take it inside and put it in the parlor?"

He shook his head but did as requested. In a minute he was back and climbing behind the wheel. I must have dozed off for a bit, because the next thing I knew we were pulling into a brightly lit parking lot with the letters *ER* in bright-red neon shining from the white-brick building at the lot's rear.

"Wait here," he told me unnecessarily. "I'll see if they've got a wheelchair."

Fortunately, the clinic was slow, today being Monday. A little more than an hour after Harry wheeled me inside, my ankle had been x-rayed and wrapped and I'd been given a prescription and a pair of crutches.

"I'm sure you've heard all this before," the clinic physician, Dr. Patel, told me, "but sprains can take longer to heal than broken bones."

She handed me a faded sheet of instructions that looked like a tenth-generation photocopy, a few of the bullet points highlighted in yellow.

"Keep the ankle elevated for the first few days while you're sleeping or sitting, and wait a couple of days before you put any weight on it. Stick with ibuprofen or aspirin if you can, but if it hurts too badly, you can fill that prescription. And let that good-looking husband of yours do the heavy lifting around the house for at least a week."

Had my pain factor not been clocking in at a good twenty-five on the one-to-ten scale, I would have hurried to correct the young doctor's misunderstanding. Instead, I smiled and nodded and waited for the nice aide to wheel me back to the waiting room so Harry and I could be on our way.

With the front passenger seat pushed back all the way, we managed to fit me and my brand-new crutches into the Mini. Harry got into the driver's seat again.

"How are you holding up?" he asked as he started the engine. "Do you want me to find an all-night pharmacy so we can fill that prescription?"

I shook my head. "I'll try to tough it out with over-the-counter meds tonight. If it gets too bad, you can go out in the morning."

"Your call. Let's get you home then."

He put the Mini in gear and backed out of the parking spot, then started in the direction of the parking lot exit.

"So how did you tear up that ankle anyhow?" he asked. "Wait, don't tell me. You tripped in the dark while you were lugging around that crazy flower arrangement."

"It's not crazy—it's a floral representation of Zen," I said, defending my creation. "I sprained my ankle while I was leaping out of the way of the car that tried to run me over."

"What?"

Harry slammed on the brakes there in the middle of the parking lot, not noticing that the sudden stop jostled my ankle and made me wince. He threw the Mini into park and turned to face me.

"Someone tried to run you over? Who?"

"I don't know. Their high beams blinded me, so I couldn't tell who it was."

I gave him a recap of those few moments of terror. When I was finished, he said, "All right, change of plans. We're going to make a little detour to the sheriff's department so you can file a complaint."

"What's the point? It happened so fast and it was so dark that I can't even say what model of car it was. And I only saw

227

the car from the front, so I didn't get a look at the license plate."

"Doesn't matter," he countered. "Maybe someone on the block has security cameras that might have caught your driver on video. Besides, you need to document what happened, in case it happens again."

Which rationale promptly sent a shiver through me. Was I now a walking—or, rather, hobbling—target for someone? "All right, I'll file a report. But can't it wait until tomorrow? My ankle really hurts."

I left that last word trembling between us just a little—not that I was faking. It really did hurt, and I really wasn't up to perching on a metal folding chair beneath fluorescent lighting, waiting all night for a deputy to take my statement.

Fortunately, that apparently made sense to Harry, for he nodded.

"I'll call Connie in the morning and see if she can send someone over so you can stay off that ankle. And maybe after you've had some sleep, you might remember something that could help identify the car."

With that, he put the Mini back in gear, and we started off again. It had been a while since I'd had someone chauffeuring me around, and normally my inner control freak would be pinging away right now. Under the circumstances, however, I was content to let Harry take the wheel. From what I'd seen, he was a far more capable driver than most, probably because he'd had a lot of practice with that beater of a tour bus.

Which observation made me think of something. But whatever that was slipped right out of my mind again as we encountered a road hump and, despite Harry's caution, my ankle was jostled again.

Once we arrived home, Harry pulled up to the outside kitchen door so I didn't have to make the hike all the way across the lawn and up the front porch steps. Even so, I would still have to make my way through the kitchen and the main hall to reach my room, which journey suddenly seemed like an obstacle course that would defeat the best of athletes.

Harry took one look at my struggles and made an executive decision.

"You can practice with your crutches tomorrow. Put your arm around my neck."

"Really, I can do it," I protested halfheartedly, even as I let him heft me up again and carry me inside.

Mattie and Gus rushed to greet us, the Aussie whining in concern as she followed us into my room.

"It's okay, girl," I told her from my perch a few feet above her. "Your mom just had a little accident." To Harry, I added, "Can you set me down by my dresser so I can grab some sweats to change into?"

"You sure you can manage?" he replied, sounding doubtful.

"No worries. I've got it. But maybe you can grab my crutches and bring them back to me while I get ready for bed."

I hopped the few steps to my bathroom and did the usual, then changed into cutoff sweats and an oversized I ♥ Aussies

T-shirt. By the time I had downed a couple of ibuprofen tablets and hopped back out into the bedroom again, Mattie and Gus were flopped atop the bed and Harry had returned with my crutches.

He'd also turned down the dog-free side of my bedcovers and propped up all but one of the pillows in my collection against the headboard. The remaining pillow he had placed where my feet would go so my ankle would be elevated as I slept.

But that wasn't all. He had brought in one of the baskets that usually held afternoon snacks for my guests. Now, however, it was filled with a cold bottle of diet soda, a carafe of filtered water and a matching glass, a small bag of pretzels, and a couple of leftover chocolate chip cookies from the last batch I'd made. The welcome basket sat on my bedside table alongside my lamp, which he'd turned on for me.

"Wow," I said—a bit inadequately—as, using the crutches, I hobbled to the bed. "That's really nice. Thanks."

He shrugged. "I didn't want you wandering to the kitchen in the middle of the night. And see, your TV remote's right there, and so is your phone. I'll flip off the overhead lights on my way out. If you need anything in the middle of the night, give me a call. Or you can just yell. I'll sleep in the parlor so I'll be close by."

"Harry, that's really sweet of you but totally not necessary," I told him as I propped the crutches against the table and sat on the bed. Swinging about so that I was leaned back against the headboard, my twisted ankle propped on the lone pillow, I added, "I'll be fine."

"Right. That's what you said when you went off to your workshop."

His tone was noncommittal, but his serious expression said something else. He wasn't just concerned about my sprained ankle. He thought I might be in actual danger.

And, to be truthful, I was more than a bit concerned myself. If I'd been less nimble earlier on that street corner, or if the unknown driver had been more determined to finish the job, I might have suffered more than a sprain. And Harry might have had his house back after all.

Not wanting him to know I shared his fear, I suppressed a reflexive shudder and simply nodded. "If it makes you feel better, you're welcome to the couch. You know where to find the extra blankets and pillows. And Harry, thanks again for everything you did tonight."

"Not a problem. Sleep tight."

But barely had he started for the door when a totally different fiasco occurred to me. I bolted upright in the bed again.

"Harry, I forgot—I've got guests booked starting Friday night. I'll still be on crutches then. I won't be able to haul luggage or show people to their rooms. And even setting up breakfast will be a nightmare. What am I going to do?"

He turned and smiled. "You're not going to do anything but be charming to them when they walk in the front door. I'll handle everything else for you."

"You?" I stared at him in confusion. "But you've never done the checking in and setting up the breakfast before."

He slanted me a look. "Nina, I've watched you do it for weeks. I think I'm competent enough to handle putting people in rooms and laying out a breakfast spread for a couple of days."

"I'm sorry, I know you are," I replied, feeling guilty at my reflexive rejection. But then I realized something else. "Wait. Aren't you supposed to be leaving Friday afternoon with Dr. Garvin for that banquet thing of hers in Savannah on Saturday?"

"Easy fix," he assured me. "I'll tell her we've got an emergency situation and that she needs to rent me a car. She's a doctor; she'll understand. If I head out late Saturday afternoon, I'll be there in plenty of time for the event. I'll leave right after it ends and be back here sometime around midnight. It's a win-win for her too, since the car will be cheaper than paying two nights for me in that fancy downtown hotel."

"Y-you'd do that?"

"Of course. Actually, you'd be doing *me* a favor," he added with a wry smile. "It was bad enough riding around town listening to her complain about her family on the way to the reunion. I don't think I could handle a road trip with her. Now I've got a legitimate excuse to beg off."

I stared at him in amazement, suddenly close to tears. It had been a while since I'd had a man in my life who would make such a generous offer. Not that I hadn't helped Harry out before when he'd been in a bind, but actually taking over the business for a couple of days was a whole other step up. Easy as it might seem to outsiders, the reality was that the innkeeping business was a lot of work.

And so I swallowed hard and put on a smile. "Thanks, Harry, I really appreciate your offer. I won't forget it."

"I won't let you."

And with those parting words, he flipped off the overhead light and headed out the door.

Shaking my head—Harry always had an angle, it seemed—I drank some water and nibbled on a cookie. Then, scooching the dogs over, I flipped off my bedside light and tried to get some rest.

But in the darkness, I kept hearing the revving of a car engine, kept seeing the coupe idling in front of me like some malevolent metal beast poised for a final deadly pounce. Maybe all it had been was a prank gone wrong, I tried to tell myself. But if the driver *had* pounced, best case I'd be in Cymbeline General right now.

Worst case, my family back in Texas would be making arrangements to fly me home a final time.

After almost an hour spent tossing and turning as much as I could, given the limitations of my ankle, I finally groaned in dismay and sat up in bed. *No sleep for me tonight*, I told myself. But as I turned on the bedside light in preparation for some distracting television viewing, that elusive thought I'd lost while Harry was driving us back from the clinic made an abrupt return. This time, I grabbed it—and then grabbed my cell phone.

"You okay?" Harry demanded as he picked up, not bothering with a hello.

"I'm fine, considering. But I just realized something important. I'm certain the silver car I saw parked in front of Roxanna's place the day we picked up Gus is the same silver car that tried to run me down tonight."

"Last night," he corrected through a yawn. "It's after midnight." Then, abruptly sounding more alert, he added, "Wait, you're saying it was silver? Why in the heck didn't you mention that before?"

"I wasn't exactly feeling up to giving a sworn statement at the time," I defended myself. "But now that I've had a chance to think on it a bit more, I'm almost positive it had to be the same person behind the wheel."

"Go on."

"The car at Roxanna's definitely was a stick shift, because whoever was driving it kept grinding the gears when they put it in reverse." I winced a little, hearing that distinctive sound in my head again. "The car tonight made that same terrible crunching sound when they backed up."

I hesitated and took a deep breath, then forged on. "Whoever it is must know I found that ten thousand dollars. And almost running me down in the dark like that was a message to let me know that they know—and that I'd better keep my mouth shut about the money, or I'll end up like Roxanna!"

Chapter Seventeen

"I wish you'd notified us about this incident last night, Ms. Fleet," Deputy Jackson said as he wrote in his ever-present notebook. "We could've been checking the business owners already for security cameras that might have recorded what happened."

It was a little after ten the next morning, and we were sitting in the parlor. I was still wearing last night's cutoff sweats and T-shirt, though I'd washed my face and slapped on a bit of eyeshadow in addition to clipping up my hair in a messy bun. Harry had opted for an equally casual look, black jeans and a plaid flannel in shades of brown, tan, and black that on him looked surprisingly stylish.

I half lay on one of the blue velvet sofas with my ankle propped on a crewelwork throw pillow. The deputy perched uncomfortably on the matching sofa across from me. Harry hovered in the background near the door, listening in but saying nothing.

Ignoring the actor's *I told you so* look in response to Jackson's last comment, I replied, "Sorry, all I wanted to do was rest once we got back from the emergency clinic. And at the time, I didn't really have much to report. It wasn't until after midnight that I made the connection between the car I saw at Roxanna's house and the one that almost ran me over."

Unlike Harry the night before, the deputy had seemed impressed by the way I'd linked the two incidents. But now that I'd given my statement, he flipped his notebook closed.

"I'm not saying I don't believe something's going on and you might be a target. But there's not much we can do unless we can find a witness or download pertinent camera footage. I'll make sure we increase patrols in this neighborhood, and if you see any other suspicious cars, don't hesitate to call."

"I won't. But there's something else I need to let you know about Roxanna Quarry's murder."

Jackson frowned and flipped the notebook back open. "And that is . . . ?"

"Remember when you came to take my statement there at the gymnasium? Jasmine and Buddy and I were asking trivia questions to pass the time, and you knew the answer to the phobia about clusters of holes."

"Trypophobia," he said with a nod. "But what's that got to do with Ms. Quarry?"

"It's not about her; it's about Virgie Hamilton."

I pointed to my Zen flower arrangement on the table between us, elegant with its mix of anthuriums and tropical foliage and gold-painted lotus seed pods.

"Virgie has trypophobia, just like you said your sister does. The morning of the bridal expo, I saw Virgie stop by John

Klingel's florist booth next to mine. She pretty well freaked out when she saw some of those lotus seed pods."

"O-kaaay," the deputy agreed, sounding puzzled. "And this has a bearing on the case because . . . ?"

"Roxanna was strangled with her own scarf. And the pattern on the fabric was hundreds of little holes close together, just like this."

I leaned forward to pluck one of the lotus seed pods from the vase, waving it by way of demonstration.

"I even remember what Virgie said to John—*first Roxanna and now you*. She was talking about the scarf. I think she thought Roxanna wore it to taunt her. It upset her so much that there's no way she would even have touched it."

"Or maybe she just closed her eyes."

With that, Jackson shut his notebook again and stood. "Ms. Fleet, that's all real interesting, but phobias aren't facts. Maybe Ms. Hamilton can bring that up with her defense attorney. I heard she bailed out sometime last night."

Meaning John must have raised the cash after all. Which was one bit of good news, for a change. But to cover all the bases, there was still the issue of Roxanna's ex.

"I'm glad to hear that," I told the deputy. "But I was wondering about Ryan Slater, Roxanna's ex-husband. When Sheriff Lamb came by yesterday, she said you were trying to locate him. Did you have any luck?"

"We spoke to the man, and he's going to drop by the station later to give a voluntary statement," Jackson replied. With a frown, he added, "Why do you ask?"

Because he might be Roxanna's killer?

But as Jackson had already been dismissive of my lotus pod theory, I wasn't going to go too far out on this particular limb. "It's just that someone I think was Ryan called me to set up a tour of the B&B but then never showed up for the appointment. It seemed a bit suspicious."

Jackson nodded and scribbled a note, taking down the phone number that the presumed Ryan Slater had called from. That concluded the questioning, and I let Harry show the deputy out.

When Harry came back into the room a few minutes later, I grabbed my crutches and got to my feet—or rather, foot. The pain in my left ankle had subsided significantly overnight, which I hoped boded well for a swift recovery. If I kept the weight off it, the worst I experienced was a low-key throb when I moved about.

"Looks like you're getting the hang of those crutches," the actor said in approval as I took a few tentative steps. "Just don't wear yourself out."

"I won't. I'm going to spend the morning on my computer. What about you?"

"I still have to give Meredith a call about this weekend. After that, I'll probably stick around the house, maybe teach the dogs how to fetch your crutches for you."

Which I knew actually meant *I'll keep an eye on things here in case we get any unexpected visitors in silver cars.* And I suspected that Harry knew that *my* answer translated to *I'm going to poke around on the internet and see if I can learn more about this Ryan Slater person.*

While Harry went off to make his call, I made my way back to my room, feeling rather proud of how well I was moving. Not that I was breaking any land speed records for crutches, but I'd mastered going up and down the kitchen-door steps. No way was I going to try the main staircase, however. My plan was to hold Harry to his promise to take over for the weekend.

I let Mattie and Gus out into their side yard so they could stretch their legs, then made my way to my desk. I swiftly checked my B&B email, sending standard replies to basic requests for information. With the inn business taken care of, I went to pull up my internet browser, when I heard a knock at my bedroom door.

"Come in," I called.

Harry walked in, phone in hand and expression pensive. I gave him a curious look. "What's wrong?"

"I've just finished negotiating the terms of my freedom with Meredith. In return for letting me drive to Savannah on my own, I need to drop by her office tonight to help her with some remodeling, which probably translates to moving furniture."

He stuck the phone in his jeans pocket and added, "Oh, and she said to tell you she's sorry about your injured ankle. And she also wants you to know that the *ice* portion of RICE"—*rest, ice, compression, elevation*, I knew from a past first-aid class—"is no longer recommended."

"Tell her I said thanks for the good wishes," I replied, torn between sympathy for and amusement over Harry's ongoing predicament as a result of that whole Plus One thing. Harry might be a clever manipulator when he wanted to be, but it seemed he'd met his match in Dr. Garvin. "What time are you headed out?"

"I'll be leaving around six. Do you think I can borrow the Mini?"

"Sure. I won't be driving anywhere tonight."

He nodded. "Thanks. And just so you know, I'd really rather not leave you alone here, even for a couple of hours, but I don't see any way out of this."

Before I could reply to that, my cell phone, which was plugged in at my desk next to me, began to ring. I checked the caller ID.

"It's John Klingel," I told Harry in surprise. "He's probably calling to let me know about Virgie."

Gesturing for him to wait, I answered the call. "Hi, John, how are you?"

"I'm not sure, Nina," came his uncertain reply.

I frowned. "Well, that's not the answer I expected. I heard that you managed to bail out Virgie last night. Isn't that good news?"

"That's why I'm calling. You see, I didn't bail her out. I don't know who did—and I don't know where she is now."

"Wait. Are you saying that Virgie is missing?"

I glanced up to see Harry listening intently to my end of the conversation. I wasn't sure if John knew the actor, but I suspected he'd prefer to keep this particular conversation on the down low. On the other hand, after the events of the previous night, I wanted Harry to know everything I did. And so I committed a small sin of omission.

Signaling to Harry with a finger to my lips, I said, "Hold on, John. I've got my hands full at the moment. I'm going to put you on speaker so I can set down the phone. Now tell me again, what's happened?"

"I'm not sure I know," he said, his voice now echoing clearly in the room. "I didn't raise enough money for bail until this morning, and when I went to make arrangements, I was told she'd already been released and someone picked her up. The clerk wouldn't tell me who that someone was—she said the information would be public record once the case goes to trial. I thought maybe you took care of it."

I shook my head. Then, remembering he couldn't see me, I confirmed, "No, it wasn't me. I haven't seen Virgie since the expo. But I can't believe she'd disappear without a word to anyone."

"Normally, no." I could hear his sigh. "But Virgie is a proud woman. Even though she's innocent, she knows everyone knows by now about the arrest. I thought maybe she was lying low somewhere—like in a motel, or a B&B."

Harry and I exchanged knowing nods. The florist obviously thought I was harboring his ex.

"John, I promise you she's not here. But if she does show up, I'll make sure she knows how worried you are." And then, so I could scratch Virgie off the *tried to kill Nina* roll, I casually asked, "Tell me, what kind of car does Virgie drive? You know, so I can keep an eye out for her."

"You can't miss her," he said with a snort. "She drives a late-model metallic-blue Cadillac four-door."

"Great, thanks," I told him, relieved to take her name off that particular list. "Like I said, I'll watch out for her. I'm afraid that's the best I can do for now."

"Understood." He sighed again. "But Nina, I've been calling her number, and it keeps going to voice mail. I don't even want to say this out loud, but until we know who really did kill Roxanna, I'm afraid that Virgie might be in danger."

Which was a valid point, as my sprained ankle could attest to. A sudden shiver of unease vibrated through me. And that reminded me of something else. "Uh, John, any chance you have exterior security cameras there at the florist shop?"

"No. It's not exactly that sort of neighborhood. Why?"

I debated telling him what had happened to me as I left the workshop last night, but he was already worried about Virgie. Why compound his distress?

And so, thinking fast, I replied, "Oh, it's nothing major. I'm considering getting cameras for the B&B, so I'm taking an informal poll of the business owners I know."

"Actually, I think Virgie has cameras. You might ask her. If we ever hear from her again."

He sounded so doleful that I wondered why the pair had even divorced in the first place. Of course they fought, but many couples had their battles. It was when you couldn't air your grievances with your partner that the marriage was in trouble—as I had learned from personal experience.

"Thanks, John. And I know it's easy to say, but try not to worry. Virgie is a resourceful woman. And if you hear from her first, please let me know."

Once the florist had hung up, I turned to Harry. "John might be right about Virgie being too mortified to show her face in public, but who would have bailed her out besides him?"

"Probably someone in a silver car," was his flip response.

And then, when I stared at him in dismay, he hurried to add, "Just trying to lighten the mood. I'm sure someone from the Chamber helped her out. It could have been Polly—they're friends, and she could raise the funds on her own, no problem. And I agree with John. She's probably holed up somewhere and we won't hear from her until someone else is arrested for the murder."

"I hope you're right," I told him. "But it's odd that she won't take his calls. I think I'll try. Maybe it's just John that she's avoiding."

Fortunately, because of my participation in the bridal expo, Virgie's contact information was already programmed into my phone. Switching again to speakerphone so Harry could hear, I pulled up her name and tapped on the number. The call immediately went to voice mail.

"You have reached Virgie Hamilton," came the shop owner's honeyed tones. "I'm unable to take your call, but please do leave a message."

"Virgie, it's Nina Fleet. All of us are worried about you, John especially. If you get this message, can you at least text me and let me know you're okay? Thanks."

I hung up and then turned again to Harry. "Well, that was a dead end. And John said the sheriff's office wouldn't tell him who bailed her out. That doesn't seem right, does it?"

"You can find out the name of the bail bond agent," he replied, "but who put up the money isn't public record. And don't ask me how I know that."

As Harry had proved to be a font of unconventional facts in the past, I took his word for it. "I suppose it's not our business anyhow. And Virgie's no fool. She wouldn't get into the car of someone she didn't know, particularly under these circumstances."

Harry nodded, but from the look in his eyes, I was pretty sure he had something up his sleeve. I didn't bother to question him, because my sleeves had a few tricks of their own. Whoever had killed Roxanna had known her personally—and that likely meant that Roxanna's longtime business partner knew the killer too.

Which meant that chances were, Virgie wouldn't have thought twice about climbing into that person's car.

"I've got a few things to do."

"I think I'll get a few things done."

We both spoke simultaneously, then stopped and stared at each other for a moment. Harry added, "I'll be around. Let me know if you need anything."

I waited until I heard him walking up the stairs before settling again at my desk and opening my laptop. I couldn't guess whether Virgie had known Ryan Slater or not. However, given the fact that he had so conveniently shown up in town the weekend his ex-wife had been murdered, I darned sure wanted to find out what I could about the man—including what kind of vehicle he drove.

I tried social media first, inputting his name into the usual sites. But either the man didn't tweet or post or he had tight security on his accounts, because the only possibilities I found under that name were a couple of grandfatherly types and a handful of twentysomething guys, none of whom fit the likely demographic. And while I was going on the assumption that he still lived in Atlanta, he might well have moved to another city or even another state. That meant I couldn't afford to narrow my hunt to that extent. And so, leaving social media behind, I did a general web browser search for the name.

After close to an hour spent typing and clicking, I finally settled on a couple of likely candidates—Ryan Philip Slater and Ryan Thomas Slater. Both men were in their early forties and had a Georgia tie, but I couldn't connect either to a wife by the name of Roxanna.

And then, giving myself a figurative slap on the forehead, I deleted what I had been using and changed my search terms to another name—*Roxanna Quarry Slater*.

"Bingo!" I said aloud as a full page of results popped up. After another few minutes of sorting and connecting dots, I finally focused on a single person: Ryan Philip Slater from Atlanta.

A picture of him accompanied one of the links. He was a pleasant-featured man with sandy-blond hair and dimples who I guessed to be around forty years old. The photo surprised me, as I'd expected someone a bit, well, sketchier. His background appeared equally uncheckered. It appeared he was currently employed as some sort of data analyst, and as far as I could see, he had no criminal record. But I did find mention of the bankruptcy that Mason had told me about. Beyond that, his history appeared pretty innocuous. Not that a clean background meant anything when it came to murder.

I took a quick screenshot of Slater's picture and emailed it to Harry. Then, needing a mental break, I shut down my browser, grabbed my crutches, and went to see about lunch.

Harry was already in the kitchen digging through the refrigerator, where I'd allocated one shelf for his use. (I had previously forbidden him from hauling a mini fridge up to the tower room, mostly because I hadn't wanted to find him squished beneath it at the bottom of the ladder stair should said hauling go wrong.) He looked up at my sudden appearance and said, "I thought I'd make you lunch. You feel like a toasted PB&J?"

I smiled. "Actually, that doesn't sound half bad. Thanks." Sobering, I added, "Check your email when you can. I think I've located Ryan Slater. I sent you a picture so we'd recognize him if he showed up here."

Setting down the jelly jar, Harry pulled his phone from his jeans pocket and scrolled, then frowned as he checked my attachment.

"Good job, Secret Squirrel," he told me. "At least we won't be taken by surprise if he decides to make an appearance. Too bad you don't actually have those security cameras you were telling John you wanted to install. It would be nice to spot the guy first before he manages to get inside."

"Believe me, I'm seriously considering doing that now. In the meantime, if any sketchy ex-husbands show up, I'll release the hounds," I said, with a nod at Mattie and Gus. They had obviously heard the refrigerator door open from their porch and had rushed in on the chance that the sound meant snacks for them.

While I settled at the kitchen island, Harry did a credible job of duplicating my famous toasted PB&J sandwich for the both of us. We ate in companionable silence. Once the last crumbs were gone, Harry pulled out his phone again.

"You're not the only internet Secret Squirrel sleuth," he said with a smug smile. "While you were busy tracking down Roxanna's ex, I researched the late-model two-door cars available in stick shift. I narrowed those down to the manufacturers Cymbeline Autos sells. And then, since we might be talking a higher-end car that's not available in town, I looked at the Savannah dealerships too. Plus, the model had to be available in silver. I think I've got four candidates that might be your mystery coupe."

Scrolling through his pictures, he showed me the cars in question. I squinted at each one, trying to determine if one of them better matched my memory of the car I'd seen. Finally, I gave a helpless shake of my head.

"What happened to the good old days when you could tell a Ford from a Chevy from a Mercedes?" I demanded. "I swear these cars all look alike."

Harry snorted. "Sorry, Grandma, but car manufacturers have been stealing design ideas from each other for decades. This isn't a new thing."

"Well, bottom line, every one of these pictures looks like the car I saw."

"Tell you what," he replied. "Let's give you another day to rest up, and how about tomorrow we take a drive around town? We might just luck out and spot the car."

On that note, we cleaned up the kitchen. Afterward, Harry took the dogs outside for the promised training session, while I retired to my room and decided to try to take a shower. Keeping my ankle dressings dry took more effort than I expected, even though I'd wrapped my foot inside a spare trash can liner. By the time I had dried off and changed into fresh clothes, I was feeling worn out. I lay down on the bed and closed my eyes for what I assured myself would be just a minute.

I woke up to the sound of knocking at my bedroom door. I glanced at my alarm clock and saw in dismay that a whole lot of minutes had passed. As in, I'd basically slept away the entire afternoon.

"Nina, are you okay?" Harry called through the door.

I sat up with a groan. "I'm fine. Come on in."

The door opened, and Mattie and Gus came flying toward me. Harry followed more slowly. "You've been out like a light for more than three hours," he told me with a smile. "I checked on you earlier, and you were still snoring up a storm, so I figured it was best to let you sleep."

"For your information, I don't snore," I loftily told him. "But thanks for letting me sleep. I guess the pain took more out of me than I expected. Are you headed out to help Meredith now?"

"In a couple of minutes. I checked the fridge, and it looks like there's some leftover chicken salad. Do you need me to fix you a plate before I go?"

I shook my head. "Seriously, I feel a whole lot better now that I took a shower and got some sleep. I'll be fine. I might even practice walking on both feet later on."

"Well, keep your crutches nearby," he warned me. "I shouldn't be gone for more than a couple of hours, but I'd hate to come back to find you sprawled on the floor like in one of those Life Alert commercials."

"I promise to take it easy," I said with an answering grin. "You're the one who needs to be careful. Don't let Dr. Garvin make you move a bunch of couches and cabinets. I need you healthy for my guests this weekend."

"I promise to stay in tip-top shape. Now, can I have the car keys, Mom?"

Giving him a wry shake of my head, I dug the keys out of my purse. I handed them over, then grabbed my crutches and followed him to the front door so I could manually lock it after him. My door key was on the key ring I'd given him, so he could get back inside later tonight without me. The dogs rushed after us, mostly because their tummies were telling them it was suppertime and they wanted to make sure at least one human was staying behind to feed them.

Harry had already opened the driveway gate, so I waited while he backed the Mini out to the street, then got out and closed the gate again. Watching the ritual, I decided that along with the security cameras, it was probably time to install an electric gate. I'd check with some of the neighbors in the next few days for a recommendation.

But I'd barely thumped my way to the kitchen to pull out the dog food when I heard a sudden knock at the front door. Harry must forgotten something, I told myself, and had left the Mini running, meaning he didn't have a key to get back in with. It was a bad habit I knew he'd clung to from driving his tour bus around.

I thumped my way back to the foyer, leaving Gus behind to keep chomping his chow. Mattie, however, followed me, showing her disapproval at this interruption of her meal by barking up a storm now.

Ready to lecture the actor about the keys-left-in-the-car thing, I told the Aussie to hush and whipped open the front door—only to find myself staring at a familiar face that most definitely was not Harry's.

"Uh, hi." The man addressed me through the screen door, which now was the only thing separating us. "I'm, uh, Ryan Slater."

Chapter Eighteen

The first thing I noticed was that, while Slater was still an attractive man, he looked older than the picture of him that I'd found. His face was thinner, his dimples more like creases, and some obvious gray was now mixed in with the sandy blond.

The second thing I noticed, because he was wearing cargo shorts, was that he was an amputee, his right leg below his knee replaced by a prosthesis. But that disability didn't mean he wasn't capable of strangling his ex-wife with a scarf—or of running me down with his car.

"You're Roxanna's ex-husband?" I managed, clutching the doorjamb for balance while Mattie growled beside me. "What do you want?"

"I, uh, just need to talk to you. You're Ms. Fleet—Roxie's friend—right?"

Warily I nodded, glancing past him toward the driveway. The pedestrian gate leading to the sidewalk was shut, as was the main gate, meaning he'd politely closed it after him. That or he'd snuck in after Harry opened it and waited until the actor had left to come knocking.

But as I swiftly debated whether to confront the man or slam the door in his face and call the sheriff's department, I heard an unearthly howl that I realized was Gus running to join us.

Slater's face broke into a broad grin that abruptly took ten years off his age. "Gustopher!" he called. "Is that you, buddy?"

The Goldendoodle shoved past me and leaped up onto his hind legs, his big fuzzy front paws plastered against the screen door as he danced and barked in obvious ecstasy.

"I can't believe it," Slater exclaimed, his nose pressed to his side of the screen and his hands splayed against Gus's paws. "You're such a big boy now. My widdle fluffer puppy is all growed up."

Fluffer puppy?

I slanted the man a look. The last thing I'd expected Ryan Slater to be was some marshmallow of a guy who talked baby talk to a dog. And if I wasn't mistaken, those were actually tears in his eyes.

But then suspicion returned.

"Gus, down," I said, grabbing the Goldendoodle by the collar and doing my best to pull him off the screen. To Slater, I said, "All right, what's going on here? This is Roxanna's dog. Why are you pretending you know him?"

Slater gave me a quizzical look. "But I do know him. Can't you tell? Gustopher is my dog."

"Nice try, but no," I said with a shake of my head. "Roxanna told me she got him after the divorce. He was a rescue."

Slater nodded. "We got him as a puppy from a place called Second Chance Doodles in Atlanta. They're a rescue specializing in Goldendoodles and Labradoodles and even regular old poodles. He was only three months old. Someone gave him up because he was too rambunctious.

"And him was, wasn't him?" he said as an aside to Gus, who wriggled in joy.

Then Slater's features hardened. "I know you don't have any reason to believe me, but Gus is the only reason I'm here. I mean, I was devastated when I heard about what happened to Roxanna. Even after everything she did, I never wished her any harm. But Gus was the only thing I wanted from the divorce, and she deliberately took him from me. And now I want him back."

And then when I hesitated, not entirely convinced, he went on, "I went straight to her house as soon as I heard. But when I got there, you and some guy were already loading Gus in your car, so I followed you home. Then I called you that day pretending to be interested in staying here so I could talk to you."

"Right, and you didn't show up that next morning like you promised."

He shrugged. "There was a sheriff's department car in your driveway when I came by, so I kept on going. I knew they wanted to talk to me about Roxanna, and I was fine with that, but I wanted to get Gus back first. I-I thought maybe you'd figured out who I was and that's why the cops were there."

Then he reached into his pocket and pulled out his phone. "Look, I have pictures of him from when we first brought him home."

He held up the phone so I could see as he scrolled through several dozen photos of him and a Goldendoodle puppy with the same apricot-colored curls as Gus. A few of the shots were of the pup and a mugging Roxanna, the sight of which made me smile even as the pictures hurt my heart just a little.

"And that's not all," he told me. "I taught Gustopher a bunch of tricks. If you'll open the door a little more, I'll show you."

"All right," I agreed. "But I'd better not see any tricks from you."

Keeping Mattie at my side, I hobbled back so I could open the front door all the way. Through the screen, Slater called, "All right, Gus. Sit. Down. Roll over."

The Goldendoodle performed each command in swift order.

"That's nice, but Mattie knows all those tricks," I pointed out. "Heck, every dog does."

He nodded.

"Okay, how about this? Gus, give me high five," he said, and held up his hand while the Goldendoodle raised a matching paw. "Good boy. Now, up."

Gus sat up on his hind legs.

"Good boy! Now, Gus, hop like a bunny!"

Hop like a bunny. That's the same trick I had Gustopher show Harry.

I caught my breath as the Goldendoodle promptly rose up and, front paws tucked close to his chest, bounced in place like a curly rabbit.

"Good boy!" Slater cheered as Gus dropped back to a sit, tongue lolling in a doggy grin. And then, with a boyish grin of his own, the man asked, "So, do you believe me now?"

"I don't think I have much choice," was my wry reply. "If you want to come on in for a few minutes, Mr. Slater, we can try to figure this out."

"Sure. And please, call me Ryan."

"All right. And I'm Nina."

I opened the screen, and Gus promptly leaped at Ryan, almost bowling him over. The man laughed and awkwardly knelt while the pup eagerly licked his face, curly tail wagging up a storm.

"Gus, be polite," I halfheartedly warned the pup, smiling at this happy little reunion. Given that he was obviously thrilled to see his long-lost human dad, it looked like the Goldendoodle had a home now. Of course, I'd check in with Sheriff Lamb first before handing him over.

"Why don't we sit in the parlor," I told Ryan, indicating the direction with my crutch. "Would you like an iced tea or some coffee?"

"I've got everything I need now," he replied, getting to his feet again and gesturing for Gus to follow.

I let him take the lead, first double-checking to make sure I still had my cell phone tucked into my jeans pocket. I was pretty sure now that Roxanna's ex was on the up-and-up, but just in case, I wanted a lifeline to the outside world should things unexpectedly go sideways.

Once in the parlor, we each settled on one of the blue velvet couches. Gus sat beside Ryan with his head on the man's knee, gazing up at him adoringly. Mattie plopped down at my feet, shooting her canine friend a peeved look. Obviously, she didn't want to share Gus with this stranger.

"Nice place you have here," Ryan said with an approving look around while he absently petted the pup. "If I ever get married again, I might want to stay here for real." Then he nodded in the direction of my injured ankle. "So, what did you do to yourself?"

"I fell getting out of the way of a car that I'm pretty sure was trying to run me over."

He stared at me with what appeared to be genuine alarm. "Whoa. Did the cops catch the person?"

"Not yet," I told him, not mentioning that until a couple of minutes ago, I'd been pretty sure he'd been the one behind the wheel. "Fortunately, it's just a sprain. I should be able to start walking on it again in the next day or so. In a couple of weeks I'll be mostly back to normal."

And then, since we were talking injuries, I asked, "What about you? Were you in the military or something?"

He shook his head. "I'm afraid it wasn't anything that heroic. I was in a car wreck the year before Roxie and I divorced. My right leg suffered a lot of trauma, and the original doctor who treated me recommended amputation. Then Roxie found this surgeon who claimed she could save the leg.

Long story short, we went with her and tried a bunch of differ-ent treatments over a couple of months."

"That must have been tough on both of you," I said with a sympathetic nod.

"It was. But we both were sure the new doctor knew what she was doing. Then I developed gangrene. I got scared and went back to my original guy. He told me I was lucky, coming back when I did. He said that if they didn't amputate right then, I would be dead in a few days. So I said the heck with all the mumbo jumbo treatment I'd been doing and told them to cut it off."

He paused and hiked up the right leg of his cargo shorts so that I could see a cluster of bright-green shamrocks tattooed above his knee. "After I healed up, I had this tat done to remind me that I might have lost a leg, but overall I actually *am* pretty lucky."

He ended his story with a shrug and a smile, and I could see that he really did consider himself fortunate.

I smiled back. "I know what you mean. I was this close to being a hood ornament, so getting away with just a sprain was pretty darned lucky for me too."

Then I hesitated, wondering if I dared ask him about the bankruptcy. That and if he knew anything about Roxanna's hidden key, as well as her hidden money. But before I could, my cell phone abruptly rang. I pulled the phone from my pocket and looked at the caller ID.

Harry.

I frowned. He would have just arrived at Dr. Garvin's office, so why would he be calling me already?

"Sorry, I need to take this. I'll just be a second," I told Ryan. And then, answering the call, I said, "Hi, Harry, what's up? Harry?"

He didn't reply, but I could hear a murmur of voices on the other end. Obviously, the actor had accidentally pocket-dialed me. I started to hang up, and then I heard his voice clearly say, "You really don't need to threaten us like that."

I froze. Had Harry really said what I thought I'd just heard? Swiftly, I put the phone on mute and then switched it to speakerphone. Once again, it was simply a murmur of voices.

"Is something wrong?" Ryan wanted to know.

I nodded and put a finger to my lips, even though I had the call silenced from my end. "I think my friend Harry is in trouble," I whispered, straining to hear anything more that might confirm my fears.

And then came a voice I recognized as Virgie's honeyed accents, now sharpened in what sounded like fear. "How many times do I have to tell you, I don't know anything about this file of Roxanna's that you're taking about!"

I waited another moment, and then the connection abruptly ended. Had Harry realized he'd dialed in error and simply hung up? Or had he ended the call so no one would realize he'd secretly phoned me? With everything that had happened the past few days, I had a really bad feeling it was the latter.

I stared at Ryan, who looked understandably confused. Rather than launch into a long explanation, I simply said, "I've got to get to Dr. Garvin's office to find out what's going on there, but Harry has my car. Can you drive me there?"

"Sure," he said, much to my relief, and stood.

I stuck my phone in my pocket and scrambled to my feet as quickly as I could, given the crutches. And then I remembered something.

"Wait. I don't know her address. I need to go online and look it up."

"Not so fast." He gave me a sharp look. "You said Dr. Garvin. Are you talking about Dr. Meredith Garvin?"

I nodded, and his expression hardened again. "Don't worry, I know where to find her. Let's go."

How he knew the doctor—let alone her office address— I wasn't sure, but I didn't pause to ask. For the moment, I was more concerned about Harry. We headed out via the kitchen, as that meant fewer stair steps for me to navigate, though Ryan had obviously mastered that sort of challenge long ago. Mattie and Gus were a greater obstacle in getting out of the house. Both pups, sensing something was wrong, barked and jumped as they tried to convince us they should come along.

Finally, minus dogs, we were at the front pedestrian gate. But I stopped short when I hobbled out to the sidewalk and saw the expensive two-door parked at the curb.

"Y-you drive a silver car?" I asked, staring in dismay at the vehicle whose bright paint job glowed in the dying sunlight. From this angle, it looked far too similar to the car that had tried to run me down the other day.

Ryan latched the gate behind us and then gave me a quizzical look.

"Yeah, I know, everyone and their dog drives a silver car. It's a bit flashy, but it was a present to myself once I was finished with my rehab," he said as he opened the passenger door for me. "I had a beat-up old Jeep four-wheel drive that I loved, but it was too hard driving a stick anymore, so I traded it in."

Automatic transmission, I thought in relief as I settled into the cushy bucket seat and dragged my crutches after me. If nothing else, that eliminated him from the *tried to kill Nina* list.

Ryan climbed into the driver's seat with far more grace than I'd managed in settling in on the opposite side, and we took off into what was rapidly becoming dusk. I pulled out my phone and checked it in case Harry had tried sending a message. Nothing.

I was almost certain that the pocket dial to me had been no accident—not when the formerly missing Virgie was apparently with him. And from the little I'd been able to hear of what was happening, it seemed that they and Meredith were being threatened by some unknown someone. I needed to let Harry know his message had been received. At the same time, I didn't want to accidentally tip off whoever was doing the threatening. And so I texted him an innocuous thumbs-up emoji.

Ryan saw me fiddling with my phone and asked, "You think we should call the sheriff's department and have them meet us there?"

I thought about it for a moment, certain I'd prefer to walk into the situation with Deputy Jackson alongside me—and then shook my head.

"You heard pretty much everything I did. I don't think Sheriff Lamb would send out her version of a SWAT team over a couple of people arguing. And hopefully this will turn out to be a big nothing anyhow."

Except that Virgie had mentioned Roxanna's name. I shivered. I knew that the sheriff had arrested the wrong person for Roxanna's murder. Which meant the true killer was still out there—maybe in Dr. Garvin's office.

Ten minutes later we were pulling into the small medical center complex not far from Cymbeline General. A line of business offices painted a crisp hospital white housed non-emergency care, according to the sign posted. They were identical, with a short blue awning over each entryway and neat brick planter boxes holding tall, slim evergreens flanking each door. The parking lot in front of the offices was empty except for a couple of cars at the far end.

One was my bright-green Mini Cooper, which meant we were at the right place. And as we angled closer, I could see the second vehicle parked on the other side of my Mini. It was a low-slung, high-end gray sports car that gleamed silver beneath the glare of a nearby nighttime security light.

I gasped. Seeing it in person again beneath the artificial light, I had no doubt this was the same car that had been at Roxanna's house the day of her murder. The same car that had threatened me as I walked from John's florist shop. And as

Virgie drove a metallic-blue Caddy, I knew the sedan wasn't hers. Which could only mean that whoever had almost run me down was there in the office with Harry and Virgie.

"Park over there!" I told Ryan, pointing to an office a few doors down. "I don't want anyone to know we're here."

And then, as the puzzle pieces abruptly fell into place, I grimly added, "Particularly not Dr. Garvin."

He nodded and eased into a slot a couple of offices down. Then, shutting off the engine, he turned to me. "You want to tell me what's really going on?"

"Sorry, Ryan, I'm just now connecting the dots," I replied, aware that my heart was beating faster. "Whoever drives that gray sports car is the person who tried to run me down the other night. And that's the same car I saw at Roxanna's. I'm pretty sure the car belongs to Dr. Garvin—and if it does, I have a feeling she's somehow connected to Roxanna's murder."

"Murder?" Ryan gaped at me, his features abruptly looking ashen in the car dome's faint light. "I-I was told it was an accident . . . a stunt gone wrong. You're saying someone deliberately killed her?"

"I'm sorry, I thought you knew. The medical examiner's report confirmed it. She was strangled."

"And you think Dr. Garvin killed her?"

He stared at me in disbelief as I nodded, and I waited while he took a few deep breaths. Then, seemingly back in control, he said in a grim tone, "I guess it's time to call the sheriff's department after all."

I reached for my cell phone and then hesitated. While I was rapidly rethinking my original decision not to call Deputy Jackson myself, we still didn't have any evidence beyond the overheard conversation and a few educated guesses—hardly enough to justify accusing anyone of murder. Then I caught sight of the gray sedan once again, and an idea came to me. I might not have evidence of murder, but I definitely had new information regarding my almost hit-and-run.

Fortunately, the deputy's business card was still in my purse from when he'd questioned me at the expo. I swiftly dialed his number, relieved when he answered on the second ring.

"I'm on the other side of town right now, Ms. Fleet," he told me once I'd explained about the car and given him the address. "I'll get there as quick as I can. You sit tight until then, hear?"

"All right," I agreed. Then, exchanging glances with Ryan, I added, "And be careful when you get here. I think the person who tried to run me down is somehow connected to Roxanna Quarry's murder."

Once I'd hung up, I glanced back over at Ryan again. "It's going to be a while until Deputy Jackson shows up. I don't think we should wait on him."

"I agree," he replied with a nod, his jaw set. "But what are we going to do, bust in like the cavalry or something?"

I gave my crutches a doubtful look. I might be able to bludgeon someone with one of them, but I definitely wasn't going to be busting in anywhere. And chances were that

Meredith had thought to lock the door, so we weren't going to simply stroll in either. We had to figure out a way to get someone to unlock the office door from inside.

"I've got an idea," I told Ryan, and quickly surveyed the parking lot.

It was a weak plan at best, but all I could muster up under the circumstances. Fortunately, it was dark enough now that the area outside the glare of the security light was in shadows. If Ryan and I plastered ourselves up against the office's outer wall behind either of the evergreens, we'd be mostly hidden unless someone was looking directly at us. And all we needed to do was wait for Harry to open the door for us so we could slip in.

I swiftly explained my idea to Ryan. I could tell from his expression that he wasn't convinced that the plan would work, but he agreed we didn't have many other options. Neither of us voiced our major fear—that Meredith might have already done something drastic in the time it had taken Ryan and me to get there.

Once we were in position, I pulled out my phone. And then, hoping against hope that Meredith would let him take the call, I dialed Harry.

To my relief, the actor picked up on the first ring.

"Hey, Harry," I cheerfully said. "How's it going?"

"Everything's fine so far," he replied in an equally cheery voice, which I took to mean that Meredith hadn't done anything crazy yet. "Look, we're pretty busy here. Can I call you back later?"

I heard a slight hollowness behind his voice, and I guessed he had me on speakerphone—probably at Meredith's direction. That way she could monitor the conversation and make sure he didn't put out a call for help. Which was exactly what I had hoped for.

"Oh, hey, I understand," I replied in the same upbeat tone. "This will just take a second. I think I left a box in the trunk of the Mini. It's got some folders and paperwork I picked up at Roxanna's place the other day. I promised Deputy Jackson I'd bring it to him. You know, for evidence. Do you mind checking to see if the box is still there?"

The line went silent for a moment, and I pictured a pantomimed exchange between Harry and the doctor. Then Harry said, "Sorry, Meredith was talking to me. Sure, I'll go take a look. I'll call you back later and let you know, okay?"

"All right, thanks," I said, and hung up.

Sticking my phone in my pocket, I leaned back so that I could see Ryan through the gap between the bush and the wall. I gave him a thumbs-up and waited for the door to open. A moment later I heard the distinct click of the dead bolt turning, and then Harry walked out the door into the parking lot.

I resisted the urge to call out to him in case Meredith was waiting at the door, listening. I didn't dare text him either, as chances were she had taken his phone. Instead, I simply waited while Harry went through the motions of opening the small trunk and looking inside. A few seconds later he slammed the trunk closed again. He casually glanced either way, and I couldn't tell if he had seen me or not. But when the office door closed behind him again, the lock didn't click after him.

"We're in," I whisper-called to Ryan.

I left one of my crutches propped beside the planter and, tucking the remaining crutch under my right arm, hopped over to where Ryan waited. He caught hold of my left arm, just in case. And then, like tag-team runners who'd forgotten to let go, we slipped into the office after Harry.

Chapter Nineteen

Ryan had described the office's layout to me on our way over, so I knew what to expect. He'd also answered my question about how he knew Dr. Meredith Garvin, which tied together most of the loose ends surrounding Roxanna's death. But I put that aside for the moment as I paused just inside the doorway to get my bearings.

The lobby was divided into a larger waiting area, which was separated from the records and check-in area by a chest-high counter with sliding frosted windows that could be closed for privacy. Those were open now, revealing a doorway to the wide back hall. A similar door led from the waiting room to the same hall. Here were the exam rooms, two to either side of the hall. Everything was painted in soothing tones of beige and sand that matched the slightly darker tile floor. A series of pastel abstracts hung along all the walls, giving the place an almost spa-like feel.

Ryan and I eased ourselves along the hallway—which for-tunately was carpeted—until we reached the last exam room.

Its door was open, so we hid ourselves there. Beyond the patient area lay two more rooms: Meredith's private office and, closer to us, a storeroom.

A door was open to the latter. The light was on, and at odds with the file cabinets and shelves that neatly lined the walls were a short two-door cabinet and a sturdy hand truck that had been left sitting in the middle of the floor. An exterior door at the storeroom's rear stood ajar, revealing an alley-like rear parking lot. A small rental box truck with a ramp was parked there. And just beyond the truck I glimpsed the front end of a metallic-blue Cadillac.

It seemed that Meredith hadn't lied about needing help moving something. And, unfortunately, I had a bad feeling I knew what that something was.

We could hear Meredith's voice coming from her office, and she did not sound happy. I pointed to Ryan's phone, which was clipped to his belt.

Leaning closer, I whispered in his ear, "Start recording."

"Really, Harry, that's too bad," Meredith was saying. "If those records had been in the trunk, maybe we could have worked something out. Not with Virgie, of course—she still has to go—but you and I could have made an excellent team."

"I appreciate your vote of confidence," Harry replied, sounding as cool as the clichéd cuke, "but just so you know, that whole team thing wouldn't have happened. Now why don't we put our heads together and figure out a way that all of us can go home. No harm, no foul."

A bang that for a moment sounded like a gunshot but had to be something heavy being flung to the tile floor made us all jump.

"You're not listening, Harry," the doctor replied, sounding oddly calm despite the momentary lapse into rage. "Maybe you can go home, but I can't. It's gone too far now."

"It hasn't, Meredith. We can—"

"Of course, I blame myself for the whole fiasco with Virgie," she continued, as if he hadn't spoken. "She never should have woken up and started banging on that cabinet. I misjudged the dosage I gave her, though in my defense, she lied about her weight. But I'm afraid the only way we can clean up this mess now is for us to fall victim to one of those unfortunate mass shootings that you read about in the newspapers all the time."

Shootings! I choked back a gasp. Things had escalated well beyond threats. Willing Jackson to hurry, I strained to hear more.

Meredith was still talking. "First, Virgie killed her partner. And once she made bail, she came after me because she suspected I knew something. Unfortunately, my fiancé happened to be here with me, so he ended up collateral damage."

The unmistakable metallic click of a pistol's hammer being pulled back was echoed by a small shriek from Virgie.

Meredith laughed.

"How ironic that Virgie provided her own murder weapon. I found this pretty little revolver stashed in the console of her car. She even has a concealed-carry permit in her wallet. Of course, there's only five shots, but I—I mean, Virgie—won't need them all."

"Meredith, this isn't you," Harry replied, the earlier cool air replaced by an unmistakably urgent tone. "You're a surgeon. You've spent your career saving lives."

"Oh, don't worry, Harry, I'll make sure everyone knows I did my best to save you—but, of course, you'll be too seriously injured to survive. Rather like Roxanna. Though I promise you will die a hero. I'll tell everyone that you wrestled the gun away from Virgie before she could shoot me, that you saved *my* life. Now, let's all move into the storeroom. I'd really rather not mess up my office."

"She's going to do it," I whispered, sending Ryan a terrified look. No time to call 911, even if I could have done so without Meredith hearing me. And even if another deputy was closer than Jackson, they couldn't get here in time to prevent a tragedy.

Which meant there was only one thing I could do to try to stop it.

I whipped out my cell phone and waited as first Virgie and then Harry walked out of Meredith's office. The doctor followed, Virgie's stylish pearl-handled revolver pointed at the pair. Once she had cleared the door, I hit redial.

The 1960s-era television theme "Secret Agent Man" abruptly blared from Harry's cell phone—his ring tone for me.

The unexpected sound was enough to break Meredith's concentration. The pistol wavered at the same instant that Harry whipped around and saw me and Ryan. He grabbed Virgie and gave her a shove into the storeroom. "Run!"

And that's when I lifted my crutch in both hands and clocked Meredith squarely across the face.

Unfortunately, the lightweight aluminum barely stunned her, while the momentum of the swing overbalanced me. I tumbled to the floor and rolled, twisting my bad ankle again in the process. I barely had time to register the pain, however, for I looked up to see the doctor's furious face as she aimed the pistol my way.

But Ryan was right there, knocking her arm aside just before she fired so that the bullet hit the far wall instead. With a snarl, Meredith turned the pistol on him.

"You!" I heard her shriek before she fired twice in succession.

Ryan dropped, but I couldn't see where—or even if—he'd been hit. And then Harry was back, grabbing her gun arm and trying to pry the pistol from her hand. She fired again, so close to his face that I was sure she had grazed him. His grip loosened, and she jerked her arm away and scrambled back.

And then, like a scene from a bad action movie, Virgie came marching out of the storeroom again, her steel-gray curls fallen from their usual bun and looking positively medusan. Pointing dramatically at Meredith, she clipped out, "Drop that pistol. Now!"

Meredith grinned a cold little grin, raised the revolver even with Virgie's chest, and pulled the trigger.

I heard a metallic click. And another.

While the rest of us stared at the pistol in disbelief, Meredith sputtered, "N-no! How?"

Now Virgie was the one who grinned. Trying without much success to pat her hair back into place, she said in honeyed tones, "It's a five-shot revolver, but my daddy, bless his heart, always taught me to leave the hammer down on an empty chamber. There were only four bullets in the gun."

And then, like a proper southern belle, she fainted.

* * *

"How's your ear?" I asked Harry a while later. "Still ringing?"

"Like a bell," he replied with a grimace. "The paramedic said I should be back to normal in a couple more hours. What about you? Is your ankle still hurting?"

I gingerly flexed my foot, which was propped up on the chair opposite me. "Let's just say I'm going to fill that pain prescription Dr. Patel gave me at the twenty-four-hour pharmacy."

We were sitting in the waiting area of Meredith's clinic being interviewed one by one by Sheriff Lamb and her team. Virgie had been taken across the street to the ER strictly as a precaution, given her fainting spell—that and the fact that she'd spent the past day drugged, courtesy of Meredith.

Fortunately, despite my initial fears, the only damage to Ryan had been to his prosthetic leg. Somehow the doctor had managed to graze it with one shot, knocking him off his feet. And the irony of that situation was that Meredith Garvin had been the very physician whose experimental treatment had cost Ryan not only his leg but almost his life.

Ryan was being interviewed by Deputy Jackson now. The questioning was being conducted in the reception area behind the frosted windows, since everything from the patient area on back was now a crime scene.

As for Meredith Garvin, the doctor had already been handcuffed and carried off to jail. I suspected that, unlike Virgie, she wouldn't be given the chance to make bail.

Harry and I both lapsed into silence, mostly, I suspected, because we were feeling a bit of shell shock over what had just happened. I knew I was. Being almost killed twice in less than a week tended to do a number on a person.

But when the quiet grew too oppressive, I glanced over at Harry. "You might have mentioned that Meredith drove a gray sedan."

"Well, in my defense, you kept talking about a silver car," he replied. "And since I saw Meredith trying to revive Roxanna, it never crossed my mind she was the one who . . . you know."

I nodded. "It was a smart move on Meredith's part, diverting suspicion like that." And then, with a small shudder, I added, "I don't even want to think what would have happened if you hadn't managed to do that stealth-dial thing. What if I hadn't picked up?"

He shrugged. "I imagine that our gossip king, Mason Denman, would have already called you with the news of my tragic death. Right about now you'd be deciding how best to mourn my passing."

He paused and slanted me a look. "You *would* mourn me, wouldn't you?"

"Of course," I said with a smile. "I mean, with you gone, I'd have to find someone to help out with my guests on Friday. And then I'd have to figure out what to do with all your stuff up in the tower room. Oh, and I'd probably get stuck having to find a buyer for your bus, though I'd probably give it to Reverend Bishop. And—"

"Fine, I get it," he cut me short. "I've passed through your life like a will-o'-the-wisp, my light flickering and then vanishing like it was never there. How did Sir Walter Scott put it— *unwept, unhonored, and unsung.* Of course you've got your new friend, Ryan Slater. He seems like a fine fellow, not half bad looking, not afraid of a fight. You could do worse."

"Harry, I was kidding," I hurried to reassure him, a bit worried by this sudden lapse into morbidness. "Of course I'd miss you. I mean, you saved my life."

"Well, I couldn't afford to lose my landlord, now, could I?"

Before I could manage a reply to that, the half door to the reception area opened and Deputy Jackson peered out. "Ms. Fleet, do you think you can manage to step back here a minute so we can take your statement?"

"Sure," I told him, and grabbed my crutches. Going over my latest brush with death had to be better than listening to Harry's jibes.

Ryan, meanwhile, stepped out of the makeshift interrogation room. His smile was weary as he passed by me and muttered, "Go get 'em, Tiger."

I smiled in return, not bothering to glance back at Harry as I followed the deputy behind the frosted glass.

The statement-giving thing took longer than I'd expected. But Jackson praised us for our quick thinking in having Ryan record the entire conversation we'd overheard, though he was less pleased with our part in the Wild West shootout that, despite Meredith's best efforts, had not ended disastrously for anyone but her.

"What part of *sit tight* did you not understand, Ms. Fleet?" were his exact words.

And though technically I was supposed to be doing the talking, Jackson let a few things slip. Such as that the entire tragedy had begun when Roxanna, needing quick cash to support her new boyfriend, had attempted to blackmail Meredith over Ryan's botched medical care.

In the weeks to come, I would piece together the rest of the story from local gossip and some of the actual players themselves. Eventually I would understand that Roxanna truly had not known about the embezzlement until days before the expo. The crime had actually been perpetrated by Jason: a yearlong campaign of small thefts as he hacked into the expo's joint account and siphoned cash for the seed money he needed for a recording venture that Virgie had refused to back. His goal met, he had given the money to Roxanna to hold—apparently overlooking the fact that half the money was technically Roxanna's. Even so, she had jumped into action on her boyfriend's behalf, looking for a quick ten thousand that she could repay to the joint account while still leaving him with his start-up cash.

I'd also learned that despite having bankrupted Ryan upon their divorce, Roxanna had long since blown through whatever money she'd walked away with following the split. Thus, she'd had no cash with which to play investor with Jason herself. Which explained the Ford she drove and the modest house in which she lived.

One thing had come to light immediately, however. Apparently, despite Meredith's sterling reputation with the Reverend Dr. Bishop and others, she was already being investigated by the medical review board over two cases similar to Ryan's. She had found herself in an untenable situation, with both her malpractice insurance in danger of being revoked and her medical license at risk. Roxanna's attempts to blackmail her had come at a tragically wrong time for both women.

As for Meredith, she hadn't waited to be hauled down to the sheriff's office to confess. Even as Deputy Jackson put her in handcuffs, she admitted that she had deliberately gone to the bridal expo to confront her nemesis a final time about the blackmail attempt. There she had surprised Roxanna backstage as the latter had been about to load the prop cake with the dozens of flowers meant to spill out of it during the fashion show finale. And when Roxanna had persisted in her monetary assault on the doctor—even claiming as a desperate last-minute bit of insurance that Virgie, as her business partner, knew about the files—Meredith had snapped.

I wasn't quite myself in that moment, I'd overheard her coolly admit to Deputy Jackson, reminding me of a character from some lurid Southern Gothic novel. She'd gone on to explain how she had grabbed Roxanna's scarf, throttling the other woman with it before shoving her into the prop cake and returning to the expo floor so as to throw off any suspicion.

And it had been she who trashed Roxanna's house the following day in a desperate search for the files.

But according to Ryan's statement, he had the only copy of the records that Meredith had desperately tried to find. Not only had she searched Roxanna's place looking for those files, but she had focused on me as well. Knowing I was a friend of Roxanna's and having seen me at the house twice after the murder, she'd assumed I also knew something about the blackmail scheme.

By the time Deputy Jackson and I finished talking, I felt as worn out as Ryan had looked. I hobbled my way back to the waiting room. Ryan glanced up from the sports magazine he was reading and gave me a smile. "They let you go?"

"Free as a bird—at least until the next time I need to make a statement," was my wry response. "Where's Harry?"

"That redheaded deputy—Mullins, I think was his name—took him outside to get his statement, since you were taking so long. He finished up about fifteen minutes ago."

I peered out the glass door to the parking lot. Harry wasn't there—and neither, for that matter, was Ryan's silver sedan.

"He wanted out of here, so I suggested he take my car back to the B&B," Ryan hurried to explain as I gave him a quizzical look. "I told him I'd drive you back in yours. I-I hope that was okay?"

I nodded. "Perfectly okay."

But even though I appreciated Ryan's kind gesture, I couldn't help but feel a bit hurt that Harry had gone off on his own rather than waiting on me. Though maybe he'd had good reason to do so. Now that I'd given Deputy Jackson my statement, my earlier tension had lessened enough that I regretted being so flip with him earlier. I'd almost forgotten that he was still grieving over Roxanna—or at least, the Roxanna he'd once known—and that he wasn't quite himself.

I hadn't helped matters by letting him think I didn't care about him, when quite the opposite was true.

All of a sudden, I was in a rush to get out of there too.

"Let's go," I told Ryan. "It's already been a long night."

We drove back in companionable silence, Ryan at the wheel. When we reached home, his car was parked at the curb and the driveway gate was open. The porch lights were cheerily blazing, and I could hear Mattie and Gus's faint welcoming barking as we pulled up in the drive.

"Harry said he'd leave my keys on the kitchen island," Ryan said as he put the Mini in park and turned off the ignition. Handing my keys to me, he added, "I can wait here while you get them, or I can walk you to the door."

"I think you just want to say good-night to Gus," I said with a smile. "Why don't you walk me in, and you two can have a quick snuggle. And tomorrow we can talk to Sheriff Lamb about letting you take Gus back with you to Atlanta."

We went inside, and Ryan and his Goldendoodle had another happy reunion.

"It's hard to leave him again," the man said, after they'd finished a few minutes of gentle roughhousing, "but the hotel would kick me out if I tried to sneak him in. I'd better say good-night before I'm tempted anyhow."

"He'll be going home with you soon," I assured him. "Mattie enjoys the company now, but deep in her little Aussie heart, she's an only dog."

"Well, maybe we can come back to town for a puppy play-date sometime soon," he said, grabbing up his keys.

And then, to my surprise, he leaned over and gave me a kiss on the cheek.

"Sorry, I didn't mean to overstep," he said, seeing my reaction. "I'm just so grateful for everything you've done."

"You mean taking care of Gus? I was happy to do that."

He shook his head. "Yes, that, but everything else. You were a good friend to Roxie. Not just while she was alive, but after. You cared that she was gone, and you wanted to find out the truth about what happened to her."

He smiled then, but his smile was tinged with sadness.

"I'm not blind. I know Roxie had flaws . . . a lot of them. Heck, she kicked me to the curb once she decided she didn't want a one-legged husband. But there was another side to her, one that was fun and sweet and caring. And even when she took me for every penny she could, even when she took Gus from me, I never stopped loving her."

"Wow," I said, a bit inadequately. "It's too bad she never realized what she had. I have to say, I'm almost envious of her."

"Hey, you've got a good guy with Harry. He's not bad-looking, and he's sure not afraid of a fight. You could do worse."

I laughed a little. "That's pretty much what he said about you."

"Yeah?" Ryan shrugged. "I guess all of Roxie's exes are pretty decent sorts."

"You know about Harry?" I asked in surprise.

His smile turned rueful. "She always told me he was the one who got away. So, Nina, you might want to hang on to him."

I nodded. "I'll think about it."

He gave Gus a final pat; then, lightly tossing his keys and catching them again, he said, "I'll wait to hear back from you about when I can pick up Gustopher. You want me to close the driveway gate on the way out?"

"No, we're fine. I don't think anyone will come prowling around tonight."

Like a good innkeeper, I stood at the kitchen door and watched while Ryan made his way down the drive. I waited until I saw his headlights turn on and heard his engine as he pulled away. Then I locked the door behind me and hobbled my way to the main hall, which was ablaze with light.

"Harry, are you there?" I called up the stairs. "Harry?"

When I heard no reply, I left my crutches propped against the wall and made my precarious way up the steps, clinging to the railing as I took the risers one at a time. Once I reached the top, I hopped my way to the secret panel that served as a door.

"Harry," I called, rapping firmly, "would you please answer me?"

I opened the panel and promptly saw that the closet-like room that housed the ladder stairs leading up to the tower room was dark, as was the narrow landing above. Even so, I reached in and flipped on the light. "Harry?"

Once again, there was no reply. Had my ankle been up to it, I might have climbed the steep stairway just to check and be certain. But I'd lived long enough in the house to know the difference between quiet and emptiness. And except for Mattie and Gus, I was alone in the house.

I hopped my way back to the stairs and pulled my phone from my pocket, then called Harry's number. The call went directly to voice mail, meaning he'd turned off his phone. Meaning that he didn't want to talk to anyone—or at least not to me.

More than a bit worried now, I hopped my way downstairs again and grabbed my crutches. Just in case, I hurried to the back door and flipped on the exterior lights. Dogs at my heels now, I peered out into the night. But the covered patio and Shakespeare garden both were empty, as was the expanse of yard beyond.

Slowly I closed the door again and shut off the lights, then turned to the pups. "I think he's really gone," I whispered.

And then, all at once, I realized where he must be. I hurried back to the kitchen as quickly as I could and snatched up my keys again.

"You pups watch the house," I told them. "I've got to go out for a minute, but I—no, we—will be back soon."

I only hoped I was telling the truth.

I made my way to the Mini and drove out into the night, checking my phone at every stop sign in case I'd missed hearing a text come through. It was a quarter hour later when I reached my destination, the Heavenly Host Baptist Church.

It felt like weeks since I'd last stopped by to talk to the Reverend Bishop, though I realized in surprise it had been only a few days. And I'd never been to the church at night, so this was the first time I'd seen the red cross on the church's sign actually lit, its crimson glow more eerie than comforting in the dark. I drove around back to the parking lot where Harry's bus was parked. I idled a moment, then pulled the Mini into the slot next to it and switched off the ignition.

At first, I thought I'd guessed wrong, because I didn't see any light coming from beneath the curtained windows. And then I spied a faint bluish glow, like the screen light from a cell phone.

Since it was but a few steps, I climbed out of the car and hopped my way to the bus door. "Harry, it's me, Nina," I called, knocking. "Can I come in and talk to you?"

For a long minute, I was afraid he wouldn't answer. And then I heard him say in a noncommittal voice, "It's open."

Warily, I pushed open the door and climbed inside. The fabric divider behind the driver's seat was drawn, and I fumbled in the dark a moment before I found the spot where the curtains met. The last time I'd been aboard the bus had been during the Shakespeare festival in August. But now that it was late September, the night was temperate enough for comfort without turning on the small air conditioner he had mounted in one window.

The bus looked more like an airport shuttle than a tour bus, with the original face-forward rows resituated so that they ran the length of the vehicle on either side. Unlike in the past, when Harry had actually lived in this space for a time, it was empty now of any personal belongings save for a couple of batik throws tossed across the seats.

Harry lay atop one of the seat rows, head and shoulders propped against the bus's rear wall. He was scrolling through his phone, the bluish light sharpening and shadowing his features.

I perched on the opposite row, waiting for him to set the phone down and acknowledge me. But when it became obvious that wasn't going to happen, I ventured, "Harry, can we talk a minute?"

"Talk all you want," was his reply, his gaze still fixed on his phone.

"Fine," I said. "I'll talk, and you can listen. Harry, I'm here to apologize. Earlier, while we were waiting to give our statements, I was flip and dismissive of your feelings, and I'm sorry. My only excuse is that it was a pretty harrowing night. All I was thinking about was how scared and angry I was. I hope you can forgive me. And I hope you'll come back to the B&B."

"Apology accepted," he said, still staring at the screen. "I probably could have behaved a bit better myself. Like you said, it was a harrowing night."

I heaved a small sigh of relief. "Thanks. That means a lot to me. And you'll come back to the B&B now?"

"No."

For the first time since I'd set foot on the bus, he set down the phone and looked over at me.

"I'm not coming back," he said. "Not to stay. Don't worry, I'll still be there to help you this weekend, like I promised. But once you're healed up enough to manage on your own, I'll move my things out. You'll have the place all to yourself again, just like you've always wanted."

But that wasn't what I wanted—not anymore.

"Harry, you don't have to leave. Really. I . . . I like having you there."

I thought I saw him smile just a little—or maybe it was the light reflecting over his features as he picked up his phone again.

"I know," he quietly said, his gaze once again fixed on the screen. "And that's why I can't stay."

I sat there a moment longer, not quite believing what was happening. Finally, feeling very tired and beaten and alone, I got to my feet.

"Good-bye, Harry," I whispered, and walked out of the bus again.

And it wasn't until I was driving down the dark streets again that I allowed the tears I'd been holding in check to finally roll down my cheeks.

Chapter Twenty

"Heads up, Nina," Gemma called, rushing past me into the dining room while carrying a covered foil tray. "The ceremony is going to start in fifteen minutes, and we still have food to set up. Have you seen Jasmine?"

"Right here, Mom," the girl called, hurrying in after her with a tray of her own. Like her mother, she was dressed in her official catering uniform of black slacks and white blouse topped by a white vest, though the Tanakas were also there as guests. "This is the last tray," she confirmed, then asked, "Did Papa already set up the cake?"

"It's all set," I assured them both.

I pointed to the three-tiered wedding cake perched atop my vintage silver cake stand in the middle of the dining table. The layers were covered in white buttercream frosting, with rows of piped-on ribbons and cascades of roses in pale yellow and white. While I'd known Daniel was a fabulous baker, I had never seen a decorated cake from him before. I'd been even more impressed when he had confessed that this was one of his first attempts at a traditional wedding cake.

The cake topper, however, was courtesy of John Klingel. Rather than the typical bride and groom, he'd created a tiny bouquet of real flowers—miniature white roses and delicate greenery wrapped in lace and tied with tulle ribbons—to grace the cake's top tier. Even better, the fairy-tale-like creation matched the full-size bouquet that his soon-to-be (for the second time) bride, Virgie Klingel, would be carrying down the aisle.

I was almost as excited for this wedding as the bride and groom, for Virgie and John's nuptials would be the first actual wedding held at the B&B. True, there would be only twenty-five people, including me and the Tanakas, but given that the entire event had been planned in less than a month, I was pretty pleased with how everything had come together. Even the weather, which could turn on a dime in late October, was sunny and only a bit crisp this Saturday afternoon.

A few days earlier, I'd jokingly suggested to the bride and groom that Mattie serve as best dog. They'd laughingly declined the offer, though to my surprise John had brought a little collar corsage for her along with the rest of the flowers. Even better, the photographer had taken a few cute shots of her in all her floral glory before Mattie retired to my quarters for the duration of the ceremony.

Leaving Gemma and Jasmine now to finish setting up the food, I made a quick run out to the covered patio. White wooden folding chairs, each with a big white satin bow tied on the back, were arranged in rows, leaving an aisle in the middle for the bride to make her entrance. Jack Hill—owner of Cymbeline's best ice cream shop and carpenter on the side—had finished my official wedding trellis just in time for the ceremony. Now it was adorned with tulle streamers and flower garlands—those being, again, John's own creations. The trellis was situated at the entry to the Shakespeare garden, which provided a scenic backdrop for photos.

Most of the guests had arrived by now and had taken their seats on the patio. I did a quick head count inside and out. Only a few hallway stragglers needed to be ushered outside, and then the ceremony could commence. I glanced over to see the wedding's officiant, the Reverend Dr. Bishop, dressed in his usual expensive black suit and white collar. He appeared to be laughing at a not-safe-for-weddings joke as he chatted with the best man—who happened to be the bride's son.

Jason Hamilton, dressed surprisingly stylishly in sharp-creased black slacks and a pale-yellow silk shirt, had turned a figurative corner following Roxanna's murder. He'd confessed the money thefts to Virgie, who had let him off the hook far more easily than I might have done. But the fact that he'd had nothing to do with Roxanna's blackmail attempts or her subsequent murder—indeed, seemed truly grieved by the latter—had gone a long way to mending the rift between mother and son. And from what I'd heard from Virgie, she'd gifted him the money for his new recording venture once he had approached her with a savvy business plan.

But Jason's hadn't been the only confession to come out in the aftermath of the tragedy. Virgie had finally told her son and her ex-husband a long-held secret—that Jason was not the offspring of some man she had supposedly married on the rebound following her divorce but was John's own son. That had been the violation of their "marriage of convenience" rules that John had told me about at the bridal expo. In the beginning, they'd both agreed that children would never be part of the equation. But when Virgie had unexpectedly found herself pregnant, she'd realized she had changed her mind. And fearful of what would happen once John found out, she had hurriedly divorced him and then made up a fictional new husband, even changing her last name to keep up the ruse.

Much to Virgie's surprise, after John had gotten over his initial shock at the news, he'd asked her to marry him again, eager to try to put together a family with her after all the years spent apart. Of course, Jason had been far less keen about accepting a new father out of the blue, but he had agreed to support his mother in the marriage.

"There you are, Nina," Polly Hauer exclaimed, shaking me from my thoughts as she grasped my arm. Dressed in a stylish yellow silk sheath and matching velvet-trimmed silk bolero straight from Virgie's shop, Polly was the matron of honor and official wedding planner.

"The bride is ready," she hurriedly told me. "And the parlor is working out just fine for a changing room. Now, once we get the last guests seated, I'll let John and Dr. Bishop know to take their places. Oh, and where's our musician? I want to hear some wedding tunes."

And then, turning a critical eye on me, she added, "I must say, that copper-colored suit you're wearing looks fabulous on you. It's too bad you don't have a date for the wedding. You know Virgie told you that you had a plus one if you wanted it."

"Thanks, Polly," I replied, summoning a smile. "I think since this is my B&B, I need to be paying attention to the guests and not worrying about having a good time."

Though, to be honest, I'd considered giving Ryan Slater a call and asking him if he wanted to attend the wedding. Even after he'd picked up Gus and taken him back to Atlanta, we'd stayed in touch via email. While there weren't any romantic sparks between us—at least, not on my side—I had come to consider him a friend. In the end I had decided that a wedding date might send the wrong message and determined to enjoy the event solo.

"Suit yourself," Polly replied. Then, pulling out her phone, she showed me her stopwatch app. "Ready or not, I'm starting the fifteen-minute countdown. Everyone better be in place, because when the alarm goes off, the bride is walking down the aisle."

"Yes, ma'am!" I said with a grin and a salute, then headed back in to round up the stragglers. Which I could do quite readily these days, as my sprained ankle was only a little twitchy now and then.

Among the wanderers were Mason and Lowell, the latter having finally finished the appraisal on my ghastly oil painting, which he'd ended up buying from me outright. In honor of the wedding, the pair were dressed in matching black tuxedos, though thankfully Lowell had not opted to copy his boyfriend's signature pompadour.

"The place looks great," Mason assured me, while Lowell merely nodded his smiling approval. "All right, all right, we'll go sit down now so you can get this show on the road."

With the slackers shooed, all that remained was a final check of the dining room. I took a look and saw that Gemma and Jasmine had done a stellar job, the food having been arranged atop my vintage china and crystal and silver in a delightful gustatory tableaux.

"Beautiful!" I told the pair as they made a few final tweaks. "But we're about ready to start, so come take your seats. Is Daniel ready with the music?"

"Right here."

Daniel wore black slacks like his wife and daughter, though instead of the white shirt and vest, he sported a black-and-white aloha shirt. In his arms he cradled one of his ukuleles—this one a gorgeous mahogany instrument inlaid with abalone around its sound hole. I knew from its larger size that it was what Daniel had told me was a baritone. Like the name implied, it had a deep and rich tone that was far more full-bodied than those of the small ukes he tended to play at the diner.

"Polly wants a little mood music to warm up the crowd before the bride and groom come in," I told him. "You think you can oblige?"

"On it," Daniel said with a grin and a nod as he followed his wife and daughter outside. A few moments later, I heard the beautiful but plaintive notes of some island song drifting in from the garden.

At that, I heaved a sigh. All that remained was to tell Polly we were ready for the happy couple, and then I could grab a chair along with the rest of the guests. But before I could head to the parlor to give her the word, a familiar voice behind me said, "Looks like you haven't started yet. Good. I was afraid I was late."

Harry?

Slowly I turned, not quite believing it was really him. But it was. At least, I thought it was. For this man wore a perfectly fitted tuxedo, his dark hair gelled into a slicked-back but still edgy style that made his even features look sharper, craggier. One hand was casually tucked into a pocket as he stood there surveying me.

I stared back at him in silence for a moment; then, as realization hit, I couldn't help a fleeting smile. "Don't tell me, you're the Retired Secret Agent."

He inclined his head just a fraction. "Double-O Harry Westcott, at your service."

And then, breaking character, he said, "You told me once that next time you were invited to a wedding, you wanted your plus one to be the Retired Secret Agent. So, if you're interested, he's here. Unless you already have a date?"

I hesitated, not quite believing he'd remembered that exchange, or that he'd made the effort to follow through. Slowly, I shook my head.

"No, I don't have a date," I told him. "But Harry, I haven't seen you for almost a month. I thought you'd left town. I thought you weren't coming back."

"I thought I would . . . and that I wasn't. But then I began to wonder if I'd made the wrong decision. I knew the only way I'd know for sure was to come back here again."

"Darn it, Harry," I replied, dismayed to find myself dangerously close to tears. "I can't talk about this now. The wedding is about to start."

Just on cue, from behind the parlor's closed doors, I heard Polly's alarm go off. I hesitated a final time—and then made a decision of my own.

"Hurry up," I told Harry, grabbing his arm. "We need to take our seats now!"

Somehow we ended up in the last two empty chairs remaining in the last row. John was standing beneath the trellis, looking happy and proud in a dark-gray suit with a pale-yellow shirt and a darker-yellow tie. Jason, looking more than a bit uncomfortable, was at his side. Dr. Bishop stood there as well, an open Bible in his hands as he beamed approvingly at the gathering.

And then Daniel abruptly cut short the cheerful island music he'd been playing. While a smiling Polly started down the aisle, bridesmaid bouquet in hand, he switched to a heartbreakingly beautiful instrumental version of the classic Elvis tune "Can't Help Falling in Love."

As the music washed over me, I began to hear the plaintive lyrics in my head. All at once, the weight of the past few weeks seemed to crash down on me. Roxanna's untimely death . . . Meredith's spiral into callous murder . . . the spunky Buddy now virtually motherless, though fortunately her father had eagerly taken her in . . . Ryan's confession of lost love . . . even the announcement of Cam's upcoming nuptials. Silent tears began streaming down my cheeks at all the pain and loss, and I was helpless to stop them.

And then I felt Harry's hand on my shoulder. It was the briefest of gestures, a kind but momentary touch designed only to offer comfort. Yet it was enough. I straightened in my chair, swiped at my eyes, and smiled as Polly joined the trio at the trellis.

The song ended in a moment of silence. And then, with a harp-like flourish, Daniel launched into a dramatic version of the wedding march.

We all stood as Virgie appeared in the doorway, looking radiant in a cocktail-length dress of heavy yellow silk as she started down the aisle. Once she reached the trellis, taking her once and future husband by the hand, we all resumed our seats. Dr. Bishop cleared his throat, waiting for silence.

Finally, with another beaming smile, the reverend began.

"Brothers and sisters, the Lord works in mysterious ways. Sometimes people who think they don't belong together finally realize that they do. And when that happens, it is a time for celebration indeed."

He paused, gazed about at the guests for a moment, then said, "Excuse me, brothers and sisters. Can we get an amen here?"

I saw a few smiles, heard a few nervous chuckles, before Jason took a step forward, pumped a beefy fist, and shouted, "A-men!"

"A-men!" the rest of the guests happily called out, drawing an approving nod from Dr. Bishop.

"Amen," Harry quietly echoed beside me.

I silently nodded. And then, just because it felt right, I scooted a bit closer to him and linked my arm through his, deciding that I did rather like weddings after all.

Acknowledgments

A big bouquet of thanks to my friend John Klingel, a former award-winning florist. Not only did he allow me to borrow his name for this third outing with Nina, but he also provided great info from his fun beginner's book on flower arranging, *The Frugal Florist*. Any errors in this story regarding the flower biz are mine alone.

And special thanks to my longtime stylist, Sheri. Not only does she keep my hair lookin' good, but she was the first to tell me about trypophobia. And just as I promised her, I used that gem in my next book!